TO KILL A GODDESS

RACHEL TORK

For the readers who prefer their romance served with a side of tragedy
(and dragons)

TRIGGER WARNINGS

Memories/flashbacks involving the murders of close family members, brief mention of sexual assault (not directly relating to the FMC), some battle gore, and themes of heavy grief

Sir Lanor: *LAN-or*
Sgàilsuil: skahl-shool
Sir Helq: *HEL-K*
Ilav Thil: *EE-lav thill (like "hill")*
Mòr Maslach: "more" MOSS-lach
Commander Jadis Eton: *JAY-dis EE-tuhn*
Vane Evva: *"vein" EE-vuh*
Yella: *YELL-uh*
Vulcan: *VUL-kuhn*
Juno: *joo-no*
Janis: *JAN-iss*
Sol: *"soul"*
Bella: *BEH-luh*
Nya: *nye-uh*

Dragons & Dragon Names
Vemon: *VEM-un*
Fesper: *fess-per*
Olariu: *oh-lah-roo*
Thessilnn: *THEH-sah-lin*
Heles: *HEL-es*
Valhamnor: *VAL-ham-nor*
Keenie: *KEEN-ee*

Places
Mise: *myze*
Aren: *AIR-un*
Meesling: *mee-sling*
Arcadia: *ar-KAY-dee-uh*
D'anna: *DAHN-uh*
Alesia: *Uh-LEE-sha*

PRONUNCIATION GUIDE

PEOPLE

Soren Cavell: *SOAR-en kuv-el*

Princess Cion Livii: *SEE-un li-vee*

Prince Nell: *"knell"*

Kelshie: *KEL-shee*

Thurn: *like "burn"*

Nyx: *Nix*

Thanatos: *THAH-nah-toss*

Mona: *MO-nuh*

Thelia: *THAY-lee-uh*

Jasmen: *JAZ-men*

Anabeth: *AN-uh-beth*

Sir Gellings: *JEL-ings*

King Johannas: *Jo-han-es*

Queen Lona: *LO-nah*

Princess Chelsa: *CHEL-sah*

Kronos: *kroh-nohs*

Prince Kellmere Hale: *KEL-meer "hail"*

Princess Hessa: *HESS-uh*

PROLOGUE

*T*HE *PALACE HALLS WERE A MAZE. Guards stood around every corner, each holding a heavy spear and sporting dark armor forged by dragonfire. It was nearly impossible to locate the throne room, much less get to it.*

But he had been here before.

Once, long ago, he had been dragged this same way, his blood smearing the gleaming marble.

He was smarter now. Time had forced him to become so, even if coming here was one of the most reckless things he had ever decided to do. For her, he would risk it. She had to survive this, and he was willing to walk straight into the lion's den for even the chance that she might live to see tomorrow's sunrise.

Even if he did not. Even if that was breaking the promise they had made to each other. Because the thought of her lifeless again, eyes wide open...

He was at the entry hall now. For just a moment, he glanced back, and somewhere deep down, he knew he would not see this hall again. He would not see anything again, not beyond the confines of the throne room ahead.

"Tell her I love her," he murmured, glancing up at the ceiling. "And that I'm sorry."

Then, he shut off the pathway. If he heard any of them now, he was afraid he would turn back. He had to do this. The god had said there was a chance.

His footsteps echoed as he stepped out into the open. There was one way into the throne room now: sheer force. The guards immediately tensed when they spotted him, their weapons held high. He lowered his chin and smiled before leaping into action.

Three of them were dead within the minute. The other two put up a valiant fight, but they were young and no match for over a hundred years of brutal training. As the last guard fell, though, he felt no sense of victory. The true battle lay behind the throne room doors, which were now slowly swinging open.

The first sound he heard was laughter. Slowly, he stepped inside the vast chamber, blade raised.

The king sat on his throne, all the way at the end of the room. Surrounding him were more guards, likely older and more viciously trained.

"I thought I might see you," the king mused. "Guards, do get rid of the pest for me."

They rushed towards him, and he ducked, barely missing the sharp edge of a blade. Another nicked his cheek and then sliced his bicep, but the guards were falling all the same.

The king watched, a sort of bland amusement on his face as he drew closer and closer. When the last guard fell and he was at the edge of the dais, breathing heavily and blood-spattered, the king stood.

"Rather impressive to see how time has molded you. It's a shame it will all go to waste for her."

"For her..." He caught his breath, chest heaving. "For her, anything."

Gold and silver flared in the king's eyes. *"Very well."*

A shadow swept through the sky above them, circling over the glass ceiling—not a dark one, but a beast with scales luminescent like the moon…

No.

He must have said the word aloud, because the king laughed again before lunging towards him. At the same moment, a stream of brilliant, white-hot fire crashed through the ceiling. Glass rained down upon them, and a familiar roar reverberated through the air.

He grunted as the king dragged him back. He could feel the blade at his throat, and when he reached for his magic, it was dull and lifeless.

The dragon crashed through the ceiling, landing on the ash-stained floor with a resounding boom. And atop her…

Eyes aglow with blazing silver searched the room through the chaos just as his body jerked.

The king's dagger was embedded in his chest, the blade resting inches away from his heart. He tried to tell her to run, but the words were lost as their gazes locked and she slid off the dragon's back.

The tip of the blade grazed his heart.

His heart, which beat only for her.

CHAPTER I

Warmth surrounded her, encasing her completely. She pretended it was the gentle heat of the summer sun. Yes, if she kept her eyes closed tight enough, she could smell the wheat swaying in the gentle mountain breeze, hear the birds calling back and forth in the jicaba trees that grew by the creek.

There was no more pain, no more blood. His screams had faded away, his broken fingers no longer reaching for her…

No—she had promised. She tried to turn back before the warmth disappeared, but it was too late.

Even as darkness consumed her, the last thing she felt was crackling heat.

Soren rubbed at her eyes with her free hand, trying to brush away the exhaustion weighing them down. She hadn't slept well again last night. The dreams she'd had since childhood were becoming more vivid, and with them, her sleep less restful. She could remember them more clearly than ever, and though she had once wished for that clarity, she now hated it. The images and feelings she remembered only brought her confusion.

She dropped her hand as she reached the door at the end of the hall, tucking it back under the linens and knocking thrice. No one answered, and she pushed it open, assuming the princess was out. Her mind began to wander to the vivid smell of a wheat field she had never been to, but as she stepped inside, all thoughts of sleep or her dreams ceased.

The princess was on the floor, crimson staining the pale skin of her palm.

At the first sight of blood, Soren froze. If the wound was anything fatal or dire, she would immediately be implicated just for being the first one in the room. Those enslaved under the crown had been blamed plenty of times for even minor wounds inflicted on those they served; the punishments doled out rarely matched the severity of the injury— or lack thereof.

But as Soren forced herself to move, hurrying over to the princess' bedside, the warrior princess of Aren began to laugh. Soren halted, a death grip on the clean linens in her hands. Princess Cion smothered her mirth, tucking a strand of long, dark hair behind her ear as she tried to compose herself. Closer now, Soren could see that, though there *was* blood dripping from her hand, it was hardly more than a shallow cut directly in the center of her palm.

"I'm sorry, Soren." The princess shook her head, looking down at her torn skin. "I just feel a little ridiculous."

Soren forced herself to take a deep breath and walk lightly over to where she sat on the floor of her airy bedchambers.

Princess Cion's chamber was in the back of the palace, overlooking the edge of a narrow cliff. The drop from her balcony was dizzying, enough that Soren tended to avoid the outdoor sitting space if she could. Lucky for her, the princess usually preferred to spend her free time *in* the lavish room.

"Are you alright, my princess?" Soren asked carefully, tucking the airy material of her skirt and kneeling in front of her.

As one of the princess' four handmaidens, Soren wore a finer dress than most servants in the palace, but she did not mistake it for kindness or rank. It was merely to appear pleasing to the eye in front of the royals.

"I'm fine," Princess Cion said, her voice leveling as her laughter died. "Really, I was eating an apple and my hand slipped. But please, to anyone else, I received this wound training." She shook her head, the light catching the green in her hooded eyes. "How embarrassing. The 'warrior princess' cuts her hand carving a piece of fruit."

She snorted softly, shifting, though not standing; the silky fabric of her red wrap dress slithered across the gleaming darkwood floor that had been polished this morning, while the princess had been at breakfast. Servants of lesser rank had completed the task, scurrying around Soren and the other handmaidens as they prepared a bath for the princess in the accompanying bathing chamber.

Soren remained kneeling next to the princess, her head

bowed as she said, "If you do not mind, I ask that you stay here, princess. I don't want you to get dizzy and fall. I'll retrieve some water and clean bandages, and I can send for Jasmen to wait with you while I'm gone, if you'd like?"

Princess Cion shook her head, closing her kohl-lined eyes. "Not Jasmen. I'll be fine, just go retrieve the supplies, please."

None of the other royals ever said 'please' to a servant. It simply wasn't the way of things. But Princess Cion wasn't like most in the palace, at least to those she liked. Soren had always felt uneasy about being on the princess' good side. Favor could change at any moment.

She rose and hurried out of the bedchamber, her slippered feet whispering across the wood as she stepped out into the empty hallway and softly shut the door behind her.

The royal wing sometimes felt like a tomb.

No one dared to raise their voice above a soft whisper, so as not to disturb the most important family in all of Aren—not that any of them spent much time in their chambers beyond sleeping. Princess Cion was usually training or studying scrolls, her brother, Prince Nell, taunting servants or *pretending* he knew how to wield a crossbow, and their younger sister attending lessons. The king and queen each had agendas of their own: the king, attending to a war outside the palace walls, the queen tending to her own battles within them.

There was a supply closet nearby; they were scattered discreetly throughout the palace for the servants, stocked with clean linens, brushes for cleaning, and sometimes a few medicinal supplies. When she reached it, Hector, one of

Prince Nell's personal servants, was already there, a pile of bed linens in his arms.

"Excuse me," she said, and he stepped out of the way as she retrieved a few bandages and a small ceramic bowl.

Hector eyed the bandages then Soren. "Is someone hurt?"

She glanced at him. He was Misean too, with tawny, bronzed skin, dark brown hair, and blue eyes, features that always, no matter how they showed their loyalty to Aren, made others distrust them because of the ongoing war between their kingdoms. King Johannas was always wary of spies. Just this last week, two servants had been detained, one of them publicly executed for aiding rebel movements within Aren's troops.

"Princess Cion, but it's just from training earlier," she lied smoothly.

Hector hesitated then nodded. "Ah, I see." He paused again, glancing around before he leaned in and murmured, "This is the third time I've had to change His Highness' sheets in the last four hours. He's quite ill."

Soren's eyes widened. "Will he be alright?"

Hector only shrugged, chewing on his bottom lip nervously. "I should go."

She relented, nodding and letting him go, but her heart beat rapidly as he walked away. She focused on her breath, trying to calm the nervous anticipation.

Half of her wished for harm to Aren's heir. It would weaken the crown and therefore give Mise an upper hand in the war. Her birth kingdom had been slowly slipping, losing more battles from what she could pick up through whispered rumors amongst the servants. Some said the war was close to an end now.

But the part of her that had been trained to loyalty shied away from any feelings of revenge. She served Princess Cion, and her brother's death would ultimately harm her. Soren did not want harm to come to anyone.

Though, deep down, she knew that was a lie.

There was that *feeling* inside her chest that she had long tucked away, the one her own mother had once told her to hide.

It tasted of ashes and power.

She buried it quickly—it was too dangerous to feel such emotions. It could crack the encasing of ice she always kept around her heart, and if that broke, she was lost.

Composing herself, she tucked a stray strand of silvery-white hair behind her ear. The color was not Misean by any standard, and it had always drawn some attention to her. But years in the palace had thankfully allowed her to blend in with the others, fading into the background, where it was safest.

She hurried back to Princess Cion's chambers, knocking softly.

"Enter!"

The princess was sitting on the floor when she pushed the door open, staring calmly out the doors of the balcony. She must have opened them while Soren was gone. Cool air filtered in, fresh and pine-scented. Beyond, the peaks of Ellys mountains towered all around them, watchful guardians of Aren's mountainside capital city.

"Your Highness," Soren said, bowing.

Princess Cion looked up, lips twitching. "You were

quick," she said. "You do know I am not truly injured that badly?"

Soren's cheeks warmed, irritation and shame mingling. She shoved both aside. "Of course, princess. May I see your hand?"

The princess held it out, and Soren knelt in front of her. Carefully, she examined the shallow gash, and after making sure it wasn't worse than it looked, she cleaned it and wrapped it gently in a bandage.

"There, my princess."

Princess Cion looked at Soren thoughtfully. Her striking green eyes, flecked with hazel and gold, had always reminded Soren of a forest in the height of summer.

"Soren," the princess began. "Tell me about where you're from."

Soren looked at the princess sharply, her throat tightening, but she kept her breaths steady and even. "I am from Mise, Your Highness."

Princess Cion sighed. "I *know* that."

Soren shifted her aching feet. "I was very young when I was taken—" She cut off, scolding herself for the small mistake in speech. Anything could be construed as treason.

Princess Cion didn't say anything; she just stood and Soren followed her, eyes trained on the floor.

The princess took Soren's hand with her uninjured one and said, "Soren, you can say 'taken.' You don't have to spew some benevolent nonsense that your life here is better or that you're glad you're a servant."

Slave, Soren almost corrected, but she held her tongue. Instead, she merely murmured, "Yes, my princess."

Princess Cion shook her head. "Never mind my questions. I know it must be painful for you. Come. I want you to attend me while I train today."

Soren was silent as she helped the princess dress in training garb: thick leather pants and a scaled, armored vest over her tunic. Dragon scales, Soren had been told, just like the dragon that someday soon would be bonded to the princess.

She was destined to be a rider.

Only the best in Aren were conscripted to be chosen as riders. They all came from noble families, training for years before the Choosing, a ceremony during which a dragon personally selected them. If not chosen, the rumor was, they died by dragonfire.

But Princess Cion would be, undoubtedly. It had been predicted by a Sister of the Arcane when she was a child. The Sisters' prophetic abilities were of the last remnants of the magic that had disappeared from the continent nearly a hundred years ago. No one knew why or how. According to the histories, one day, it had just…disappeared. Aside from the Sisters, the bond between a rider and a dragon was the closest thing to magic these days.

Princess Cion strode towards the door, and Soren fell into step behind her, ducking her head in a familiar act of submission. She had seen enough servants struck because they were 'looking around' too much, despite the order that they were supposed to *also* be constantly vigilant for threats to those they served.

The royal wing was still empty and nearly silent, but as they passed Prince Nell's chambers, Soren could hear the violent retching from within. Princess Cion glanced at the door, and for just a moment, concern flickered across her features. It was quickly replaced by her usual, even calm. Soren didn't dare comment on the prince's illness.

They descended the main stone stairwell that connected the wing to the rest of the palace. Sunlight shone in from tall, arched windows, illuminating the rich material of woven tapestries and colorful rugs. The afternoon light shone off the spotless white marble floors, and the air smelled like jasmine. The palace was a bright, beautiful place.

Even Soren could admit that.

She often wondered if Kelshie was somewhere beautiful, even if she knew it was unlikely. Her elder sister had been sent off to be trained and shoved out onto the battlefield, fighting for the king who had slaughtered their family and friends. And here Soren was, living under the same roof of that very king, serving his house and even becoming friendly with his daughter.

She quickly pushed the thoughts away before they could swallow her whole and stepped into the entrance hall with the princess.

The vast, high ceiling was covered in a mural, a depiction of the goddess Nyx and her consort, Thanatos. For a flash, she looked up and let her gaze catch on the silvery-hued eyes of the gods as they stared down at her, at all of them.

Night and Death personified.

She had always wondered why King Johannas' ancestors had commissioned the two gods in particular to be their watchers. Out of the eight principal gods who reigned in Arcadia, she would have thought Kronos, their king, or Sol, the god of light, would be more popular choices. Still, she always had an appreciation for the mural, despite its general lack of color and brightness.

Before the princess could see, she tore her eyes from the mural and followed her down one of the many winding hallways that branched off from the grand entrance hall. The simple stone corridor they turned down led out to the training yard where Sir Gellings, the princess' personal trainer, was waiting.

The palace guards did not use this yard; instead, it was almost always empty for the princess. Dust from the packed dirt beneath their feet made its way between Soren's toes as she headed to her usual spot.

She perched on a rough wooden stool as the princess picked up a slim sword from the rack of weapons, testing the balance in her hand before she approached Sir Gellings.

The knight, a tall, weathered man with a bald head and scarred face, bowed to the princess, his own heavy sword in hand. As usual, she sighed in irritation at his formalities, and he ignored her mockery.

Quickly, though, the humor left their faces.

Soren watched closely as they began to spar without a word. They moved so *fast*. It reminded her of a deadly dance. She often found herself wishing she could move in such a manner.

Princess Cian won the third round, grinning and breathing heavy as they lowered their weapons.

Sir Gellings voice was a rough bark as he told the princess, "Good. Three laps around the yard."

The princess groaned but did as he said, jogging around the expansive circle. Sir Gellings caught Soren's eye, and his mouth tightened in disapproval, his hazel eyes narrowing. Quickly, she dropped her gaze, looking down at her hands, slightly calloused from work. When she looked up again, the knight stood in front of her, still holding his sword.

"Are you or the princess in need of something, sire?" Soren asked quietly, meekly even. She sounded as she should.

The knight 'smiled,' though it was much more of a cruel grimace. "You were watching us."

Soren's chest tightened. "Yes, sire. I am always watching Her Highness. It is my duty to attend to her needs and, if need be, protect her."

"And have you ever been trained?"

He was laughing at her.

Heat crawled up her neck onto her cheeks. "No, sire," she said, tamping down a sudden urge to lash out. "Not with a blade or a bow."

"But you know other things, don't you?"

Soren froze. This was not something the knight should know—what the queen used her and a few of Princess Cion's handmaids for. Soren had been trained in several arts of the night, but the queen usually called upon her when poison was preferred. She could detect it, identify it, though the queen had never made her use it against someone. Still, Soren knew she was in no way blameless, sure the queen had used Soren's knowledge for hurting others, perhaps even killing them.

She had never been caught, but another girl, Amelea, had been, three seasons ago, and put to the execution block. She was fully aware Queen Lona used her and the other handmaidens as buffers for her own evil-doings. If they were caught, it could be blamed on a rogue slave or servant, not the crown itself.

"I am not stupid, girl," Sir Gellings said in a low voice. "I know many of the handmaidens of this palace are not just that."

Soren looked away, resisting the urge to raise her chin or give any other show of defiance. Silence was likely the best option at the moment.

"Gellings!" Princess Cion called.

The knight turned. "Yes, my princess?"

"Stop harassing Soren and come and train me like you're being paid to do!"

Sir Gellings let out a gruff breath but nodded, his gaze lingering on Soren for a moment longer before he turned.

A few hours later, while Soren and her other handmaidens helped the princess bathe in water scented with fragrant petals and milk, she asked, "What did Sir Gellings want with you, Soren?"

Soren swallowed as she gently poured water over the princess' long, silky black hair. She had to be very careful what she said in reply.

"I think he saw me watching you train," she told the princess, massaging a floral-scented oil into her roots. "He asked if I had any interest in it."

Princess Cion twisted, facing Soren. "And do you?"

A surprised laugh bubbled up, but Soren tamped it down. "Of course not, Your Highness. My duty is to serve you alone."

Mona, Thelia, and Jasmen all eyed Soren warily. They must have lacked discreteness, because Princess Cion noticed and said to all of them, "You're not in trouble, Soren. I was just curious."

"Of course, Your Highness," Soren murmured, rinsing the rest of the soap and oil from her hair.

Once the princess was done bathing and the water was drained, Soren and Mona went to retrieve Princess Cion's dinner while Thelia helped her dress.

As soon as they were alone, Mona hissed, "What was that about?"

Soren pressed her lips together. "The knight who trains the princess, Sir Gellings—he knows. About what Her Majesty has us do. He inquired about it today."

Mona's eyes widened. "You need to tell Her Majesty. *Immediately.*"

"The knight is important to the princess," Soren murmured. "You know what will happen to him if I say anything."

"Do you want to be caught?" Mona whispered harshly. "Do you want to be blamed for—"

"No!" Soren whispered harshly. "Of course not."

"You care too much for them." Mona's voice was barely a whisper. The words were dangerous, and they both knew it. "Remember who they are. Remember what they have *done.*"

Soren glanced at the closed door to the prince's chambers down the hall as Mona's words washed over her. Sudden, cold fury overwhelmed her; of course she remembered. They were trapped in the kingdom of a tyrant king who had overreached. And when Prince Nell eventually rose to power, she knew it would only get worse. It would almost be better if he died now and Princess Cion or her sister took the throne.

She would stop it if she could, but she was powerless. They all were.

"We should get her dinner," Soren said, voice flat.

She suddenly felt so numb, so devoid of emotion. Defeat did that to a person, she supposed.

"Yes, we should, and—"

But Mona cut herself off as Hector practically stumbled from the prince's chambers, his eyes bloodshot and wide, his lips pale. Both Soren and Mona stilled when they saw his dazed expression.

"Hector," Soren said, taking a step forward, holding out a tentative hand. He was trembling so hard, each breath was audible. "What is it?"

"He's gone," Hector breathed, not looking at them but at the night sky beyond. "The gods took him."

Soren froze, her hand midair, and Mona muttered, "Holy gods."

Hector shut his eyes, taking a shuddering breath before insisting, "Forget I said that. You cannot know. No one can, not yet."

"I thought it was merely an ailment of the stomach," Mona whispered.

Soren cleared her throat then tugged on Mona's hand and said in a voice steadier than she felt, "We need to retrieve the princess' dinner. She will wonder what is taking so long."

Hector cleared his throat. "Yes, you should go. And not a word to the others, either of you. I'm going to notify His

Majesty, but I'm sure he'll want discreteness for as long as possible."

The two of them hurried away from the hall, where Hector was opening the supply closet and retrieving a clean sheet.

She and Mona took their usual route, cutting through a servant's passage and crossing the laundry chamber before entering the kitchens. Wordlessly, they retrieved the princess' tray, neither of them looking at each other nor anyone else.

By the time they had returned to the royal wing, Hector was gone, the door shut again. But now, there was commotion inside the prince's room as they passed. Soren could hear the voices and the sounds of people shuffling about. Hector must have informed the king and queen.

When they entered Princess Cion's chamber, her eyes were shining and wide, her brow pinched with concern as she wrung her hands in her lap.

"What is happening?" she asked as Soren set her dinner on the small table by the balcony doors. "I heard people running in the hall to Nells' room."

Soren did not say anything, but Mona's hands shook as she poured the princess a silver goblet of red wine. Outside in the hall, the sound of someone wailing pierced the air, and Princess Cion rose to her feet immediately.

On some protective instinct, Soren moved in front of the door, blocking the princess' way.

"Let me through, Soren," Princess Cion said in a hard voice.

Thelia glanced at Mona in confusion as Soren said, "I think you may want to wait, Your Highness."

"Soren. Move. *Now*," the princess ordered, her eyes shining with unshed tears.

Soren had no choice but to step aside.

The princess stepped out into the hallway, her steps slow and tentative. It reminded Soren of when she was on the defense during training. She sensed danger and was preparing to handle it, except that this was not the kind of danger one could run from or fight.

"Should we follow?" Mona said softly.

Soren met the other handmaiden's blue eyes—Misean eyes—and nodded once. Thalia and Jasmen lingered in the bedchamber, nervously twisting their hands in the fabric of their dresses. Soren and Mona stepped into the hallway just as Princess Cion pushed the half-open door to the prince's bedchambers wide.

"Out!" Soren heard the queen shriek from inside. "Out! Get her out now!"

Soren rushed forward without thinking, running to the princess' side just as she stumbled back into the hallway, averting her eyes from what surely lay inside. But just before the guards closed the door, a tug in her chest had her looking up.

The prince was indeed dead.

His skin was paper-white, stretched over his face too tightly, his mouth twisted in a gruesome expression that looked like a silent scream. Wide open, his lifeless eyes were bloodshot and strained, nearly popping out of his head. And on his brow, there was a strange mark. It looked like it had been inked on with midnight ash, contrasting sharply against his pale skin.

The door shut, and Princess Cion fell to her knees in the

hallway. Soren caught her as she collapsed, shaking with silent sobs. As she stroked the princess' dark hair back from her forehead in soothing, calming motions, she realized why she had recognized the mark.

She had seen it just today, in the entrance hall, on the ceiling. It was the same mark that sat upon Thanatos' head. A moon, broken apart by a blade.

Nyx's mark.

Prince Nell of Aren had been claimed for death by the goddess of night herself.

CHAPTER 2

GENTLY, Soren guided Princess Cion out of the hallway and back to her chambers. Mona and Thelia had already made the bed, and Jasmen coaxed the princess into the soft piles of pillows and fresh sheets as if she were a child.

Once she was settled beneath the blankets, she stared up at Soren and said in a crackling voice, "Soren, I want you to bring Lady Anabeth."

Soren furrowed her brow. "The scribe's daughter, Your Highness?"

Princess Cion nodded, her lower lip trembling. "Please, Soren. Do this for me. Find her."

Soren bowed her head, not questioning the request further, especially not now. "Yes, Your Highness. I'll return with the lady as soon as I am able."

Princess Cion said nothing; she just sank deeper into the pillows. With a quick glance at the others, Soren hurried from the room. She had no idea where Lady Anabeth was or why the princess wanted to see her. She knew the two were friends, but they had never seemed particularly close. She must have read their relationship wrong, though, if the princess wanted her in a moment such as this.

She tried the library first, only finding Master June, Lady Anabeth's father. His head was bent over a thick record book, and he was making tiny marks next to what looked like scrawled names. He looked up as she approached, his brown eyes a liquid hazel in the candlelight, wire glasses perched on his long nose, his simple linen robes rustling as he stood.

"How may I help you?" he asked in a soft-spoken voice.

Soren bowed her head. "Master, I come with a request from Princess Cion."

Master June's expression did not change. He simply nodded. "I believe my daughter is currently in her chambers."

Soren paused, hesitating. The master seemed to be aware of whatever was between his daughter and the princess.

He must have seen the terseness in her expression, because he said simply, "It is not my story to tell, Soren."

She met his kind eyes, her own rounding. She knew who he was, but that he knew her by name was odd. There were hundreds of servants in the palace, and she was no one of note.

He stood, offering her a hand. "You are surprised I know who you are."

Tentatively, she took it, so surprised at the interaction that she blurted out without thinking, "Yes, Master. I am."

His lips twitched. "The goddess Nyx marked our late prince tonight. You saw the mark, did you not?"

Unease stirred low in her gut, but she whispered, "Yes. How did you know?"

He lifted a shoulder. "You know how information spreads within these walls. Like a blazing fire." He paused, searching her eyes with a sad expression she did not understand before adding, "The gods of Arcadia abandoned us many years ago. It is curious that such a mark should appear at all."

She bit her lower lip, worrying it between her teeth. The candle on his desk flickered, wavering and casting shadows around the library.

"I suppose so," she said after a moment. Then, remembering her task, she pulled back her hand and curtsied low. "I should be going, Master. The princess awaits."

"Yes, of course," he said.

She turned, but as she did, he said quietly, "Memory is such a strange, fickle thing. Pay mind to those dreams you have."

Soren froze then turned slowly and looked back at the scribe. "My dreams, Master?"

His eyes twinkled in the flickering light. "Nothing of consequence, Soren. Not yet, it seems. You should go retrieve Ana."

His words did nothing to put her at ease, but she bowed and left, heading to Lady Anabeth's chambers.

As she walked, her mind raced. How did the master know about her dreams? They had haunted her nearly every night for as long as she could recall. She hardly remembered them when she woke, usually only an image or lingering feeling. The dreams were not memories, at least not her own. In the privacy of her mind, she had always surmised the dreams were pieces of someone else's life, as foolish as she knew that likely was.

All throughout the palace, servants and lords alike hurried with their heads down and their faces grim. It seemed Master June had been right about one thing: the news of Prince Nell's death had spread quickly.

When Soren reached Lady Anabeth's chambers, she stopped in front of the wooden door and knocked twice, announcing, "A request from the princess, my lady."

The door swung open almost immediately to reveal Lady Anabeth in an orange silk night robe. Her black hair hung in a sheet of silky strands down her back, and brown, slanted eyes pierced Soren's gaze, a single brow raising. It was a shade unnerving, how intently the lady looked at her, as if she could see right through Soren.

"Yes?" she asked in a light, delicate voice.

Soren swallowed. "Her Highness Princess Cion requests your presence in her chambers."

"Why?"

Soren shifted nervously as Lady Anabeth smoothed her long fingers over the robe. Her red-painted nails gleamed, catching the candlelight.

"It is not my place to say, my lady."

Lady Anabeth pressed her lips together in a thin line but nodded. "Give me a moment."

She turned, shutting the door before Soren could give a reply. When it opened again a few minutes later, Lady Anabeth was wearing a soft purple day dress, and slippers clad her previously bare feet.

They began to walk side by side in silence until Lady Anabeth asked, "How did you find me?"

"Oh." Soren cleared her throat. "I asked your father, Master June. I apologize for the intrusion at this hour, but this is a rather…serious matter."

"Ah," Lady Anabeth said, watching as a few other servants hurried by, one of them crying softly. "And you still refuse to tell me what this 'serious matter' is?"

Soren took a deep breath, calming the anxiety churning in her stomach. "I think it would be best if the princess spoke to you about it, my lady."

They entered the royal wing, and Lady Anabeth stopped short as she saw the people gathered around the closed door to the prince's chambers. Her hand raised to her throat, fingers tracing over a thin gold chain that dipped below the neckline of her dress.

"Come, my lady," Soren said softly.

Lady Anabeth's voice was thin as she replied, "Alright."

Soren led her the rest of the way down the quiet hall to the princess' chambers and knocked once before opening the door. "Your Highness, I have returned with Lady Anabeth."

The door was flung open, and Mona came into view, her voice frantic as she said to Soren, "I need your help. Now."

Soren glanced at Lady Anabeth, whose delicate face had paled. They both hurried inside to find the bed chamber empty.

"Thelia is with her. They're on the balcony," Mona told them.

Soren's breath caught, the hairs on her neck raising. If she understood Mona correctly, if the princess jumped from that balcony…

They would all be dead too, but not before being

punished in the most severe manner possible for letting the princess do such a thing.

"What is happening?" Lady Anabeth demanded now, the panic in her voice mirroring Soren's.

"Ana?"

They all turned as Princess Cion spoke. She stood in the doorway to the balcony, her nightgown floating around her, making her look ghostly in the moonlight. Behind her, Thelia mouthed something, but Soren could only make out one word.

Jump.

Lady Anabeth rushed forward, and Princess Cion did too, her body crumpling as she fell into her arms. She sobbed, and Lady Anabeth stroked her hair just as Soren had done in the hall not so long ago. But there was something different about the way Lady Anabeth held the princess, something tender and intimate.

"Shhh, Cion," Lady Anabeth murmured. "It's alright, I'm here. I'm always here."

"H-he's d-d-dead!" Princess Cion gasped. "And now I am—" She cut herself off, shaking her head.

Soren's eyes widened as she realized it. She had been so preoccupied with retrieving Lady Anabeth, she hadn't even thought of what tonight truly meant for the princess.

Now, Princess Cion was the heir to the throne of Aren.

The realization hit Soren like a blow to the stomach, and she felt for a moment as if her lungs were robbed of air. What would happen now? Princess Cion *had* to bond with a dragon. That much was clear from the prophecy. But would King Johannas send his heir into the dangers of the war?

She realized another harsh truth as she watched Lady

Anabeth hold the princess. The princess would be expected to marry and produce heirs for the royal bloodline now. Whatever this was between her and the scribe's daughter would have to end, or at least change.

Suddenly, the princess' tears and panic made more sense. She was not just mourning a brother, who had mostly been absent, a neutral figure at best to her.

She was mourning a *life*.

"You may leave us," Lady Anabeth said, looking around at Soren, Mona, Jasmen, and Thelia. "Go to your quarters for the night and do not return until morning."

"Yes, my lady," they all murmured, curtsying low before hurrying out of the chamber. None of them spoke, not until they reached the servant's hall.

When they arrived in the dim cold of the quarters, they were surrounded by several other staff, all asking the same thing.

"Is he dead?"

Thelia and Jasmen slipped away to their room before they were forced to answer.

Mona glanced at Soren, who took a short breath and told them, "He's gone. I saw it with my own eyes. Now, leave us be."

The others cleared away, and Mona followed Soren to the cramped room they shared. It contained but two narrow wooden beds and one tall, worn dresser by the doorway that held their clothing. A narrow window hung between their beds, looking out upon a courtyard where kitchen shipments were received. They usually kept the curtains drawn.

As soon as they were alone, Mona said sharply, "You

shouldn't have told them the prince is dead. It wasn't your place."

"They'll know anyways come morning," Soren replied wearily, beginning to fumble with the ties of her wrap dress.

Mona looked sidelong at her and said, very quietly, "We need to keep a low profile. All of us. The king will be on edge."

Soren knew just who 'we' meant.

All the Misean servants were children who had been brought up as slaves in the palace, with minimal memories of their home kingdom. But King Johannas was always on the lookout for reasons to punish them, especially when he was in a mood. The next few weeks were bound to be dangerous, for them especially.

"I know," Soren said quietly.

Even as she kept her face neutral and her voice calm, inside, she felt as though she wanted to scream.

Traitor.

The word repeated itself in her head like a terrible mantra. Somewhere out there, her true people were fighting tooth and nail to keep their kingdom from Aren's grasp in a war that had carried on for decades.

When the gods abandoned them over a century ago, Aren had fallen into a great drought. As a mountain kingdom with a drier climate, only magic had once kept their crops from dying. When it was gone, the food supply quickly dwindled. Mise's land remained fertile and lush as it had always been. But when King Hammod of Mise refused to aid Aren, knowing full well his smaller kingdom could not support the enormous beast, King Johannas took it as an act of war. He decided if Mise would not give, Aren would take.

And take, they did.

The war had been going on for nearly thirty years now. Mise still stood only because the neighboring desert kingdom of Meesling had agreed to aid their military effort in exchange for a marriage alliance, and likely a share of resources along with it. Even so, from what Soren had heard, both Mise and Meesling were barely holding the line.

She pushed away the thoughts of war and her own betrayal, though. They were too overwhelming, and the helplessness she felt when she let them sink in helped no one.

So instead, she let her mind calm and mechanically pulled off her dress, tugging on a coarse nightgown. Silently, across the room, Mona did the same. They took turns in the tiny bathing chamber, and then Soren settled into her bed. Mona blew out the single, waning candle atop the dresser, plunging the room into cool darkness.

Just before Soren fell asleep, Mona whispered, "Be smart as you have always been, Soren. Do not let the events of tonight turn your head to any grand notions."

"Don't worry," Soren muttered sleepily. "My hope died a very long time ago."

In the morning, she and Mona rose at dawn, as usual, then hurried to the royal wing. When they arrived, all was quiet. It was almost *too* quiet.

Thelia and Jasmen were already at Princess Cion's door, waiting with her breakfast. They stayed in a different wing of the palace; the Misean servants were kept separate from the others.

"Have you gone in yet?" Soren murmured to Thelia, who shook her head, an odd, amused expression tugging at her lips.

It was then Soren realized why they were waiting. The sound of soft, feminine moans came from the princess' chambers. A few moments passed, and the moans grew louder. Jasmen clapped a hand over her mouth to keep the giggles from escaping as Mona glanced at Soren, her brows raised.

Soren sighed then said to them all in a harsh whisper, "Not a word about this to the queen or king, even if they were to ask. We serve Princess Cion first."

Three pairs of eyes darted her way.

Mona was the first to nod and reply, "Of course."

Thelia and Jasmen quickly made quiet noises of agreement. Then Jasmen, in that soft-spoken, wary of hers, asked, "Should we knock? Before someone else hears them?"

Soren took a deep breath, worrying her lip between her teeth before saying, "I think we should."

They all looked at each other until Soren muttered, "Alright, fine. I'll do it." She gave three sharp raps on the door and announced, "Your Highness, it's Soren and the others. We are here to dress you."

The moaning abruptly stopped. After nearly a minute, the door cracked open, and a rosy-faced Princess Cion appeared behind it.

"Apologies, Your Highness," Soren said. "We…wanted to give you privacy but also needed to warn you others in this wing are likely to wake soon."

Princess Cion's mouth tilted to the side in a half-smile. Despite the events of last night, it seemed Lady Anabeth was able to lift the princess' spirits.

"I understand, Soren. There's no need to worry, though."

She stepped back, allowing them in. Lady Anabeth was brushing her long hair, examining her features in the mirror as Soren stepped inside the chamber. She hardly gave the handmaidens a glance, as if unconcerned by their presence.

Soren busied herself readying the oils and milk for the princess' bath while Mona, Thelia, and Jasmen served her breakfast and pulled back the curtains.

A knock sounded on the door, and Soren hurried to answer it. A boy, probably about thirteen, stood there, two full pails of steaming water in his arms.

"Water for the princess' bath, miss," he said in a trembling voice.

She nodded curtly, reaching out. "Thank you. I'll take the buckets from here."

"Are you sure, miss? They're heavy," he said, his pale blue eyes earnest.

"I'm sure." She paused, examining him. "Are you new? I've never seen you before."

The boy hesitated but replied, "Yes, miss."

Soren feigned a soft smile then leaned in and murmured, "Don't try to run. They'll catch you and kill you before you can even beg for your life, understand?"

She pulled back, still smiling as she took the pails of hot

water. The boy's eyes were wide, but he only bobbed his head and hurried away down the hall.

She shut the door, Mona eyeing her suspiciously as she hauled the buckets to the bathing chamber. Thelia helped her carefully pour the water into the bath, Jasmine adding the oils, milk, and rare honeytwine flower petals. The flower was said to have originally come from Arcadia, the land of the gods. If the legend was true, they were one of the last relics of an age quickly fading into the past.

Mona and Jasmen helped Princess Cion out of her silken robe and into the bath. Soren, who always washed the princess' hair, poured soap from a glass bottle into her hand before gently massaging it into Princess Cion's scalp.

"I want you all to know," Princess Cion began, tilting her head back, "I am alright. I know last night may have frightened you. It frightened me too. But I refuse to be afraid."

"Will you still ride?" Thelia blurted out. "Now that you're Aren's heir?"

Mona shot her sharp look, but Princess Cion only sighed heavily. "I will. The prophecy said I must, and even my father cannot deny such a hand of fate. I will likely serve my duty in the war effort and then return to take the throne when the time is right."

"I see," Thelia said. "Apologies, Your Highness, if I was too direct."

Princess Cion chuckled. "Do not worry, Thelia. I'm not about to report you to my mother."

Thelia bowed her head slightly in thanks, but Soren saw her hands shake before she could steady them.

"Princess," Soren began quietly. "Should we keep word of your relationship with Lady Anabeth discreet as of now?"

Again, the princess sighed. "For now. And Soren," she turned, water dripping from her now-rinsed hair, "my Choosing ceremony is in a week. It will occur, even with my brother's passing, and I'd like you to attend to me as we travel to the temple and afterwards."

Soren blinked. "You… Do you mean to say you would like me to stay with you once you enlist and begin your service?"

"If that's alright?" Princess Cion said, raising a brow.

Soren cleared her throat. "Of course, Your Highness. I serve you wherever you wish to go. I am just surprised is all. Honored, but surprised."

Princess Cion twisted back around in the bath and reached for a bar of honey-lemon soap, this time speaking to them all. "I value all your aid and the work you do for me. I hope there are no hard feelings amongst you given my choice for Soren to come with me. I will be back someday, and then soon, you will be serving not just a princess, but a queen."

Mona, Thelia, and Jasmen all smiled and bowed their heads, but Soren could see the envy in Thelia and Jasmen's eyes. Mona, on the other hand, looked like she was concealing poorly hidden relief. Soren thought she knew why.

She had been chosen to aid the princess while she fulfilled her duty as a rider, fighting for Aren. She would have to be close to Misean soldiers. She might even have to stand by and watch them die, and, if needed, she would be required to protect the princess from them.

Heaviness already weighed on her at the task ahead.

Princess Cion finished washing, and then they helped her into a heavy, midnight-black mourning dress, the fabric so different from her usual wear. The thickness of the material was an Arenean tradition—a cage to keep sorrow in the body and a shield to ward off spirits as they passed.

Soren affixed a veil in front of the princess' face, Lady Anabeth watching closely from her seat by the vanity.

"I feel like a ghost," Princess Cion said quietly, slowly turning as she eyed herself in the mirror.

"You look beautiful," Lady Anabeth said sternly. "And remember, you hold much of the power now. You are their heir."

Princess Cion sucked in a sharp breath, clasping her hands in front of her. "I'm ready."

Soren and the others bowed their heads as they trailed after the princess. When they emerged into the hall, each and every servant and slave they passed did the same. Whether they truly felt any sorrow for the late prince or not, there remained a heaviness in the air. Much of it was probably an act, but here, they did not have a choice. Submission meant survival.

Princess Cion walked down the length of the royal wing, her head held high. Several highborn ladies stopped as she passed, bowing and whispering condolences. She ignored them all, keeping her expression fixed and stern under the veil.

They walked with her all the way to the Great Hall, where King Johannas and Queen Lona waited on the heavy, gold-rimmed thrones lined with spears said to have once belonged to Kronos himself. A shiver raced up Soren's spine as she eyed them.

She thought it would have been terrifying to live at a time when the gods still walked the mortal realm freely, when the dragons came into being, forged by Vulcan, the god of fire, their seed of life from Sol himself. What was even more terrifying was that King Johannas came from a line that *had* lived in a time akin to that. His father, the princess' grandfather, had lived when magic from the gods still existed. The previous king had seen mortals hold the power of magic, had once held a piece of that power himself. The king's crown was even crafted into jagged streaks, reminding them all of what his bloodline could do.

Lightning had been his father's magical affinity many years ago. Soren supposed the crown was a reminder of the power his family once held, a reminder to all of who they dared tally with if they disobeyed the king.

The king and queen wore the same traditional black mourning clothes as the princess. Soren had once heard the thin veils over women's faces were not just to keep away ill spirits but also meant to conceal their tears.

The queen's eyes were red-rimmed, but her midnight hair was swept back from her face and under the veil, her makeup flawless as ever. The king's face was set in grim determination as the princess approached. Various lords and ladies lingered in the alcoves and balconies around the room, watching and waiting. Even little Princess Chelsa, the youngest royal at only nine, stood just below the dais, trying not to fidget.

Princess Cion bowed low in front of her parents. Soren,

Mona, Thelia, and Jasmen lowered to their knees, lingering just behind her, watching and waiting, always. They were Princess Cion's ladies to the grave, and through forced loyalty and conditioned fierceness, they protected her. Soren would not admit, even in the quiet of her own mind, that her devotion to the princess extended beyond any conditions of enslavement or servitude.

The king raised a hand, indicating for them to rise. As Soren stood, she caught a glimpse of the above, where Nyx and Thanatos gazed down upon them from the painted ceiling, surrounded by star-speckled heavens and half-moons in which godlings hung and frolicked. But as soon as her gaze caught on Thanatos' brow, she quickly looked away. If she was caught lingering too long—if anyone was now—there would be grave consequences. She was sure the king took the mark as a personal message, and anyone who dared to question the occurrence would find themselves without a head.

Ahead, the king gazed across his throne room, a flat expression on his face. He never showed any awe over the grandeur spread before him—never seemed to behold the gleaming marble floors or the enormous pillars coated in creeping ivy or even stop a moment to enjoy the master-piece painted above them. Instead, he merely sat smugly atop the throne. Still, Soren had noticed the way he tended to grip the handrests. It was as if he was afraid someone was going to rip the power from him at any moment.

When his eyes finally landed on the princess, he said in a booming voice, "Speak, daughter."

Princess Cion took a short breath, too audible in the still, quiet air of the hall. She needed to keep her nerves at bay. Each soul here was watching, waiting for her to rise or fall in the wake of her brother's death.

"My king," she began. "I come with a request."

The princess knew King Johannas was well aware of what she wanted. Everyone in this room, including Soren herself, knew that. But she was purposely feeding him power to appease him, at least at first. Even amongst members of the royal family itself, there were games to be played.

"Continue," the king said, quieter now, though nothing about his tone was gentle.

Princess Cion lifted her chin slightly, just enough to display her own bit of power. "When I was a child, one of the revered Sisters of Arcane prophesied I was destined to be a warrior, to ride astride the greatest beasts to ever grace the sky. All I ask now is that I am allowed to fulfill this destiny."

King Johannas sat back in the throne, his brow narrowing. "You are not ill-witted, daughter. I know this to be true. So, I ask: why even make the request?"

Princess Cion's nostrils flared slightly, and Soren tensed.

Hold your temper, princess, she thought. *Do not play into his mockery.*

"I request this," the princess began evenly, "because even royals such as us cannot change the winds of fate. They will direct us to where we are meant to be, no matter how we might try and resist."

"So you think me a fool?"

The princess bowed her head again. "No, my king."

King Johannas paused, and the room held its breath.

Perhaps this was it, the moment the warrior princess of Aren simply became the 'heir.'

"I will allow you to undergo the Choosing ceremony and live out your 'fate' as a warrior," the king finally said. "But after you serve your allotted three years in your station, you will return to begin formal training as my heir."

Soren watched disappointment flood Princess Cion's features then promptly disappear. It was carefully practiced, the immediate concealment of her emotions. The princess knew she would be a fool not to take her father's offer, as no others would likely come from his lips.

She lowered her eyes to the floor. "Thank you, Father."

The king stood abruptly, and so did anyone else seated in the hall. He gave Princess Cion a hard look before sweeping off the dais into the council room behind the Great Hall.

His command was clear: *Follow.*

Princess Cion's throat clicked audibly next to Soren. This was far from over. Still, she kept her head held high as she strode towards the heavy door. Queen Lona stepped off the dais, immediately surrounded by her own ladies. She caught Soren's eye for a brief moment.

Soren knew what it meant without any further indication or words. The queen was in need of her services. Her throat tightened at the prospect, but she set the fear aside for later. She would go to the queen in her chamber tonight, perhaps while Princess Cion was dining.

Little Princess Chelsa eyed her sister's handmaidens curiously, as she always did, her gaze lingering on Soren the longest, as it always had.

Soren had no idea why the small princess was so interested in them. She was proper in a way all mothers of high society longed for their daughters to be. With long, dark tresses perfectly waved with hot irons each morning and fine silk dresses she slipped into without ever fussing, she was the definition of prim.

Soren often heard other servants, even Misean slaves, talking sweetly about the princess. And truthfully, Soren could not fault a child for the bloody war that raged hundreds of miles away. She would be a monster and a fool to do so. Then again, plenty of men in power let their hot-headed anger rule their decisions. It had always seemed odd to Soren that politics were the one place women were sparse in, that *they* were the ones said to be too emotional.

The sweet-faced princess swept past her, led away by a nanny and paraded out of the hall. With her, Soren let all wild thoughts of politics and battle and passion drift away too. She needed to focus.

Soren and the other handmaidens reached the door, and Princess Cion turned. Out of the group of her most trusted ladies, only one of them would be allowed in as her cupbearer. Who the princess chose always signified trust and who held the most of it currently. Soren had never been chosen in the past, though in fairness, there had not been many occasions. But now, the princess looked straight at her, green eyes filled with intent.

"Soren," she murmured. "Come inside."

Soren bowed her head immediately in thanks, as was the custom, before stepping ahead and pushing the heavy door open for the princess. Once they were both inside, Soren paused. She had never stepped into the small council chamber before, but it was as opulent as she had imagined.

Chairs made of soft, woven wood lined a long table, both made from rare Golden Nectar trees, said to have originally come from Arcadia. The surface of the table was covered in a long runner of turquoise-stained silk and laden with silver goblets and pitchers of sweet berry wine.

The large, arched window looked out across the cliffs beyond, creating a dizzying effect. It felt oddly as if she were standing on the edge of the world as she glanced outside. And perhaps, in a way, she was. This was the room where decisions that had caused the deaths of thousands of her people occurred. Now, it would be the room where the princess' life was surely to change forever, though Soren had little idea of how.

"Sit, Cion," the king said, taking a spot in his own chair at the head of the table.

The princess perched delicately a few seats away from him, leaving room for the masters of coin, war, and trade closer to the king. Royal guards stood on either side of the door as it shut, their long, curved swords readied for any dangers that might lurk nearby. Their capes were a gleaming shade of jade, pressed with the royal crest: a rare Vemon dragon eclipsing the sun. It was a great symbol of power, as Vemon were the largest, and often most powerful, of their kind. It was fitting, she supposed, for the biggest kingdom on the continent. After all, Aren held eleven districts within its borders, whereas Mise held only five and Meesling three.

"There is more to this agreement," King Johannas began.

Princess Cion was ramrod straight in her chair, and Soren, with the other slaves and servants, kept to the shadows at the edges of the room, only stepping forward if wine was requested.

"I understand, Father," the princess replied quietly. "Will you expand?"

The king chuckled dryly. The sound sent a small shiver up Soren's spine.

"You have always been the most headstrong and passionate of my children," he said thoughtfully. "Which makes for a good warrior. You will do well on the battlefield, especially once you are astride a dragon."

"But?" Princess Cion dared, raising a single, sculpted brow.

Soren curled her fingers into a fist, hating that she cared what the king said next. She *wanted* to loathe these people, but she had known the princess since they were children, serving her since they were practically just playmates. And now, Princess Cion Livii, with her easy smiles and snarky quips, was going to ride into battle and murder hundreds of Soren's people astride whatever terrifying beast chose her.

For the briefest of moments, King Johannas paused, and in the hush of that breath, his gaze dragged over to the shadows where Soren stood. His amber-speckled eyes narrowed as they snagged on her.

Soren had never considered herself remarkable, and she had done her best to never catch the eye of the king. Up until this moment, she had been invisible, but she wondered what he saw as he looked at her now.

Like most from Mise, she had tawny skin that grew a shade darker in the heat of the summertime. She was short and slight but not overly muscular, since her work for the princess was not particularly labor-intensive. Her clothing was simple, just twisted pieces of fabric that crossed over her torso and fell to her bare ankles. The only adornments she was allowed were the small bronze studs in her ears and the single, gold-tinted ring in her nose, and even that was only permitted because she served in the royal household. None of her jewelry or clothing was truly fine; it was made to look presentable to reflect properly on those she served, but at the end of the day, she was often left with ripped bits of fabric she had mend herself or tarnish on her nose ring.

The only feature that had ever pinned her as different was her silver hair, tucked back into two long braids. A birth defect, she had been told by her parents.

Even so, there was no reason for King Johannas to be looking at her, but there was no mistaking the heavy weight of his attention. When the king singled a person out, they knew it, and it was almost never a good thing.

Soren resisted the urge to duck her chin or shift her feet. It would be over soon, and he would look away. She was nothing and no one, simply another orphan picked up from a burning village in Mise. There were many who had come before her and many who would surely come after her if this war continued the way it was.

King Johannas did look away, and she was entirely certain the whole exchange only lasted a few seconds, even if it felt much longer. Still, those brief moments left a feeling of acrid heaviness behind, as if his fathomless stare had been branded into her very being. She tamped down her fear as he began to speak again.

"But you are my heir now. That comes with certain duties and responsibilities, including marriage."

Princess Cion opened her mouth, but the king lifted his

hand before she could speak. "I have let you carry on for too long, Cion, like a child with a plaything they have outgrown. It is time to take on your true responsibilities as a member of the royal household."

"Father, please—"

"Perhaps, if you were not such an essential piece in carrying on the royal bloodline, you could dally as you pleased with scribe's daughters. But this is your role, Cion."

Soren watched the princess' face slowly drain of color at the mention of Lady Anabeth, but she said nothing this time, letting her father continue.

"This is what will occur, my daughter. You will attend the coming Choosing ceremony and bond to a dragon. Your term as a rider will run three years, or until you are injured in any matter of severity. Upon that time, you will return here and marry Prince Kellmere Hale, heir to the throne of Meesling. Your dragon can remain in the capital if it wishes."

Soren could not help the small puff of air that escaped her. Several other servants in the room had similar reactions. Prince Kellmere was currently engaged to Princess Hessa of Mise. The marriage pact was a large part of the reason Mise still held any real chance against Aren and their dragons.

Meesling had wyverns in their ranks. They were smaller than Aren's dragons, and there were fewer of them, but without Meesling's support, without their extra resources and wyverns, Mise was lost. King Johannas had to know this. King Nektas, Prince Kellmere's father and Meesling's king, had to know this, which meant Soren was privy to a secret betrayal.

To her credit, Princess Cion did not react with much

shock or surprise. Perhaps she was just used to her father carrying out such acts of cruelty.

She bowed her head and said in a low voice that was anything but submissive, "As you wish, *my king*."

Soren knew the princess well enough to know this fight was far from over. She wondered if King Johannas knew that too. By the tick in his strong jaw, Soren ventured to guess so.

"Know," the king said as he stood, his gravelly voice thick with the promise of violence, "that if any one of you spills the secrets laid out in this room today before they are ripe to the world, you will not simply be executed."

And with his threat hanging in the air, he swept from the room, his heeled boots clicking against the stone floor. The other small council members stood too, and for a brief moment, Soren memorized their faces.

The Master of Coin, a small man with a white goatee, tiny circular glasses, and quizzical brow. The Master of War, with his hulking form, shining bald head, and terrifying thin-lipped smile. The Master of Trade, with his opulent jewels, long black braid, and sparkling green eyes. They were as much responsible as King Johannas for what was sure to be the end of the war. Someday, if Soren was ever free, she might describe these men to an assassin. It was a fool's dream to even hope for freedom now.

Not ever before today.

But *now*.

Now, with her kingdom's princess in danger where she stayed in Meesling, unaware of the end of her engagement. Now, with the coming end of the war and the taste of defeat a bitter sting on her tongue. Now, she finally felt something after years of numbness.

The dream ended, though, the moment Princess Cion said, "Come, Soren."

Soren dipped her head, reality crashing down upon her in violent waves. She was no warrior, no spy or assassin.

She was what these people had made her.

Nothing at all.

CHAPTER 3

THE THIN WHITE veil obscured her vision. She hated it, but she hated the man looking at her through it even more.

"You've grown to look like your mother," the god king said dryly.

She lifted her gaze to his crackling amber eyes. "Does that bring back memories?"

Kronos' jaw tightened, and he stood to his full height, looking down on her with a sneer. "I prefer my betrothed to not have an attitude."

"Well, I prefer not to be here."

His hand struck her cheek before she could even blink again, quick as a bolt of lightning. She bit off a cry as she stumbled back. Blood stained the veil as she ripped it from her face. Kronos looked at her blankly, his eyes flat and his face expressionless once more.

"You're dismissed."

She narrowed her eyes but did not give him the dignity of a reply or a bow, fleeing the throne room as quickly as her feet would carry her. When she was finally free of the palace grounds, she broke into a run, heading for the barrier. She didn't stop when she reached it, leaping through the shimmering wall of magic and landing in a heap in mortal lands.

She wept in a farmer's field until nearly sunset.

For nearly a full moon cycle, this repeated. Kronos called on her, claiming he needed to 'examine' his promised bride. Her mother, not wanting to incur the wrath of him or Sol, sent her. Each time, she mouthed off to Kronos, and each time, he struck her. She healed quickly, but the reminder of the power he held over her cut deep.

She didn't understand why her mother bowed to such a king. Nyx was just as responsible for the entire realm's existence as her brother.

Perhaps it was her father's fault. It was laughable to think a power like Death would make one weak, though in the end, she knew it wasn't power or life or death.

It was love.

Perhaps her marriage to Kronos was part-blessing, because she would never love her future husband.

As her tears dried, she vowed this would be the last time she wept in this field. It was childish and soft and—

"You're not invisible in this field, you know."

She startled, looking up. A man towered over her, his face partly obscured by the sun. She scrambled to stand, but he crouched down to stop her, reaching out but not touching her. The thoughtfulness in that simple lack of contact struck her to her core. He could have assumed she wanted or needed to be touched by him, but instead, he thought to pause.

"Don't. I shouldn't have bothered you."

Backlit, she still couldn't quite see his face, but there was something off about his aura...

This man was no mere mortal. He couldn't be. All magic had a presence, even amongst humankind, but he was not buzzing with it as most did, no.

He was aflame.

CHAPTER 4

Soren awoke with a jolt, lying frozen in bed for a few hazy moments before rising at the soft knock on the door of her and Mona's quarters.

The dreams were worsening with each night.

When she was very young, she had once told her mother she was dreaming of the gods. She had only patted Soren on the cheek and assured her it was only natural for her imagination to wander to what was greater. But now, as the dreams grew more persistent and vivid, she began to wonder if it *was* something more. Perhaps a goddess from beyond the barrier dividing their worlds was somehow sending her visions?

It was a foolish thought, one she tamped down swiftly. If the dreams were becoming stronger, she just had to become better at ignoring it all when she woke.

When she opened the door a crack, a servant whispered, "Her Majesty the Queen requires your service, Soren."

She held back an audible curse; she had completely forgotten about her summons earlier in the throne room.

Ignoring the hot flare of unease, she forced herself to reply, "I will make my way to her now."

She quickly donned slippers and a thin robe before hurrying through the halls, her practiced footfalls near-silent. When she reached the queen's chambers, she knocked twice, tapping on the wood with her fingernails.

"Enter, Soren," the queen murmured from the other side.

Soren obeyed, standing in front of the queen, who still lay in bed. She bowed low, strands of silver falling in her face.

"My queen, how may I assist you?"

The queen sighed. She was still wearing her mourning garb, even as she lay in bed. "Do not fret; it is not an errand. It will only take a moment."

"Yes, my queen," Soren said, her head still low. "How can I be of help?"

"Rise, Soren, and come. I am in need of your gift."

Soren did so, approaching the queen carefully. On the bedside table sat two vials, identical in color and each in a silk cloth.

"Which one?" the queen asked, her voice soft but firm.

Soren's lips parted in a rush of air, nodding and placing her fingers on the first vial. She felt nothing. But as she touched the other...

A tidal wave of darkness swept over her. Screams echoed in her mind, accompanied by distant wailing—the consequences of this substance might inflict.

"That one?" the queen pushed.

Soren sucked in a breath and pulled her hand away. "Yes, my queen."

The queen nodded, evidently satisfied. "You may go now."

Soren bowed again, murmuring, "Sleep well, my queen."

The queen did not reply, still examining the vial. Soren took it as a final dismissal, turning and leaving.

The 'gift' was why the queen had recruited Soren in the first place. Once, as a child, she had dropped a cup of Princess Cion's tea, screaming as sounds of terror echoed in her ears. She was nearly executed when she told the guards it was poisoned. But when they brought her before the queen, the woman tested her instead of ordering her death. Soren had passed with flying colors—the queen asked her which vial could kill a man, and she remained one of the many servants secretly in her service ever since.

Still, her loyalties were to the princess first, and, seeing her light on, she hurried to the kitchens. When the cup of calming herbal tea was prepared, Soren returned to find the light still there.

"Who is it?" the princess called from the other side after Soren knocked softly on her chamber door.

"My princess, it's Soren. May I come in?"

There was a long pause. With all that had happened today, she wondered if the princess was up for more of a reason than sleeplessness. She was likely deciding whether it was safe to let Soren in. There was no reason for her to fear. Soren was sworn to silence.

When the princess called, "You may come in, Soren," she entered, finding the princess sitting at her vanity table, scrolls and ink scattered across its surface.

"My apologies, princess," she said, her voice low and

quiet. "I brought you some herbal tea. I saw your light was on."

Cion raised a brow. "And what were you doing in the royal quarters at this hour?"

"Your mother," Soren replied quietly, keeping her gaze cast downward. "She needed someone to assist her."

Cion narrowed her eyes. "You are loyal to me first, though, yes?" she said, taking the warm cup from Soren.

Soren bowed her head. "Always, my princess."

"Good," Cion said shortly. "I need your assistance."

Soren nodded at the crumpled scrolls and pots of ink. "You are writing a letter, my princess."

Princess Cion smiled. "You are very observant, but…yes."

She stood, crossing her arms over her chest. "Though I am not a poet nor a scholar. I need the assistance of someone used to wielding words as opposed to blades. You used to write letters for me when I was a child. I ask you to assist me in the same way now."

Soren's brow creased at the faint memory. Her script had always been neater than the princess', her words more careful.

"And what should I know about this letter, princess?" she asked after a moment's hesitation.

"I am writing to my betrothed," Cion began, her eyes flicking to the closed door.

The room was shadowed, but moonlight filtered in from the balcony doors, leaving a glimmering trail of pale light over her ruffled bed sheets.

"I want to introduce myself. My passions, the things and the people I care for—it is important for a future husband of mine to know these things. I also want to acknowledge he must have passions and priorities too," she continued. "Different than mine and already in place, since we come from separate kingdoms. Different places have different customs, I know. I want to honor this and protect his passions, so long as he is willing to help protect mine."

Soren said nothing, but she understood. The princess wanted to bargain with the Prince of Meesling. She wanted protection for those they loved. For her, Lady Anabeth. For the prince, Princess Hessa of Mise.

Soren had heard rumors the prince and princess were actually in love, despite the arranged betrothal. Now, she knew the rumors must be true, though their love was useless now that they were being ripped from each other. Or perhaps Prince Kellmere knew of the betrayal. For Princess Hessa's sake, she could only pray he would at least try to protect her and that Princess Cion would bargain for the same.

"I understand, princess," Soren said quietly. "May I?"

Cion glanced at the pile of scrolls. "Please."

It took Soren under an hour to compose the perfect coded letter to the Prince of Meesling. As Cion held it in her hand, eyes skimming the last words, Soren asked, "Is it adequate, my princess?"

Cion's lips twitched. "In another life, you might have made an excellent spy, Soren."

Soren ducked her head, a small spark lighting in her belly. It was just the faintest hint of a feeling, something less than subservient. Beneath the soft, practiced smiles and quiet words, Soren kept a beast at bay. It roared at the iron shackle on her ankle and sniffed the air at Princess Cion's words.

Yes… it hissed, urging her to take the opportunity, *any* opportunity to escape and run free.

She hushed it like it was an obstinate child.

"If that is all, my princess," Soren said. "You should try to sleep, if only for a few hours. Dawn will be breaking soon."

Cion glanced outside. The faintest hints of light stained the horizon, just barely peeking between rocky slopes and jagged mountain sides.

"Post the letter," Cion said, her eyes still on the landscape beyond. "Send it off with one of the military ravens before anyone wakes to ask questions."

"Yes, my princess. Do…try to rest."

Princess Cion glanced back at her, and for a moment, her eyes narrowed, as if she was seeing something Soren couldn't. Standing there in her faded nightdress and fraying slippers, she bowed her head, hiding the beast beneath her skin. She hid her nature well, despite the odd look the king had cast in her direction the other day. She hoped it was just a coincidence.

Still, as she left the bedchamber, sealed letter in hand, there was a strange flutter in her chest. It was an intrinsic feeling telling her some change was on the horizon.

She ignored the primal warning bells and hurried to the aviary.

~

Soren watched the enormous raven take flight, its feathers blue-black in the infancy of morning. At the top of the palace where the aviary lay, she swore she was on top of the world. Given that D'anna sat nestled among some of the highest peaks in Aren, she supposed the thought wasn't entirely far off from truth.

When she had first been brought to the capital as a child, many of those with her had become sick from the altitude change. She had merely felt dizzy with a terrified sore of awe. Several of the balconies in the palace jutted over cliffs that fell hundreds of feet. She had no idea how the building had been constructed. With the aid of magic, if she was a betting woman.

But she was not. In fact, she could not afford to gamble away any chances. Her life depended on it, and if she wanted to ever have any chance of finding Kelshie or Thurn...

She knew in her heart her little brother was likely gone. He had been far too young to be of any use to Aren when they were all taken, and she had heard such horrible stories about what became of Misean babies.

But perhaps Kelshie was in one of the war camps. Maybe, with Princess Cion, Soren could find her. It was foolish to expect such a thing, but it was the first thread of hope she'd felt in nearly a decade and couldn't bring herself to let go of it just yet.

And then, there was the letter she had just sent off into the crisp morning.

The princess was committing treason by attempting to undermine her father in any way. Soren knew her rebellion was for entirely selfish reasons, all of them having to do with the scribe's daughter. Still, it gave her hope that perhaps Mise's princess could at least be spared in the mess sure to follow Meesling's betrayal.

For just a few more moments, she gazed at the horizon as the raven became a speck. Once it was gone from sight, she finally left the aviary behind, hurrying across the vast tension bridge connecting the main residential wing and the rest of the palace. It swung slightly with each step, and she ignored the sharp bite of unease in her stomach at the movement. She was afraid of the height, just as she was afraid of being caught today. Many men claimed to be fearless, but it was usually a falsehood. Soren had learned mastering fear was the way to truly conquer it, not by pushing it away or denying it.

It was why, as she rounded the corner off the bridge and saw a guard posted there, she did not freeze or panic. She simply kept walking, her body curved in the expected submissive stance of a servant or slave.

"You." The guard's voice was gruff and stiff with command.

She turned slowly, her eyes downcast. "Good morning, sir."

"What were you doing on the bridge?"

It only took her a few seconds to think of a story, half-truth, half-lie. "I was delivering a letter, sir."

"To whom? Only certain people are allowed in the aviary at this hour."

She nodded. "Yes, sir, I know. I was delivering it to Sir Gellings' quarters nearby. The princess will be unable to attend her morning sparring session due to poor sleep."

The guard eyed her. "I see. You did not go into his chambers like this, did you? It would be unseemly."

She bit back a smile. As if she would want anything to do with Sir Gellings, of all people. Still, she kept her face neutral as she replied, "No, of course not, sir. One of the other servants in that wing promised to give it to him upon his waking."

The guard sighed heavily, looking around. "Alright then. Hurry back to your quarters and dress. I am sure you will be needed soon."

Soren bowed her head and hurried away, her heart beating hard and fast. It had been a close call, and the princess would be unhappy about having to skip her lesson, despite her true lack of sleep. But she had not been caught, not truly, and that was all that mattered, for more than her sake.

As she walked quickly back to the room she shared with Mona, she avoided the main halls and stairways where she knew some of the staff would already be readying for the royals to wake. When she finally stepped back into the cramped quarters, Mona was awake, washing her face, a basin of water below her.

"Where were you?" she asked sharply as soon as Soren shut the door.

"Business for the queen and then the princess," she replied, her voice thin with exhaustion. "Do not worry; all is well."

Mona pressed her lips together before she said in a hushed tone, "You *must* be careful, Soren. The princess has chosen you to accompany her, which means more eyes on all of us. This is not the time to take risks…but if you must do so, be smart."

Soren could only mutter, "You don't think I don't know that?"

Mona looked away, busying herself with dressing and plaiting her dark hair into two tight braids. Soren quickly washed and changed into day clothes, swapping out her thin slippers for soft, woven sandals.

"Soon, you'll be wearing riding boots," Mona said softly from behind Soren in the age-speckled mirror. "How grand that will be, not to get pebbles and dust in between your toes all day long."

Soren forced herself to smile, though the mirror reflected more of a grimace. Still, she kept her voice light as she replied, "It will be, won't it?"

Mona returned her tight smile, clasping one of Soren's hands. The two of them were not friends by any means, but Mona had been Soren's roommate since they arrived here, and they had always served the princess together. And most importantly, they were both orphans from Mise. For Soren to succeed, in a way, was a step for Mona as well, for all of them. It was why Mona warned Soren to be careful too, because any failure of hers could impact other Misean servants in the palace.

Soren did not often let herself cave into fear. But in that quiet, still moment, one of the last she would share with Mona, she let herself feel it fully, watching as it reflected in Mona's eyes too.

CHAPTER 5

Too swiftly, the morning arrived when Soren was to depart D'anna with Princess Cion, to journey further into the rugged Eastern Peaks that made up an enormous portion of their district.

Deep in the mountains sat the dragon's keep, where the eggs were laid and kept until they hatched. Nearby, the Sisters of Arcane kept their council in a sacred temple said to be a place closest to the gods.

Soren was given thick, warm riding clothes and sturdy leather boots. She dressed early, before the princess awoke, counting her breaths as she braided her hair and laced up her boots.

When she was finished and there was nothing to further delay her leaving, she cast one last glance around the room that had been anything but a home these last thirteen years. She was a woman now at twenty and two, and if she was not a servant, she would likely be marrying soon. But a different life had been thrust upon her.

She picked up the light pack containing all her things:

clothes, a pair of worn sandals, her jewelry repair kit, a set of needle and thread, and a small, time-worn river rock. It was her only memento from home; the rock had been in her pocket the day she watched her mother's head leave her body; the day her father's blood had stained the soil a shade too dark; the day Kelshie had screamed at her to run, but she had simply stood there, frozen, her feet digging into the forest mud.

Shaking off the fractured memories, she stepped into the hallway bustling with servants off to attend to their early morning chores. Standing amidst the chaos, she let herself wonder what exactly she and the princess would be facing in the war camps. She wasn't a fool to think these were going to be a pleasant three years, but at least it was not this hallway, full of fear and waning hope, kneeling on already-bruised knees.

She would not be free out there, but perhaps she could pretend to be.

When Soren arrived at the princess' chambers, Mona, Thelia, and Jasmen were already there, packing the last of her things into an ornate trunk and braiding her hair.

As soon as Soren stepped inside, Princess Cion twisted in the vanity seat and said, "Good morning, Soren. Are you ready to depart?"

Soren bowed her head. "Indeed, my princess."

Princess Cion nodded curtly, but Soren could see the burst of bright excitement sparking in her eyes despite the events of the last few days.

"Good. Prepare yourself; this journey is sure to be quite taxing physically, especially since you have not ridden much on horseback before."

Soren gave the princess a small smile, veiling any nerves that threatened to appear on her features. Princess Cion turned away, facing the mirror once more, Thelia and Jasmen attending to her as Mona stood by if needed. Soren's attention drew downwards, to where Mona's fist was clenched at her side, just slightly tucked behind her wrap skirt.

Soren tried not to read too much into it. She knew she carried the fire for each and every Misean slave in the palace as she traveled with the princess—she could either snuff out the flame of rebellion or feed it.

Both were terrifying prospects.

Princes Cion stood, looking at herself once more in the mirror before turning. "It's time."

Soren bowed her head, a strand of hair falling into her eyes. "Yes, my princess."

The princess walked forward and lifted Soren's chin with a finger, tucking the hair behind her ear. "I am glad you will be with me, Soren."

"I am glad to hear it, my princess."

Cion smiled and made for the door. The four of them fell into step behind her, heads bowed and eyes trained on the floor as they followed her into the hall, past the empty chambers where the princess' brother had often tormented servant and slave girls.

Through the arch that signaled they were entering the king's hall, where his and the queen's chambers lay.

Down the long corridor that separated the royal wing from the rest of the palace, steep cliffs on either side of the breezy, open arches.

And finally, descending a set of sweeping marble stairs that led to the grand entrance.

Each step felt monumental to Soren, and she had the odd sense she might never walk them again. It could very well be true. She and the princess were about to enter dangerous territory.

The smell of jicaba tree blossoms wafted in on a cool mountain breeze, and harsh, early morning sunlight illuminated the airy space. The king and queen awaited them, along with a party of knights clad in thick leather armor, yellow bands on their left arms signaling their station.

"They will accompany us," Cion said quietly to Soren.

Soren nodded. "I see, my princess."

Cion walked slowly to her parents and then bowed low in front of her father. Soren followed her motion, a few paces behind.

"Rise, both of you."

Soren ignored the unease in her belly. The king was addressing her too now, and he met her eyes as she straightened. She did not dare look away, not this time. Instead, she merely murmured, "Your Majesty," keeping her voice soft and reverent.

The king tilted his head, examining her before turning his attention back to Cion. "A Misean servant. Interesting choice, daughter."

Cion kept her back straight and her voice firm. "She is the most loyal and capable of all my handmaidens."

The king's brow rose. "Let us hope she remains that way."

Soren bowed her head submissively, and the queen laughed softly. "Do not worry, my dear. I have observed all her handmaidens with scrutiny over the years, having picked them myself. This one will fare well serving our daughter on this long journey."

The king merely grunted, but Soren could feel his gaze still upon her. It made her feel as if she had done something wrong, but she had no idea what.

"Sometimes, special people are used for bad things."

Soren shut her eyes ever so briefly, banishing her dead mother's voice from her mind. It was amongst a handful that were not permitted residence in her thoughts. Not anymore.

The king's attention finally shifted.

Soren uncurled her fist, ignoring the bite of pain from how hard she'd dug her nails into her palm, and praying no one saw the single droplet of blood that fell to the shining floor.

No one paid her, or the blood, any further mind.

Cion led her out the familiar sweeping, gold-painted arch, a door that had only ever been an entrance and never an exit. Soren had to crush the fledgling cry of victory in her chest as she stepped onto the wide, packed road surrounded by mountain greenery and wildflowers.

The queen stepped forward, and Cion stiffened as she pulled her daughter close, kissing her brow then murmuring in her ear, words Soren could not catch. Cion stepped away quickly, her eyes narrowed and her jaw clenched. The queen's thin smile remained, but Cion's composure had fallen. Soren wondered if the display of affection had merely been a way to mask a threat.

As always, the king watched them closely.

Not wanting him to catch on to the princess' sudden

anger, Soren took a step towards the princess and quietly said, "My princess, the horses await."

Soren's words snapped Princess Cion out of whatever shock had overcome her moments before. She lifted her chin, tightening her trembling lips, and walked to the two horses as the knights followed suit to mount their steeds, one approaching Soren.

"My name is Lanor," the knight said, his kohl-painted eyes bright. "I will be assisting you with your horse. Our princess tells me you have not ridden much prior to today."

Soren bowed her head. "No, sir. Just once or twice, as a child."

Lanor nodded. "I'll help you mount her, and then I'll ride beside you so you may learn the basics as we go."

"Thank you, sir."

Lanor chuckled, offering her a hand. It was half-gloved in rough, worn leather, open at the fingers so she could see the many callouses adorning his flesh.

"So formal. What is your name?"

She hesitated before taking his hand, and he gave her a gentle smile. "I won't bite, I promise. Just take my hand and stick your foot in that part there, hanging off the side, then swing your other leg over. Easy enough."

Soren swallowed thickly, looking at the enormous black mare above her, kicking the dust up with her hooves.

"Yes, sir," she finally relented, taking Lanor's hand.

He nodded. "Step on my other hand with your foot. One, two…"

Soren froze.

"*One, two—*"

No.

Not that memory.

Not today.

But she was helpless as the image of her mother's death assaulted her. The soldier, the one who called himself Jadis, had counted down so casually before his companion had swung his blade. Kelshie had screamed, the sound mingling with the wet smack of their mother's head hitting the forest floor…

She sucked in a breath, banishing the memory, and hopped up on Lanor's outstretched hand, hauling herself clumsily onto the mare. Lanor and a few of the other knights laughed before Cion shot them a dark look.

"Apologies, princess," they all murmured.

Lanor hopped onto his white-speckled horse easily, just as a processional hymn began to play loudly behind them. Traditional send-off music, local to Aren; the same song Soren sometimes heard playing in the streets as soldiers marched off to battle.

The beating of the drums lined up with the wild thumping of her heart.

"One, two…" she whispered, her eyes on the horizon.

A trumpet cried out.

"Ahead!" a knight at the front of the party cried.

"What was that?" Lanor asked, that easy half-grin still on his face.

Soren glanced at him. "Nothing, sir."

He laughed again, something he seemed to do quite a lot. Soren couldn't decide if it bothered her or not. She couldn't decide anything about the knight, not yet, which unsettled her. People were generally easy for her to read, but this knight…

He was handsome in a rugged sort of way, with typical features of a man born in Aren: short black hair, pale skin, brown, upturned eyes, a tall stature. He boasted many scars, an honor for a knight or warrior, and he was muscular under the armor, but he needed to shave. There were dark circles under his eyes. Perhaps these knights were not treated as well as they appeared at first glance.

"Take hold of the reins." His voice startled her out of her observation. "Pinch your legs slightly and lean forward."

She followed his instructions and held back a yelp as the horse moved. It was an odd feeling, being up this high and not in control. She wasn't sure if she hated or loved it.

"Good," Lanor said, smiling. "Get comfortable. We have a long journey ahead."

"So I've been told, sir."

Lanor laughed. "So she *can* make a joke, and so soon into our journey together."

Soren looked away, facing ahead toward the streets of cheering people quickly approaching. Of course, King Johannas would make a spectacle of the princess leaving. Another celebration to add to the appearance of glory surrounding the war.

Still, even with the cheering faces and pumping fists, Soren saw it in their hollow cheeks and desperate eyes: these people were hungry. Some for food, some for a savior, many for both. They thought perhaps Princess Cion would be their champion, but Soren knew that wasn't true. The princess was here for entirely selfish reasons.

A few caught sight of Soren and spit curses her way. When a pebble collided with her cheek, Lanor intercepted it, angling his horse in front of her and shouting, "Enough! She is with the princess!"

"Misean whore!" a woman screeched.

"Another pup?"

"Barely."

She shuddered at the memory. Perhaps the woman was not wrong. Soren was powerless against these people; she had heard many stories of servant girls being taken advantage of against their will…

In dark rooms.

Alone.

With no one to hear their cries.

That was how hope died.

"Ignore them," Lanor called over the shouts. "They don't know what they're saying."

Soren lowered her gaze. "They do, sir. But it's alright. They're just looking for someone to blame."

"You are…" she looked up as Lanor trailed off then continued, "oddly observant and well-spoken for a slave."

She gave him a practiced smile. "I was brought up as a handmaiden for the princess my whole life. It required me to have certain skills others might lack."

"Of course," Lanor said, dipping his head her way.

She hated that she still could not decipher his intentions.

CHAPTER 6

THE EASTERN PEAKS WERE MERCILESS. The cold grew more bitter by the hour, and by the third sunrise, Soren could hardly dismount. Lanor had given her the name of the enormous black mare she rode midway through the second day of riding—*Sgàilsuil.*

Shadow Eyes.

When Soren heard the name, her heart began racing. It was likely just a coincidence; surely, the mare had been named after her dark coat and nothing more. Yet still, the memory of whispered folktales around a crackling fire echoed like phantoms in her mind. Kelshie had held her hand as Papa explained some creatures acted as portals between their world and that of the gods, thin veils one could not step through but perhaps see behind.

People could be shadow eyes too.

On the morning of the fourth sunrise, as Soren was braiding the princess' hair, the leader of their party, Sir Helq, announced a storm approaching.

"We should consider sheltering until it passes," he said gruffly to Princess Cion.

The princess' gaze drifted to the darkening horizon, but she shook her head. "We cannot. We must make the journey in time. This is only part of the test."

"Princess—"

"I must insist, Sir Helq."

He bowed his head. "As you wish."

The princess turned to Soren, her face softening. "Do not worry, Soren. I am fated to be chosen in two days' time. The gods will protect us as we take these final steps."

Soren had lost faith in any of the gods, much less their protection, long ago. Still, she bowed her head. "Of course, my princess. Is there anything else you require before we begin riding for the day?"

The princess paused, hesitating. "Do you…" She trailed off and shook her head. "No, Soren. I think we are ready."

Soren bowed her head once more then made her way to *Sgàilsuil*. Lanor was already atop his horse, and she bit back a request for him to help her mount, instead struggling up on her own. A ghost of a smile graced the knight's face.

"Yes, sir?"

"That was a test, which you failed."

Her brow creased. "My apologies, sir?"

He laughed. "None required, but remember, Soren, it is not a weakness to ask for help. A wiser man chooses to rely on a friend."

She nodded but could not bring herself to meet his kind eyes. They were a mocking reminder to her, for she had no friends. Despite his kindness, it was temporary. They would arrive at the temple and then part ways once the princess had her dragon. Soren doubted she would receive much kindness from then on—likely only suspicion and disdain once they were in the war camps.

"Onward!" Sir Helq called from the front of the party just as a strong wind whipped through the clearing.

She shivered, a foreboding feeling curling in her gut like a great, slumbering beast. Each step *Sgàilsuil* took pushed her closer to something dreadful. She was sure of it, even as reason tried to shout her thoughts were created by fear and nothing more. For as the storm began to rage around them, the knights shouting and forming a tight ring around Princess Cion, the suspicion that *fear* itself was the logical one now grew.

Ahead, through the pelting rain, Soren swore she saw shapes moving in the mist. *Sgàilsuil* suddenly kicked up speed, and Princess Cion screeched Soren's name as the horse shot past the rest of the party. Soren was breathing hard, the icy air like daggers in her chest. She clung to the beast as it began to buck and rear, but it was no use.

She flew into the air then landed hard on the cold, muddy earth, the impact knocking the breath out of her and sending a rattling pain through her bones.

As she lay on the ground, shaking, her breath catching in tiny heaves, the mist grew thicker. Whispers surrounded her, overlapping and insistent. Soren slowly stood on shaky feet, trying to see through the thick air.

"Hello?" she called tentatively. "Princess? Sir Lanor?"

You...

Soren froze at the sound of the rasping, inhuman drawl. Animal instincts told her she was correct. Then, there was something else inside her chest, an ember of suspicion that had perhaps always been there…

"Are you afraid, Mamma?

Soren froze.

A child's laughter echoed in the mist. The rain had stopped.

"Not of you. Never of you."

"Then of what?"

"Stop," Soren whispered to nothing and no one as the children began to scream.

Peals of harsh laughter joined in, merging and melding with the sounds of terror until it was all that remained, the cackles growing louder until they surrounded her. She sank to her knees, covering her ears. Something brushed against her back, and she jolted, bolting up and running as fast as she could through the mist, her eyes half shut. She did not want to see what had made those sounds.

She only stopped when she collided with something hard.

"Soren!"

She opened her eyes, her breath catching as Sir Lanor caught her, keeping them both from toppling over. She was in a clearing, a sliver of sun peeking through the clouds. But as she turned and saw the last tendrils of mist creeping away…

Three figures lingered at the tree line.

Waiting. Watching.

Whispering.

She shuddered, and Princess Cion set a firm hand on Soren's shoulder. "Soren. What did you see?"

"I…"

"Just now, you looked back as if something was there. What was it?"

Soren looked at the princess' hard eyes and thinned mouth, realizing the question was not a request but an order. So, she swallowed her terror and replied, "Three forms, my princess. They…whispered things to me in the mist, reminding me of memories no one alive but me should be privy to."

"Holy gods," Sir Helq breathed just as *Sgàilsuil* galloped towards them.

"I named that horse well," Lanor murmured, his face pale.

Soren wasn't sure what they were referring to and had half a mind not to ask, but the princess pushed, "What is it?"

Sir Helq swallowed hard. "Have you ever heard of the Three Sisters, princess?"

Princess Cion hesitated. "I… Yes. But they are a legend, nothing more."

The two knights exchanged a look, but Lanor said, "As you say, my princess."

"You disagree?"

Soren tamped down the temptation to ask what exactly the Three Sisters were. Half of her didn't want to know at all.

Princess Cion sighed sharply through her teeth, looking to the horizon. "The storm has delayed us. We need to move."

The knights merely nodded. They could act as friends all they wanted, but when it came down to it, the princess was their master.

On shaky limbs, Soren mounted *Sgàilsuil* once more. The princess pushed them ahead at a brutal pace, stopping for only a few hours in the night. Soren didn't sleep at all, the ground hard beneath her thin pallet and the echo of the whispers she had heard swirling in her mind.

The final day of the journey came with a flurry of snow and gray skies. The knights pulled heavy cloaks from their packs for them, though the fabric did not do much to cut through the biting chill.

About midday, in the distance, Soren spotted spirals reaching up into the sky, disappearing into the clouds.

"The temple," Princess Cion breathed, eyes shining when she saw it. "We are nearly there."

A distant roar had Soren jumping and the horses neighing uneasily. The princess smiled, though, unafraid of the promise of dragons ahead.

"Do not worry, Soren," she said. "You'll be kept safe."

"Yes, my princess," she said on instinct, her eyes on those spires.

Princess Cion laughed. "Let us finish this. I need to change before the Ceremony."

CHAPTER 7

A FEW HOURS FROM SUNSET, Soren stood behind the princess in what looked like an arena. It was carved out of the mountain itself, much of the stone oddly dark and shiny. The princess had murmured in Soren's ear that the stone had been touched by dragonfire.

A small group of women stood on an outcropping of rock above the hollowed out space, all wearing robes of fiery red, thin, sheer veils covering all but their mouths. Around their necks, they each wore a heavy bronze amulet engraved with a symbol Soren could not see from her place on the floor.

The Sisters of Arcane, the last links to the gods.

Soren hardly believed these priestesses had any real connection to the gods anymore. They had abandoned this realm long ago; it didn't make sense to pay humans any mind after sealing themselves away, even devout women such as these.

To the right of the princess, two young men stood, and on the left, three young women, each waiting to claim a dragon. Soren was sure they were sons and daughters of high-ranking nobles, or perhaps the child of an honored general if they were lucky. No one else had the right to this day. The dragons only wanted nobility and warriors.

Straight ahead, directly under where the Sisters stood, an enormous cavern entrance yawned. It was completely dark inside, making impossible to see anything that might be approaching.

"You have been chosen!"

Soren jolted as one of the Sisters, this one wearing a gold circlet on her head, shouted from above them.

"Esteemed sons and daughters, this day marks the beginning or end of your destiny. If a dragon finds you unworthy, this may be the last day you draw breath. If you are chosen, glory awaits. This is your last chance to walk away."

Soren resisted the urge to heed the Sister's words and run, instead standing still behind the princess, her shoulders curled in submission. She had little choice in being here, yet still, she didn't feel out of place. Soren didn't believe in fate, but this moment was the closest she had come to thinking it might have a hand in her life.

The Sister smiled when no one moved, saying in a low voice, "Then let us begin."

She stepped back, and as all the Sisters closed their eyes, they began to hum, the sound rich and resonant in the mountain air. A few broke off, singing a broken, raw melody that pricked the hairs on the back of Soren's neck. As the song escalated, the arena trembled slightly. Soren kept her eyes on the cavern as the first dragon crawled out into the open.

It was terrifying as it was beautiful. Dark blue scales shimmered in the fading sunlight as the dragon flexed the thick muscles of its back. Amber eyes blinked slowly, and it cocked its head as it took in the line of noble heirs. The Sisters continued their song, and then, a low, rasping voice resonated so deeply, Soren could not tell if it was aloud or in her mind.

Cowards, liars, and cheats—I see all in this line. But a few may live to see the moon rise tonight.

Next to Soren, a young slave girl trembled so violently, her breath made an audible noise. Quietly and slowly, she reached over and took the girl's hand, squeezing once. Soren swore she saw the dragon's eyes land on the movement and narrow, but the moment passed, and the dragon continued.

Step forward, Son of Lord Wixin.

The young man at the end of the line moved, taking a confident step forward as the dragon requested. Soren could see the triumphant smirk on his lips as he was picked first. Muscles rippled on his body when he moved with the grace of a warrior; just like Princess Cion, he had probably been training to be a rider all his life.

The dragon lumbered towards him, her breath blowing strands of dark hair out of the boy's face. His haughty smirk fell as she tilted her head, examining him. A pit formed in Soren's gut, and the girl next to her gripped her hand so tightly, it hurt.

You are arrogant. Self-involved. I would not risk myself or my kin for you. For when the moment comes, a rider must be ready to die with their dragon. You would flee.

The Sisters continued their haunting melody even as the dragon opened her mouth. Without another thought, Soren pulled the princess back, away from the sudden path of dragonfire. The princess did not protest, not as white-hot flame spewed from the dragon's mouth and incinerated the boy completely. He hardly had the chance to plead or even scream before he was nothing but ashes. Soren stared at the space where he had stood mere moments before, wide-eyed, pulse pounding erratically.

The dragon slowly faced the group again, something almost like a smirk pulling at the corners of her long mouth.

Ah… There are a few brave ones amongst you after all. Let us continue.

Soren realized she and the last remaining man were standing in front of the rest of the group, arms outstretched. He narrowed his eyes at her, noting the shackle on her ankle marking her as a slave before stepping back into place. Soren shrank back behind Princess Cion, who did not even look at her.

Two more dragons clawed their way out from inside the dark of the cavern, both smaller than the first. The smaller of the two was bulky, with umber scales and spikes up its neck, the other larger but slimmer, boasting scales the color of moss.

Boy.

The umber dragon flipped its tail up in the air as it spoke before dropping it down again, sending dust into the air, several of the servants jumping at the impact. The last man stepped forward and bowed deeply, the knot of dark hair atop his head falling loose. He was taller than the other man but more limber, and he wore a dark purple mourning cloth on his left arm.

My name is Olariu. We will see if you can make it through training.

The man lifted his head, murmuring something Soren could not make out, and the dragon made a rough sound, almost like a chortling laugh, before slinking back to the other side of the arena. The man rose to his feet and followed the dragon as Soren took even breaths. Princess Cion had still not been chosen, and it was becoming clear it was no guarantee.

The green dragon's ice-blue eyes tracked over the group, narrowing on the small, trembling noble girl next to Princess Cion. The dragon opened her mouth, blue flames curling in the back of her throat. But this time, as the dragon roared and a stream of white-hot fire descended, Soren did not dare pull the princess back and shield her again. Instead, she grabbed roughly onto the slave girl's wrist next to her before she could leap ahead and try to save her master.

"Ebba!" the girl shrieked.

Soren lunged, pulling the girl to the side, out of the path of the fire as it poured from the dragon's mouth.

They were all ash-stained and shaking as the fire died down. Then, the dragon narrowed her eyes on Princess Cion. Soren was breathing heavily in the thick air, her eyes rounded as the dragon spoke to the princess.

Yooooouuuu. You hold great fear, Heir of Aren.

Princess Cion's entire body froze, her eyes wide. The Sisters' song began to grow louder as Soren silently begged the princess to show bravery to the beast.

"I..." Princess Cion began, but the dragon roared, cutting her off.

Heat curled once more in the air, and without a second

thought, Soren took a step forward, feeling as if she were in a dream. The dragon went completely still, the heat building in her throat diminishing, her eyes flicking sharply from the princess to Soren.

Interesting, the dragon mused before looking back at Princess Cion. *We shall see if you can survive training, heir.*

Soren let loose a slow breath, watching as the princess followed the dragon to the edge of the arena. She wasn't sure if she should follow or not. The other slaves and servants remained, so she decided to wait with the last girl.

The arena trembled, signaling another dragon approached. At first, only one beast slunk out, about the same size as the others and burnt maroon in color. But moments later, a large shadow appeared behind it.

An enormous creature, moon-white in color, crawled out into the arena after the maroon dragon. Its eyes were an odd silver, and Soren wondered if the dragon was blind. A long scar cut over its eye, almost down to its mouth, like a permanent cruel smirk.

"Vemon," the slave girl next to Soren breathed, her eyes on the pale dragon. "They're incredibly rare."

The maroon dragon came forward first, merely rasping, *Come,* to the remaining girl. Wide-eyed, she hurried after him to the other side of the arena, keeping a wide berth of the Vemon dragon. Only servants and slaves remained now in front of the pale beast.

"It's going to kill us," a boy breathed.

The girl cowered behind Soren, the rest of the group falling in line. The Vemon dragon approached, sniffing the air.

So much fear, her voice came smoothly.

Soren realized the Sisters were no longer singing. The only sound she could hear was the thundering beat of her own pulse as it roared.

But you… *They all cower behind you, even the precious heir, fated for this path from birth. Do you not wonder why?*

It took a moment for Soren to realize the dragon was speaking to her. When she did, she raised her gaze to those silver eyes and shook her head, whispering, "I am nothing."

Indeed, this is what they have made you, Soren Cavell.

Soren left the others behind, walking slowly to meet the dragon. She did not want them caught in the dragonfire when it surely rained down on her.

But when she knelt in front of the dragon and closed her eyes, the blinding heat did not come. Instead, the dragon touched her head with her nose, chuffing, almost…purring.

Soren looked up, staring directly into the beast's eyes.

An odd feeling snarled her senses.

She had been here before.

Silver.

Under the dying moon.

Hello, Soren.

The dragon might have actually been smiling now.

My name is Thessilnn. Let us see if you survive training.

CHAPTER 8
CION

Cion kept a close eye on Soren as they filed into the temple with the others. The dragons awaited their departure to training camp, but first, as she knew was tradition, they were to be blessed by the Sisters.

The narrow, dim halls were just as she remembered: plain and cloistered, void of any decor or art. The Sister leading them was silent as she walked, as were the boy and the girl. The boy was Ilav Thil, the son of a general, the girl, Elaana Mixt, the daughter of Lord Mixt, one of three responsible for overseeing the jade mines. And then, there was…

Soren.

Soren, with her slave anklet and plain wrap dress. Her shoulders were still curved, as they always were, her eyes downcast—and she had been picked by a Vemon dragon. Little did the girl know, Thessilnn was not just any dragon. She had hatched centuries ago, rumored to have been alive before the Veil to the gods even shut. There were whispers

Aren had another ancient Vemon dragon in its fleet. In fact, she had met its rider.

Mòr Maslach.

Masked Death.

Few knew his true identity. Cion only assumed he was a man based on his voice and stature when he had been summoned to court three years prior. Yet still, she remembered he had kneeled for her father just like everyone in Aren, a deadly pet with an even deadlier mount: Heles, the only other Vemon dragon currently under Aren's leash.

Jealousy, hot and potent, poured through her as Cion walked behind Soren. Why would the gods choose to bless her with a dragon like Thessilnn? Her own dragon, Valhamnor, was graceful and cunning, but shouldn't the Warrior Princess and heir be the one with the strongest mount?

She bit her cheek in frustration, the taste of copper flooding her mouth as they stopped in front of a simple arch. Through it lay the Chamber of Whispers, where speaking was not permitted by anyone but the Sisters. The Sister leading them walked inside, gesturing for them to follow.

Cion had been here once before, when she was barely eight years old, and had heard a prophecy about herself.

"Darkness rises, an ember to meet it. And you, warrior, will taste the skies in the last days."

The words were still burned into her mind, even over a decade later. The first phrase had always bothered her, though her father chose to blatantly ignore the warning. Was the 'darkness' the war or something else? And what did the 'last days' refer to? She had never gotten answers to either question.

The Sisters of the Chamber swung a pot of smoky incense around them. Elaana had closed her eyes, a stupid move in wartime. Any one of them could be spies. If slaves could be dragon riders now, anything was possible.

Oh gods, her father was not going to be happy.

The Sisters finished their circling, and she, Ilav, Elaana, and Soren were each approached. An ancient woman leaned in close to Cion's ear and rasped, "A word for the wise, princess. Rumblings of the past are afoot. Keep your head."

The Sister pulled away, smiling softly, the worn lines of her face crinkling. Unease snaked through Cion at her words. The past was often revered, but so much of it was unknown. The woman could be referring to the gods themselves for all Cion knew.

She glanced at Soren as a Sister stepped away from her. Her eyes were wide, her lips pale with shock. Cion was beginning to understand the reality of what was occurring. Soren had a part to play in all of this, and it made her deeply uneasy.

The girl knew far too much.

CHAPTER 9

THE CLOAKED *figure watched from behind an outcropping of rock as the girl shielded the others, caring little for her own safety. He watched as she saved the princess, though neither of them knew it, watched as a dragon the shade of the moon chose her.*

Rage, hot and violent, stirred in his gut at the sight of the slave shackle on her ankle, the knowledge it would likely remain there compounding his ire.

If only they knew...

But he had to wait.

Patience had never come easily to him, but the years had forced him to practice until it was close to second nature.

Oh, yes.

He would wait.

CHAPTER 10

After the ceremony in the Chamber of Whispers, the four of them were taken to quarters to 'rest' for the night before they flew out. Soren had already resolved not to shut her eyes. She was sure any of her fellow new dragon riders would be happy to slit her throat and take Thessilnn as their own.

She didn't even trust Princess Cion. In fact, she might just trust her the least. She had seen the sour envy in her eyes after the Choosing ceremony. Soren couldn't really blame her. After all, this was what the princess was *fated* for. For Soren, this was just a fluke, and she was ill-suited to the task. She had never trained with a blade nor bow, and her body was weak from the near-idleness of court life, even as a working servant. Why the dragon had chosen to spare her, she had no idea.

The Sister leading them down the simple, winding hall stopped at a doorway. It led into a wide, airy room full of cots and bed mats. Basins of water and white towels were placed in the center of the room, cups of steaming noodles and fragrant herbal tea on a low table. Soren could smell the Lily of the Moon petals in the drink from where they stood. It was an expensive ingredient, one that spoke to who the Sisters *thought* they would be serving tonight.

Still, as they filed in, the Sister said softly, "Enjoy these last small comforts. There will be few where you are going."

The boy snorted once the Sister left, the sound cutting through the quiet. "Was that a warning?"

"Felt like a threat," the girl said snidely.

Princess Cion rolled her eyes. "Are you two really so naive that you don't know what you're getting yourselves into? The Sister spoke true. The camps, even the training ones, are no place for comfort. You'll be treated like any foot soldier while you're there."

The girl laughed, a cold sound. "Except for you, of course, *princess*. Heir too I hear, now that brother dearest went to the grave."

Soren bit back words of defense for the princess. They would be useless, and she wasn't sure the princess even wanted them from her, not anymore. Besides, Cion could defend herself.

"That's low of you, Elaana," the princess said. "And you, Ilav? Nothing to say?"

Both their faces pinched, and the princess laughed. "Yes, I know who you two are. Didn't you do your research before coming here?"

"Would it have mattered?" Ilav sneered, his eyes on Soren. "Given the trash they let in this year."

The insult hardly stung. After all, she was used to such a

thing. Even so, a notion stirred, spinning in her mind. She might still be an enslaved servant, but as far as she knew, she was conscripted as a soldier now too. If she was going to survive, she couldn't cower and bow her way through.

"I did not ask her to choose me," she found herself saying.

Ilav's brows raised. "I'm sorry, did I permit you to speak? Cion, you need to keep your leash a bit tighter on this one. At home, we whip them for such defiance—"

"Shut your godsdamned mouth," the princess cut in sharply. "Soren isn't wrong. You both know it, I know it. It's why I'm so envious of her right now. But bitterness won't help us, not out there. Thessilnn chose her of her own free will. We had one Vemon dragon in our fleet, and now we have two. That is something to celebrate."

"Not if its rider can't even fight," Elaana muttered.

Soren curled her hand into a fist, nails digging into the soft skin of her palm. But she did not speak, not yet. Every move, every word, needed to be calculated, and the anger rushing through her clouded her judgement.

Princess Cion rubbed at her eyes, smearing the makeup Soren had applied this afternoon before the Ceremony. "Can you two shut up so we can just go to sleep?"

"As Her Highness wishes," Ilav mocked with a little bow.

Soren glanced at her and said quietly, "Ignore him, my princess."

The princess she had cared for since they were both small stared at her. They were at a crossroads, but Soren was still a servant, Princess Cion still the heir to the kingdom.

She had the power to decide how they would move forward.

"Just call me Cion, Soren," the princess said finally. "It will make more sense out there, and we've known each other long enough that it will not feel odd to me."

"Yes, my pr—Cion."

Using her name felt odd on Soren's tongue, like a taboo word, something she should not speak aloud.

Elaana snorted as she took a cup of the tea and claimed a cot. Ilav ignored Soren altogether, foregoing the tea and lying back on a mat. Tentatively, Soren took a bowl of noodles and settled herself. The princess did the same, and they ate in silence next to each other. Soren resisted the urge to collect her empty bowl.

Night set in, and a Sister came by to collect their empty dishware before dimming the salt lights. Lamps like these must have been imported all the way from Meesling, where they were carved from a unique type of opaque desert rock and filled with a natural gas mined there.

Hours later, when all the others had long fallen asleep and the sunrise tinged the horizon a blazing shade of red, Soren let herself think of her family.

Of Kelshie.

Her parents.

Little Thurn.

They were all gone—her parents slaughtered by soldiers the day she'd been ripped from her village and Thurn likely murdered with the other small children deemed useless.

But Kelshie… Perhaps she finally had a chance to find her now.

A far-away roar echoed through the mountains, and the others stirred just as a Sister appeared in the doorway.

"It's time," she announced. "This is your first test. Your packs have been readied. Let us see if you will all make the journey."

Soren swallowed hard but tried to hide her fear. Her dragon was by far the biggest, but she wasn't sure if that was a help or a hindrance. She rose to her feet and quickly braided her hair before glancing at the princess—Cion.

"It's fine," she said quietly. "I want to feel the wind in my hair when I fly for the first time."

Soren nodded, following the Sister out of the room with the others. She led them down a set of rickety wooden stairs hugging a cliff, open to the outside air and the hundreds of feet below, save a few raised wooden guardrails. Ilav looked a little green as they descended.

When they stopped again, they were standing in an open stone clearing, even larger than the arena from yesterday. There, the dragons awaited, each wearing a harness, saddle, and pack. Thin rope ladders hung down from the saddles, and Soren surmised getting onto Thessilnn would most definitely be more difficult than it would be for the others.

Good thing you've never been afraid of heights.

Soren jolted as she heard the dragon's smooth, feminine voice in her mind for the first time since the ceremony.

She stared at her with those oddly familiar silver eyes.

Good instinct.

"What?" she said aloud, and Ilav laughed.

You can talk to me…quietly. Avoid the rat's mocking.

Right, Soren thought.

"It's time!" the Sister shouted. "Mount your dragon. They know where to go."

Cion grabbed Soren's wrist before she could move, whispering in her ear, "Stick with me once we get there, alright? You'll be safer that way."

She pulled away, and Soren could only nod before she rushed off to meet her dragon. Slowly, Soren turned to face Thessilnn again, walking towards her and staring at the ladder for a split second before crawling up it. The muscles in her arms and legs burned by the time she made it to the saddle, and her breath came in quick gasps, fiery hot in her chest.

Get ready.

That was all the warning she had before the dragon took off. In a blind panic, she grasped for something to grab, finding a tether at the front of the saddle. Air whooshed past her ears as Thessilnn flapped her wings. To her right, she thought she might have heard Elaana scream, but she didn't dare turn her head to look.

A few flaps later, they were soaring, the mountains on either side of them. That was, until the dragon sailed higher into the clouds and the peaks disappeared. Soren clung to her as the icy mist hit her square in the face.

Relax. You know how to do this.

Squinting through the moisture of the clouds and the wind, Soren shot back, *I do not. And it's freezing up here.*

Ah. There's some personality—finally.

Soren sighed, coughing as she inhaled the air too quickly. Next to her, another dragon—Ilav's—shot up further at a sharp angle. She thought she might have heard him shout, but it was quickly lost to the wind.

Is his dragon trying to get him killed?

A huffing chuckle. *Olariu likes to test his riders.*

He's had others before?

Just two. He is very particular.

And you?

She paused, and Soren wondered if she had pushed too far, but the dragon simply replied, *Once, yes. A long time ago.*

Even in Soren's mind, the dragon's voice spoke of pain, so Soren didn't push.

After a while, the flying began to feel less terrifying and more like riding a horse: uncomfortable but not completely foreign. A few times, she saw the other riders and their dragons through the clouds. By the time the sky had begun to turn pink with sunset, the cold remained but had turned less brutal.

They must be getting close.

Thessa.

Soren wasn't sure what had compelled her to call the dragon that.

But as the dragon tipped downward, she simply said, *Yes, child?*

Have we arrived?

They descended further, close enough to the ground that Soren could see the light of fires dotting the camp and specks of people moving around. Her stomach turned with unease. She did not know exactly what to expect, but she could guess.

She was Misean.

A servant.

A woman.

You are untouchable now, Soren.

She didn't reply, even knowing the dragon's words at least rang partly true. They could not kill her because they needed her. Just as much had been true all those years ago when she had been ripped from her family.

They approached a large, grassy clearing at the edge of the camp, figures awaiting them with torches. The people grew larger and the ground loomed, but Thessa glided to it smoothly, though her landing was enough to shake the earth. As the people saw her, their eyes widened, and Soren could see a few of their mouths dropping in shock.

Goodnight.

Soren took a deep breath. *Goodnight, Thessa.*

Shakily, she slid off the dragon's back and unfurled the ladder. Her heartbeat doubled as she climbed down, her limbs aching from the position she had been holding all day. Ahead, Cion's dragon landed, and she heard a dull thud behind her, signaling another.

But there was no fourth.

As she made it to the ground, Ilav swept past her, his hair windblown and his teeth chattering. She waited a moment to see if Elaana and her dragon were coming.

"She's dead."

Soren whirled to find the princess behind her, face pale and body trembling.

"What?"

"It's fairly common, I hear. Elaana wasn't able to stay on as her dragon took off. She fell off and impaled herself on a rock. I saw it."

Soren swallowed, her throat tight. "I see."

"Come," Cion said, speaking as she always would. "We need to meet with our commander before bed."

Soren resisted the urge to bow her head, instead keeping her back straight as she followed Cion out of the clearing. Whispers followed in their wake. She could guess what they were saying.

More eyes landed on them as they walked through the camp of small canvas tents. Some sat around small fires while others talked or simply stared. Soren supposed the three of them, the new riders, were the main attraction. Jealousy soured many of the faces along the dark path.

Cion stopped at a larger tent in what appeared to be the center of the camp. Soren watched her take a deep breath before calling, "Commander Eton. Princess Cion Levii, Heir of Aren."

Soren wondered if it felt odd to announce yourself like that. Then again, others normally did it for her.

There was no reply for a few tense seconds, and then a gruff male voice called, "You're late, princess."

Cion walked ahead first, Soren following. Inside, the tent was warm, lit by a fire in the middle, smoke funneling up through an iron tube. A large table sat on one side of the tent, covered in scrolls, maps, and open books. On the other side, Ilav sat cross-legged on a worn pillow. Only one pillow remained.

The gruff man, whom Soren assumed was Commander Eton, didn't look up as he said, "I assume you think because of your station, you will be treated differently here, princess. I would be remiss not to inform you, this will not be the case. You chose to join our ranks as a rider. There are certain expectations I wish to uphold. I do not like tardiness."

"I did not receive any indication of a specific meeting

time," Cion said crisply. "I was only told to come here once we arrived."

Commander Eton turned, and Soren held in a gasp.

"Another pup?"

"Barely," the dark-haired man said, gaze darkening.

"Jadis. We're not to touch them."

Now she had a surname for him. This was the man who cut her mother's head from her body, the same man who had torn her from Kelshie's arms. Jadis Eton.

The scar cutting his features in half was his most notable feature, but what she really remembered were his cruel, jade-green eyes. His hair had once been shorter, but he now wore it in a topknot. Whereas he had been a grunt soldier all those years ago, he was now decorated in metals worn proudly on his leather armor.

From the way his gaze skirted over her body, she knew he had no memory of her.

"Watch your tongue," he growled. "And send your slave to your tent. She isn't permitted here."

Cion smiled slightly. "She isn't."

"Isn't what?"

"My slave. At least, not entirely. I'm surprised you haven't heard the news, Commander."

Now, he did look at Soren. It was a slow perusal, his eyes narrowing as he reached her face. "The Sisters sent word, but I hardly believed the scroll." He spat on the ground. "You. A Vemon dragon picked *you*."

Soren held his gaze. "Perhaps the dragons do not hold such prejudices as our kind."

Commander Eton's eyes flared with rage, and he strode

over, towering above her. "You're from Mise. You're *weak*. I can tell just by looking at you."

"She has never trained," Cion cut in. "She'll need to be assigned a mentor, or she won't make it through basic training."

The Commander snorted. "You want me to give a Misean slave special accommodations?"

Cion did not laugh. She only said, "As your future queen, I want you to ensure the rider of a *Vemon dragon* is fit for battle. If Soren is able to do this, she and her dragon may one day be as strong as *Mòr Maslach*. Do you not want our forces to have that?"

Soren held back a shiver at that name. She had no idea who it was, but she knew what the words meant.

Masked Death.

The Commander was nearly purple with rage, but he bit out, "Fine. I will confer with the other leaders and see what can be done. Now, sit."

Cion smiled and bowed her head for a moment before sitting on the last cushion. Soren sat on the grassy floor beside her.

"Tomorrow," Commander Eton began, "your basic training begins. From sunrise to midday meal, you will be tested in various weapons of battle and in your stamina. The rest of the day will be spent testing these skills while riding your dragon. If you can't shoot a bow without falling off your dragon's back during battle, we won't have much use for you."

"Why do we need arrows if we have dragonfire?" Ilav asked.

Idiot, Soren thought.

Rat, as I said, Thessa replied.

Commander Eton laughed coldly, pacing in front of them. "Being a rider does not mean sitting back and letting your dragon take care of everything. If you think that would be enough, you have no idea the chaos of battle. You will soon, though." He stopped walking and stared directly at Soren as he added, "Out of my sight now. Training begins in the morning."

He turned away from them, a clear dismissal. Soren rose to her feet to follow Cion and Ilav out of the tent.

"Come with me," Cion said quietly to her.

Soren didn't argue as the princess led her to a tent not far from the Commander's. Inside, there were two simple sleeping mats alongside neat piles of what appeared to be folded clothing. There were no sleeping shifts in the pile, so Soren simply laid on the mat in her day clothes, pulling the thin blanket tight around her as Cion settled in too.

"I had no idea," Soren whispered into the dark. "I vow it."

Cion sighed. "I know, Soren. You do understand what this means, though?"

"As much as I can, yes. Thessa is rare."

"There is only one other rider of her kind that we are aware of."

"You said his name," Soren whispered.

Cion turned to face her, her eyes shining in the dark. "I did. *Mòr Maslach.* No one knows his true name nor his face, but he is my father's prized weapon. You may one day meet him, given what you share."

Soren did not want to meet his masked rider, the one surely responsible for so much of the death and destruction that had been rained down on her people. But she didn't say that.

"We should sleep, princess," she only whispered.

Cion did not reply, shutting her eyes. Soren did the same, and when morning came, her limbs stiff and her eyes heavy, she resolved only one thing.

To survive the day.

CHAPTER 11

A DOG.

He was a dog to a greedy master, one who had no idea he had, in truth, snared something feral—untrainable. Every move, every breath…

It was all calculated.

There were some days he despised what he had done, but all it took was one flash of memory, and the rage replaced any grief. He was blind to the atrocities before and ahead. There was only the sound…

A scream.

A ripping.

And silence. So. Much. Silence.

CHAPTER 12

SOREN WAS SEPARATED from Cion after breakfast, which had been a simple bowl of bland gruel. It was almost humorous, watching the princess struggle to finish her serving of the plain, cooked grain. Soren was, of course, used to such fare —the single advantage she had above Cion, if she could even call it that.

What am I, goat's dung?

Soren bit back a small smile. *You are only an advantage in theory right now. If I can't make it through these weeks of training, it won't matter that you chose me.*

You will.

Thessa went silent after that, and Commander Eton approached, muscled arms crossed as he barked, "Mise. Come with me."

Stares landed on Soren as she stood, leaving Cion and Ilav, who lingered close by. Fear pricked her hands as the commander led her away from the thick clustering of tents and towards the edge of camp. He was silent most of the way, only increasing her growing unease.

She jumped when he spoke, walking ahead of her and not bothering to look back. "I sent word to the king of you by dragonback last night. It's the fastest way to get a message to the capital. Unfortunately, he agreed with the princess."

The commander turned, and Soren flinched as he stepped in close, his face inches from hers now. "I don't think scum like you is worth the extra time or resources of a personal trainer. No one is, in my opinion. But I have to follow orders."

She met his burning gaze and said softly, "Indeed."

Commander Eton narrowed his eyes, surveying her closely. His head tilted, and some emotion she could not decipher flickered across his harsh features. But it was fleeting, and he stepped away and barked, "Evva!"

Soren followed the commander's eyes to the small clearing ahead. From inside a tent at the very edge of camp, a man emerged.

He was tall and broad, with pale skin, hooded brown eyes, and a gold ring piercing one of his eyebrows. Fine hair fell in dark waves just past his sharp jawline, the strands casting shadows over his face. He wore the same leather armor Commander Eton sported, though lacking in any of the decorum, and his muscled arms were covered in thin scars.

"The girl I spoke of," the commander spat, gesturing back at Soren. "Girl, this is Swordmaster Vane Evva. He's to be your trainer for the first few hours of each morning. After that, you will join the others for the rest of the day."

Vane Evva lifted his gaze to hers. A strange awareness crept over her as he met her eyes, the back of her neck prickling. The air felt oddly still, but the spell was broken quickly as Vane said in a deep voice, "We'll need more than a few hours a day. She's weak."

A furious flush crept up her cheeks, but she tamped down her emotion quickly. He wasn't wrong, and getting angry was not going to help her at all.

"She has to mesh with the other riders," Commander Eton said, his tone brokering no room for argument. "You can have her until the midday meal, no longer."

Vane's brow rose, his eyes still on her. "Fair enough."

She fought the urge to squirm as he looked at her, standing with her arms crossed over her chest. Commander Eton turned to leave, but he paused with a final warning to her.

"I've trained Misean soldiers before, and the second I saw any spark of rebellion in their eyes, I killed them. You would do good to remember that, girl."

She swallowed hard, her throat tight, but did not reply. The commander left, his footsteps fading, leaving her alone with Vane, who still stared at her. Now that the commander had gone, the curiosity in his expression flickered to something…raw.

He looked at her like it hurt.

But the trace of odd vulnerability left his face quickly as it had come. She cleared her throat, fidgeting.

"Are you going to train me?"

A soft snort escaped him. "Hm. Rather mouthy, aren't you?"

She looked away. "I apologize."

Gravel crunched beneath his boots as he took a step closer. "I didn't ask for an apology, nor do I want one.

You're going to have to cut the groveling act. It won't serve you here."

She clenched her jaw, her brow creasing as she looked at him. Her demeanor was no act; rather, it was an attitude that had been hammered into her for years. This 'sword-master' likely couldn't even imagine what her life had been like, the hardship she had faced.

"You're angry at me now."

She blinked. "No."

"And a bad liar too."

Before thinking, she shot back, "I am an excellent liar."

Fear flooded her as soon as she spoke the words aloud. What if he reported her? Could he take it as some act of rebellion? One word, and the commander would surely kill her.

But Vane merely shook his head, the corner of his lips twitching, as if he found her funny. He walked away, his back to her as he picked up a sword, slim and lightweight—or at least it appeared that way, because when he handed it to her and said, "Let's see if you have any balance," her arm bowed from the weight.

"It's heavy," she said quietly. "It didn't look like it would be."

"Mm. It's made of a special kind of steel."

She chewed on her lip, examining the blade. "But wouldn't it be more beneficial for the blade to be lightweight and easily handled? What's the purpose of it being heavy like this?"

Vane paused before replying, and she looked back up at him. Gods, he was so much taller than her. Granted, she was short, even for a woman, but she could hardly meet his eyes without craning her neck back.

"You're curious. Why?"

She bit back an apology, as he'd requested she do, and instead admitted, "I used to watch the princess train with her master. I was never given the opportunity to learn, of course, but it interests me."

"What does?"

She felt foolish as she replied, "The dance."

His expression grew sharp. "Your princess learned swordplay in a child's pen, soft and safe, without consequence if she faltered or failed. You do not have such luxury. We need to teach you to defend yourself quickly, which will allow little room for finesse or fear—especially fear. You need to get used to the idea of taking a life. Your dragon won't always be the one to do so for you."

Soren felt her face drain of color. She knew this, had since Thessa chose her yesterday. But the reality, thrown carelessly in her face, was harsher than she bargained for. He was not wrong in thinking it would be difficult for her, but he was wrong to assume she had never taken a life before.

In fact, she had taken five.

"You must not speak of this, Soren. Ever."

But Vane must have somehow seen it on her face, already unnervingly good at reading her when most could not, because his brow creased, and he said in a low voice, "You are not unfamiliar with death, are you?"

She cleared her throat softly. "I have seen it before. Most Misean slaves have."

"That's not what I—"

"Is all this talking helping me learn to kill?"

Vane went still before he leaned in so close, they nearly shared breath. A tremble rushed down her spine at the look in his eyes.

"You're going to need to learn when to use that mouth of yours. Talking back to me will only get you this."

Swiftly, before she could even register what was happening, he kicked out a foot, causing her to tumble to the ground. She flailed but went still as he pressed his weight over her limbs, the cool metal of the blade at her throat.

"Understood," she whispered.

He searched her eyes for a long moment before shoving off her and standing again. But when she tried to move, his foot stopped her. "We need to work on your strength, soldier."

She kept her mouth shut this time. He sat down a few feet from her and said with the ghost of a smirk, "You're going to hate this part."

He wasn't wrong at all. He pushed her through a circuit of strengthening exercises, and by the time he declared they were finished, her entire body burned. But the torture continued; running laps around camp until she tasted copper in the back of her throat, and then an order to top it all off.

"After sundown, before you sleep each night, you'll complete the circuit I just showed you."

"The whole—"

"Yes," he clipped out, not looking at her. "And if you want to complain, I'd be happy to add more to the routine."

Soren lowered her gaze, but she said nothing to Vane, holding in her anger as she had done all her life.

"We're done for today. Tomorrow, we meet at sunrise."

He stalked away without giving her further instructions, so she wandered to the center of camp. She found Cion and Ilav there, along with a group of five others.

"Here," Cion said as Soren sat down next to her, handing her a piece of dried jerky and a small portion of flatbread. "You missed the handouts."

"Thank you," Soren said quietly, biting into the bread.

Ilav snorted. "Why don't you just let her fail? It'll happen anyways, with or without your coddling."

Soren ignored him, quickly scarfing down her food. Just as she had finished chugging from a skein of water, one of the other five nearby said, "So the rumors are true, then. A Vemon dragon chose a Misean slave. I hardly believed it when I heard."

Soren sighed softly, and Ilav caught it.

"Is this all rather annoying for you?" he sneered. "All the attention? I'm sure you're not used to that. Is it overwhelming, being the odd one out?"

"I heard her mamma found her in the river!"

"Outsider!"

The voices in her memory began to blend with Ilav's, and an old darkness started to rise in her.

Five, she reminded herself. Five final breaths, five wailing mammas, five suspicious papas, and a warning: never let anyone see what you can do, and *never* tell anyone what happened.

She had not been tempted for so long to touch that corner of her soul. She had been taken from her home, separated from her family, beaten, neglected, forced to kneel and scrape and grovel…

So why now?

"Soren?"

She looked up, finding Princess Cion staring at her, brow creased. "You went quiet."

Soren swallowed. "It's nothing. I am simply tired from my training this morning."

"Vane, huh?" a girl said.

She, along with the four others, all wore armor that appeared to be made of scales. Dragon scales, if Soren was a betting woman. The girl had long, dark hair done in a single braid and a nose ring. She didn't look at Soren with venom, but with mere curiosity.

"Yes. Commander Eton assigned me to train with him."

The girl snorted loudly. "I wish you luck. Vane is an asshole."

"I…gathered that," Soren said before she could stop herself. Cion glanced sidelong at her, unused to Soren speaking in such a way. Soren ignored her.

The girl laughed. "I might be able to tolerate you after all. My name is Yella."

Soren dipped her head. "Soren."

Yella glanced at Ilav and Cion. "If you three are done with the meal, we should begin."

"We are," Cion replied.

Soren could feel the princess' eyes on her.

Yella jumped to her feet. "Good." She gestured behind her to the others. "The five of us are Aren's newest riders, from two seasons ago. The rule is that the newest train the newest, so for the next moon cycle, you'll be with us for half your days. After that, the real fun begins. Come—the dragons are waiting in the field."

She and the other four began walking, and Soren, Cion, and Ilav followed. All Soren wanted to do was lay down and sleep after her training session with Vane, but she couldn't afford to show weakness here, not ever.

"So, what's with the hair?" Yella asked as they walked.

Soren bit her cheek. "Just a birth defect, I was told."

"Not an omen?"

"Not at all."

The practiced lie slipped easily off her tongue.

CHAPTER 13

Thessa waited for her in the field with eight other dragons. Now that hers stood beside so many others, Soren truly understood the reason Vemon dragons were whispered about in folktales. Thessa was enormous, far larger than even the next largest, the dragon Yella bounded over to.

"Mount your dragons!" she called over a cold wind that swept through the field.

Ilav glanced at Cion, who merely shrugged.

"Just like that?" he called to Yella.

One of the other riders, a stocky man with a shaved head, rolled his eyes and muttered something to his companion, who laughed. "My bet is still on the Misean girl. She'll be the first to drop, and you'll owe me ten gala."

Soren tamped down the anger that kept trying to rise, instead walking with her chin up towards Thessa. It felt odd not to curl her shoulders in and keep her eyes down, but she was determined to survive. Kelshie might be out there somewhere in Aren's endless ranks. If she could just find her, maybe together, they could somehow escape.

A fool's dream.

Soren stiffened, finding Thessa's silvery gaze inches from her own. She had been so lost in her own head, she had not thought of the dragon's ability to see into her mind, nor had she noticed the dragon, large as she was, creeping closer.

Do not fret. My loyalty is to you alone, which is why I am counseling you.

Soren set her jaw. *She could be alive.*

Perhaps. But you have more dire issues to attend to at the moment.

"What in the gods' names is she doing?" Soren heard Ilav say.

She turned to find him and Cion looking at her, their expressions puzzled. Behind them, Yella was already atop her dragon.

"What's the issue, you three?" she called.

Cion took a step closer. "Soren, what were you doing?"

Soren stiffened. Had she done something wrong without realizing it? She cleared her throat softly. "Thessa was scolding me about something. It doesn't matter. I was just being silly, and she—"

"You can speak with her?" Ilav cut in, his eyes widening.

"I… Can't you?"

Ilav's face twisted. "Are you lying, Mise?"

Cion shook her head. "Soren has never studied dragonlore. How could she know about the mind connection?"

Soren's mind was whirring. Was this not something the others could do? She wasn't exactly keen on the thought of being singled out over something yet again. Some visibility and importance protected her, but too much could be a threat.

From atop her dragon, Yella let out a laugh. "She's not lying. Keenie conferred with Thessilnn," she said, running a hand over her dragon's tan scales.

The stocky man stared at Soren, slack-jawed, while his companion looked enraged. Yella rolled her eyes and slid off Keenie, muttering, "Pick up your mouths, you idiots," as she passed the two men. When she reached Soren, she said, "You were never taught anything about dragons, were you?"

"No," Cion replied.

But Yella didn't even spare her a glance, eyes still on Soren.

"No," Soren affirmed. "I was never allowed to read. I know how, but I have not touched a book in years."

Yella's expression tightened momentarily, but it quickly brightened again. "Right, well, there are a few things you should know. A rider and a dragon share a bond, established the day the dragon chooses their rider, but the bond takes time to strengthen. Telecommunication is something that often takes several moon cycles, or even several seasons, to become easily accessed. The dragons don't like opening themselves up to a rider who may not live."

"But we could all hear them at the ceremony," Soren said, brow furrowing.

Yella shrugged. "A necessity they allow. But I didn't hear Keenie again until the last moon cycle. Jona and Adem aren't there yet."

Their dragons sense a weakness and fear their time together will not last.

Soren flicked her gaze over to Jona and Adem, who had now taken to glaring at her. Yella patted Soren's shoulder, and she jolted at the contact. She was not used to human touch.

"But you," Yella said, a grin gracing her lips. "You can hear your Vemon dragon already."

A heavy silence fell over the training yard, interrupted only by the wind and the sound of dragons chuffing restlessly. Eyes landed on Soren and on Thessa behind her.

Eventually, Jona said, "We should begin. We've already wasted enough time."

Soren was grateful for his interruption and took the opportunity to turn, climbing up onto Thessa's back. By the time she had managed to perch atop the saddle, everyone else had already mounted their dragons.

"Follow!" Yella shouted from ahead, just before her dragon's wings spread out and pumped the air.

Soren felt her stomach dip as Thessa reared back, her wings splayed wide before taking off, trailing Yella and Keenie. The others fell in line, and they soared up into the cloud line.

"Dive!" Yella screamed over the wind.

Ilav shouted, and Soren sucked in a sharp breath as Thessa began to dip, tucking her wings in.

Hold on tight.

Wind seared Soren's eyes, tears blinding her as the air rushed past. On instinct, she leaned low on the saddle, keeping her legs tight to Thessa's body. Her muscles screamed from the effort of holding on, and as Yella shouted to bank, she nearly flew off Thessa's back from the force. Her ears popped, and as the tears cleared from her eyes, she realized they were in the middle of the Ellys mountain range, peaks on either side of them.

You did well.

Even in her own mind, Soren's voice was breathless. *Thanks for the warning.*

Thessa huffed out a chortle, gliding behind Yella and Keenie. Yella glanced back, and Soren could see her taking inventory, making sure they were all still there. Soren craned her neck to see Ilav vomiting off the side of his dragon. Princess Cion took up the back of the group, and the rest of the more seasoned riders looked merely windblown.

"Camp!" Yella called, waving them forward.

The wind tousled Soren's hair, pulled free from the braids during their dive. She pressed a hand to Thessa's scaled back and took a deep breath. For the first time in many seasons, she felt oddly at peace.

Atop a dragon, hundreds of feet in the air, she was free of the heavy shackles she had worn nearly all her life.

The dream ended as soon as they landed in the field behind the camp. She slid off Thessa, foregoing the ladder this time. Sensation jolted up her spine as she dropped to the ground, but she held back her yelp. A few paces away, Ilav was vomiting again. Even the princess looked pale as she dismounted and slid to the ground.

Yella smiled. "Fun, right? Diving like that is one of the more difficult maneuvers, so I figured we would just get it over with."

"*Bitch,*" Ilav choked out. "You're trying to weed us out."

Yella's brow rose. "This is war, is it not? I have orders to ensure a strong group of riders can lead our armies. I'd advise that next time, you just choke it down."

Ilav snapped, rushing at Yella, his face pinched in fury. She caught his arm before his fist could hit her face, twisting roughly. He yelped in pain as she held the position. "You think this is a game? I would have thought being a general's kid would give you a more realistic view."

"We are the reigning power," he gritted out. "Mise has no chance."

"True as that may be, would you like to know how many dead riders *and* dead dragons that has taken to remain true? Meesling has its wyverns, and Mise has better fed soldiers. Those things won't win them a war, but it will make it more difficult for us to end it."

Ilav grunted, pulling free of Yella's hold and stumbling back. She looked around. "Anyone else?"

No one spoke. Yella smiled again, dusting her hands off on her leather riding pants. "Good. Follow me. We're going to study flight formations."

The rest of Soren's afternoon was spent on her knees, huddled around a circular wooden table filled with unrolled parchment weighed down by stones. Yella pointed to different formations, informing them again and again that they would practice most of them together before training was up. She also drilled into their minds that memorizing the formations now was important.

"When you're out there, in the thick of battle, you'll forget it if it isn't already second nature," she told them sternly.

Soren was bleary eyed by the time dinner came around, but the knowledge that her day was far from over weighed heavy on her. She ate quickly before slipping from the group, huddled around the fire.

Unsure exactly where to do her exercises, she headed back to the field where they had met the dragons earlier in the day. It was empty and dark, clouds obscuring any moonlight trying to fight its way through. She sighed heavily, her breath clouding as she dropped down and began the circuit of core exercises Vane had shown her. Once she was done, she ran laps around the field before letting herself collapse near the edge of camp in a sweaty, shaking mess.

There's a stream just beyond the field. It's cold, but at least you won't stink.

Soren's mouth quirked up. *Thank you.*

Thessa was quiet after that, and Soren trudged across the field, finding the stream just hidden behind a small grove of trees. Glancing around several times, she made sure no one was there before she stripped down to her underclothes and slipped into the water, gasping at the icy chill. After dipping her head in once, she crept out, teeth chattering as she slipped her clothes back on over her wet skin.

By the time she made it back to the tent, Cion was already fast asleep. Soren settled down on her mat and shut her eyes, praying to gods she knew would never answer that her dreams would be kind.

As usual, the gods did not listen.

CHAPTER 14

Breakfast was not ready by the time Soren left the tent for training. Not wanting to be late and incur Vane's anger, she hurried to the clearing where they had trained the day prior. He was waiting, arms crossed over his broad chest. His gaze flicked over her, catching on a point by her shoulder. He was looking at her hair, she realized, the silvery strands braided tight and falling nearly to her waist.

"I know, it's an odd color," she said, touching it self-consciously. "Not very Misean."

His mouth bracketed with tension. "A family trait?"

She shook her head. "Not that I know of. If it was, my mother and father were dead before they could tell me much about where it came from."

Lie. She remembered asking her parents incessantly about her hair and why she didn't look like them and her siblings. They had glossed over the subject every time she brought it up.

Vane didn't react to her words the way she thought he

would, though. She expected *some* semblance of pity. Instead, he only said shortly, "Start your exercises. Now."

Fury rose in the back of her throat like a bad taste. It clouded her thoughts and her reason, making her promptly forget the threats that had been hammered into her mind at the palace.

"I was planning on it, *sir*," she quipped, raising a brow and matching his stance, her arms across her chest.

He lowered his chin, a storm in his eyes. "I am trying to help you."

"You don't even know my name."

His dark eyes narrowed. "You didn't give it, Soren."

She stiffened, taking a step back. "How do you—"

"Commander Eton told me, believe it or not."

She blinked. "I didn't know he bothered to learn it."

Vane's mouth twitched, but the amusement quickly faded. "Enlightening as this conversation has been, get on the ground before I make you."

She reined in the urge to roll her eyes at his dramatics. It shocked her a bit, this person she became around him. Fleetingly, she wondered if this was who she might be without a life in shackles. But the thought was gone quickly, like a passing breeze, and she began her exercises. Vane remained standing above her, his jaw occasionally twitching between barked orders of ways she could better her form.

When she finally stood to begin running her laps, her vision swam, but she ignored it. Vane ran beside her, his breath even while hers was ragged. Vaguely, she observed others in the camp staring as they ran by.

"Keep up the pace," he ordered, not at all out of breath.

She blinked hazily, forcing her legs to move faster, even though they felt as though they were made of stiff, heavy iron. By the time they had reached the clearing again, black dots swarmed her vision, and her body began to feel light.

"Soren."

Vane's voice sounded far away.

"Sorry…*sir*," she slurred just as her legs gave out beneath her.

Instead of the hard, muddy ground she expected to hit, strong arms caught her. A scent enveloped her, one that reminded her of sitting around a blazing campfire, warm and smoky and…

Firelight danced all around her, blazing torches lighting the chamber, where no one would find them. Tonight was theirs alone, no matter what the morning brought.

Strong hands brushed through her hair, and the torches flared.

"Careful. I'm not fire resistant."

Lips touched her neck, a soft chuckle vibrating against her skin—

With a gasp, Soren opened her eyes. Backlit by the gray sky, Vane's face hovered above her, his brow creased and his full lips set. Still half in a haze, she reached up and touched his forehead, a few strands of hair catching on her fingertips. His lips parted before he pulled away, but she caught it: the moment of vulnerability, when the hard look in his eyes softened just a fraction. There was something he wasn't revealing, some card he had yet to play.

"Are you alright?" he asked gruffly, his voice catching just slightly, just enough that she heard it.

She dropped her hand abruptly and tried to sit up, but he pressed a hand on her shoulder, stopping her.

She sighed. "I'm fine. I just missed breakfast."

Vane shut his eyes briefly and muttered something under his breath, words she could not understand.

"*Eejja caileag.*"

"What?"

He opened his eyes, and this time, he let her shove away from him. Cold rain had begun to fall, storm clouds thickening above them. The frigid water sluiced down Vane's face as his mood quickly shifted. His entire body was tense as he stood, crossing his arms.

"You are an idiot."

She ignored the scathing words and instead scrambled to her feet, still barely reaching his chest. "The language you just spoke, what was it?"

Lightning flashed, reflecting in his onyx eyes. "It doesn't matter. Next time, if you miss a meal, tell me so I can get you something."

She snorted, shaking her head. "Why?"

"Why what?"

"Why do you care to help me? Why does it matter if I've eaten or not or if I'm strong? Most here would love to see me fail."

Vane lowered his chin, water running in rivulets down his face. "If you let yourself be what they made you, Soren, you will *never* rise above their expectations."

His words took her aback. He spoke as if he knew her struggles, as if he too had once worn shackles of some kind. She wasn't foolish enough to think all chains were worn on your limbs, but she didn't ask about what his might be, afraid he would lash out at her.

"Midday meal is probably being handed out soon," she merely replied. "I shouldn't miss it too."

Vane tightened his jaw and looked away from her. "No, you shouldn't."

She nodded once then abruptly turned and walked away, her mind whirling as she left him behind in the pouring rain.

Mud and rainwater sloshed around her booted feet, but she hardly noticed it, her mind on what she had seen when she'd fainted. It had felt just like her dreams, and she was nearly certain whoever's perspective she was looking in from was the same. It unnerved her, that the visions were starting to seep closer to her waking hours.

Could it really be some god's rebellious daughter playing with her mind?

But *why*?

She pushed the question from her mind as she approached a tent where everyone was sheltering from the rain to eat. She couldn't afford to be distracted, not now, not as she faced the wolves.

After grabbing one of the last portions of dried meat and hot grain, she sat gingerly on a wooden bench next to Cion, who was soaking wet and wearing a sullen expression. Without the usual coating of makeup, the princess looked younger. Still, even as she appeared miserable, there was determination hardening her jaw.

"Not so grand, is it, princess?" Yella said from across the tent.

Cion lifted her head. "Are you done?"

Yella smirked, and Soren had a feeling the girl was just getting started in a fight she did not want to pick.

"Maybe," Yella said. "I was wondering how you've been faring without a servant. Soren was supposed to attend to you, right? I mean, that must be hard, having to wipe your own ass—"

In the blink of an eye, Cion leapt from the bench and tackled Yella to the ground. The benches tipped over, and people began to shout, some encouraging the fight. Soren watched with wide eyes, a knot in her throat as the princess hit Yella's face square in the middle. Blood streamed from her nose, but she was still smiling, even as Cion reared her shaking hand back for another blow.

"Stronger than I bargained for," Yella said between broken laughs.

Soren stood slowly, a hand on her throat. Something was wrong. She could feel the dissonant hum of it in the air, like a call beckoning some dark void closer and closer to Cion…

Death, a bodiless voice rasped in Soren's ear. She whirled, searching the tent, but turned back just in time to see the two women roll. Soren caught the flash of silver in Yella's hand as she pinned Cion to the ground. Soren yelled the princess' name, but Cion looked back at her instead of at the dagger in Yella's hand—

Someone screamed.

The room plunged into a deep darkness, the temperature falling with it. In an instant, the air felt achingly frigid. Gods, she was quite suddenly so, so cold, from the tips of her fingertips to her very center, where her heart beat quick as a desert jackrabbit's.

Five.

She could *feel* Yella's heart slowing, as if the organ was beating in her hand.

Four.

Tiny bodies lay scattered around her on the forest floor, and a woman wailed in agony.

Three.

"Are you afraid of me, Mamma?"

Two.

"Misean whore!"

One.

She was becoming exactly what they wanted.

A killer.

Please, someone whispered, the sound brushing against her very thoughts. Not Yella, but her dragon, Keenie—

In an instant, the room brightened, the only sound the pounding of the rain against the canvas fabric of the tent. Yella was curled in the corner, rocking herself slowly and muttering under her breath. Princess Cion sat a few paces away from her, face drained of color. Her throat had been nicked, but the blood was already drying against the pale skin of her throat.

"What in the gods' names is happening here?"

Commander Eton's voice echoed through the tent, and before Soren could even react, Ilav pointed at her. "It was her! She tried to kill the princess with dark magic!"

Rough hands tore at Soren, spinning her around abruptly until she came face to face with cruelly familiar jade green eyes.

"Magic, hmm?" the commander said. He laughed harshly, shaking his head. "Magic doesn't exist, not anymore. But if you tried to kill the princess—"

"She didn't." Cion's voice shook as she stood. "She didn't. Yella did. Soren stopped her, I don't know how…"

Commander Eton shoved Soren back, and someone else grabbed her from behind, though the touch wasn't as rough.

Vane.

She twisted to find his jaw set and his gaze hard. But he didn't look at her, instead focusing on some spot at the back of the tent.

The commander advanced slowly toward Yella, who was still on the ground. He stopped in front of her, crouching down and whispering, "Up, girl."

When she didn't move, he barked, "Now."

Finally, she lifted her tearstained face to look at him, but she did not stand. Instead, she moved her arm from where it had been curled in her lap, placing the curved dagger on the grass floor with a trembling hand.

The commander snatched it up immediately, eyes narrowed as he demanded, "Who sent you?"

Yella swallowed, her throat bobbing with the movement. "My cousin is Misean," she rasped. "A bastard. She escaped over the border two seasons ago."

"Her name?" the commander asked, his voice suddenly a strange, deathly calm.

Yella only stared at him, eyes wide and face pale. The commander glanced back at Vane, who nodded once then let go of Soren. She stumbled back slightly at the sudden loss of his presence.

Vane strode purposefully towards Yella, chin lowered and hand on the sword pommel at his hip. She shrank back when he knelt in front of her.

"The magic," he said in a clipped voice. "Is the boy's claim true?"

Soren felt the air leave her lungs as Yella lifted a shaking hand to point at her.

"It's impossible, isn't it?" she whispered. "But I could feel my heart slowing. It was her… It was Soren."

Vane's hard expression did not shift, and still, he did not look at Soren. Commander Eton was staring at her now, though, eyes wide in disbelief, along with most of the others in the tent.

"Death magic," someone whispered.

The spell broke eventually when the commander took a sharp breath and barked, "Mise, with me. Vane, take care of the traitor."

Soren's heart beat rapidly, and all she wanted to do was run. She felt like the child who had been caught by her mother after a terrible act. But unlike then, there was no one to protect her, and she had little choice but to follow the commander out of the tent. As she left, she could hear Yella struggling and pleading with Vane.

A few seconds later, Vane dragged Yella out of the tent, her still fighting against his hold, even though it was no use.

As he pulled her past Soren, Yella grabbed her arm roughly and hissed in her ear, "Vane is not who you think he is. Be careful, Soren."

She mouthed something just before Vane pulled her around the corner and out of sight, but Soren couldn't decipher it. The words were too foreign and oddly shaped. She didn't have much time to consider it as Commander Eton dragged her by her hair across camp through the mud. Eyes followed them as they went, and Soren wrangled the urge to let the darkness still building inside her out. It was as if it had gotten a taste of freedom and now wanted more.

She kept it in check, even as they reached the commander's tent and he threw her inside. Glowing gas lamps flickered as she hit the ground, pain vibrating up her spine.

"What are you hiding?" he growled, towering over her.

She shook her head. "I didn't know," she gasped.

It was a lie, one she had been telling herself for years now. She was not evil, even if the beckoning death swelling inside her begged differently.

The commander's heavy-booted foot struck her side, and the sharp pain of the blow knocked the breath out of her.

"You're lying," he snarled before kicking her again.

She coughed, the pain blurring reason as she struggled to find an answer. She had never considered the power she held to be a gift. It was a shameful secret. 'Death magic', someone had just called it, and they were right. But what would the commander—and the king, for that matter—do now that they knew what she could do?

Commander Eton kicked her again, and her ribs ached with the force. But even as he hit her again, fear and shame kept her mouth sealed shut.

Finally, he stopped, sighing harshly. He leaned down next to her and lifted her face with calloused fingers. She flinched at his touch.

"Who else knows about this?" he murmured, his voice unnervingly soft in the face of all the violence he had just inflicted.

She shook her head and rasped, "No one…alive."

"Because you killed them?"

Lowering her chin, she said in a low voice, "No. Because

you did. Although, I'm no pup anymore, am I, Commander Eton?"

His expression clouded momentarily, but she saw the shift the moment he remembered. A cruel smile spread slowly across his face, twisting his features.

"Ah, how could I forget?" He brushed a strand of her hair back, and she stiffened. "I do remember thinking it strange, a Misean bitch with hair like the moon. I brushed it off at the time as some defect of birth."

She remained silent, staring at him, hate burning in her chest, tempting her to unlock the cage within her. But even now, she tamped it down.

He sighed heavily through his nose then grabbed her roughly, hauling her up as he stood. She fought his grip, but he held her firm.

"You know," he said, nose to nose with her, his breath clouding the chilled air. "Your family could have saved themselves if they'd sold you out. We might have given them their lives at least in exchange for the knowledge of what you are."

"And what am I?" she dared, holding his gaze.

He smiled slowly again. "A weapon."

Her mind emptied for a few seconds, catching up with the meaning behind his words. When it did, terror flooded her at the realization of what he wanted.

"Don't worry. I won't kill you," he said, finally releasing her.

She stumbled back, and he chuckled, shaking his head.

"King Johannas will not be pleased his newest pet is Misean, but beggars can't be choosers in a world so dry of this kind of power."

"There are others?"

Commander Eton snorted. "Hardly."

"Who—"

"You will never be cleared to know that kind of information. But if you agree to help us, I'll elevate your rank and speed up your training."

A shiver raced down her spine. There was a price to be paid here.

"What else?" she pushed, her breath coming in thin gasps as she shivered.

His answering smile was wicked. "Of course, you want to know what we truly ask in return. Don't worry—there is a much more tempting prize waiting for you should you succeed."

She paused, curling her hands into fists. She could try to run or fight this, but in the end, she supposed she was farther gone than she had hoped, because she merely whispered, "I'm listening."

CHAPTER 15

WHEAT STALKS SWAYED in the warm air on either side of her, and a black beetle crawled up her calf. She ferried the shining insect into her hand before releasing it into the air, buzzing as it flew away. She watched it forlornly, her lips pinched.

"Jealous of a bug?"

She snorted softly, but it was half-hearted. "Aren't you? He's free to go where he pleases and do what he wishes."

"His lifespan is probably only a few days."

"Of freedom."

The man chuckled, his voice rough and deep. She liked the sound of it much more than she wanted to admit, even to herself. Last week, he had tried to tell her his name, but she'd stopped him. Names would make their meetings far too real, much too personal. Knowing his name would break the bubble of the dream, the one in which she could always come here and laugh with him.

"When is your wedding?"

She sighed sharply and turned to face him. "Do we have to talk about that?"

His gaze was heavy on her, his voice steady as he replied, "Ignoring it will not change your fate."

She rolled her eyes. "When are we going to talk about you?"

He tilted his head, lifting a shoulder. "There's not really much to talk about."

"Hmm," she hummed, lips tilting up. "You know what I am. Don't think I can't sense what I'm sure you can feel."

He stiffened. "It's nothing. Besides, plenty of humans have magic."

"Not like yours. It's too potent. Which parent is missing? Or are you an orphan?"

He eyed her with that same unflinching gaze. "So delicate with my wounds," he murmured, raising a sarcastic brow.

But the soft way he said it, looking at her like that, had her stomach dipping. A gentle heat spread inside her, slowly melting into an ache at her core. She shouldn't be feeling this…this want*, looking at him now, but she couldn't deny it, not as their gazes caught and her breath shuddered audibly. Something was shifting between them, and she didn't know how to stop it. Perhaps it wasn't even possible, not if she remained here.*

She stood abruptly, the wheat tickling the sensitive skin of her thighs. "I should go," she said quickly, turning and hurrying away from him.

But he caught up with her, a little breathless as he admitted, "My mother raised me alone. She passed when I was seventeen."

Pausing, she turned, meeting his earnest dark eyes. "You feel it most when you are around fire, don't you?"

His brow creased, but as she'd expected, he nodded.

"I believe your father might have been one of the bastards of Vulcan. Though, he is rather tight-lipped about his personal affairs, so I have no idea who it could be beyond that."

"I see."

She searched his face for any sign of distress, but his expression remained the same. Tilting her head, she said, "That doesn't bother you at all?"

He shrugged, though she caught the flicker in his jaw. "My place in this world remains the same."

"You'll just remain a farmhand then?"

His lips twitched. "Don't look so disappointed, princess."

She froze at the nickname. Or was it more than that? The man grinned, and she hated how much she liked his smile. It was dangerous.

"Ah, I thought so."

She took a step closer to him, narrowing her eyes. "How did you know?"

"A guess," he said, dipping his chin to look her directly in the eye. "Based mostly on your clothing and speech. I second-guessed myself because of your hands, though."

"My—why?"

He took her hand in his, his fingers and palm dwarfing hers. She shivered, her breath catching when he brushed his thumb along the tops of her fingers.

"You have the calluses of a warrior. Princesses aren't typically armed."

She dared a glance up at him again. "They are where I come from. And you're very observant."

"Mm, only of things that interest me."

Her heartbeat quickened when his hand tightened around hers, their fingers tangling. She let her eyes flutter shut, letting the solid warmth of his presence and the heat of the summer sun settle around her for just a few stolen moments. His lips brushed against her forehead, and she exhaled sharply.

"*Tell me your name,*" he whispered, his breath disturbing loose tendrils of her hair.

She lifted her head to find his gaze molten as he stared at her. A careless, thoughtless decision had her lifting on her toes, her hand curling in the waves of hair curling at the nape of his neck. She brushed her lips against his, and he groaned softly, affected by even her subtle touch.

"*No,*" she murmured just before pressing her lips to his.

He was ready for her, his broad hand sliding to the small of her back, the other untangling her hair from the loose braids. When he teased the seam of her lips with his tongue, she opened her mouth, moaning softly. He tasted like honey and smoke, and she found herself wanting more, wanting everything from him.

But she needed to let him go. She had already put him in enough danger by spending any amount of time here. And if Kronos ever found out...

She broke away, gasping. He didn't let her go far, though, pressing her forehead to hers as his breath came in broken, heavy gasps.

"*You're afraid,*" he said roughly, placing a hand lightly over her sternum. "*I can hear your heart pounding.*"

"*Mortals cannot sense that,*" she said, shutting her eyes. "*So you know for sure now what you are.*"

His lips brushed over her eyelids, and her eyes burned at the gentleness in his touch. She had to save him, had to run from this field and never look back. It was the only way.

"*I'm not afraid,*" he said quietly.

She opened her eyes. "*You should be. If he were to ever find out about this, you would wish you were dead long before you took your last breath.*"

He tensed, and she could sense the anger brewing in him like an inferno, rising to the surface of his skin. There was no mistaking it *now, the fire that ran within his blood. She wanted to douse herself in his inferno, to burn with him. Instead, she stepped back, finally creating some distance.*

"I'll be alright," she told him softly, holding his gaze.

She saw the understanding in his eyes—she was not coming back.

Still, he said to her, "Come back if you need a place to cry in secret again. I'll always be here, waiting."

She smiled sadly. "Don't waste your time. Live your life and be happy. Goodbye."

He opened his mouth, but she ran before he could stop her again. As she passed through the barrier between their worlds, she finally let the silvery tears fall, shimmering like starlight as she left the man and his fierce kindness behind.

Soren woke to find her pillow damp with tears she had shed in sleep.

Her dreams were becoming longer, more real. When she was younger, they had merely been flashes of a place or a person. Sometimes, they had even just left a feeling, but now, she saw this unknown goddess' life play before her in clarity. She knew now that the visions had to be from the past. The veil between this world and that of the gods had been shut long ago.

She rubbed the sleep and tears out of her eyes before she dressed and crept out of the tent quietly. Last night, she had waited until the princess was asleep to enter the tent, instead sitting by the creek until the moon was high in the sky. She did not want to know what the princess thought of her now. In fact, the idea of facing anyone was daunting, Vane included.

When she approached the training field, she paused. He was sitting near the edge of it, cross-legged and facing away from her. She debated calling his name, or even just turning and leaving altogether, but the deal Commander Eton had offered her weighed heavily on her mind.

You help us win this war, Cavell, and you go free.

The fate of Mise rested on her shoulders now. She could be responsible for its demise and become a free woman, or she could stand with her home kingdom and forever be hunted by Aren's king. She had quite suddenly made herself too important not to be noticed now.

Briefly, she wondered what the goddess in her dreams would do. Would she fight for herself or her people? Soren had no idea who her loyalties were to, besides the man in the field. Now that she was awake, a familiar blur settled over most of the dream. She could remember what she had seen but could not *see* it any longer.

The commander had told her if she accepted his offer—if she chose to live rather than run or be killed—she would spend most of her time with Vane. She wasn't sure how he was going to help her train with Thessa, since he was not a rider himself, but she hadn't dared ask. She had merely nodded and left quietly. The commander had let her go, free for one final night—except that she had never really been free. Freedom was a foreign concept to her. The shackle around her ankle had always ensured that.

She took a breath, and Vane shifted and then rolled his neck.

"Are you going to just stand there, Sora?"

She clenched her jaw then called back, "That's not my name!"

His entire body stilled, sudden tension filling the space between them. But he broke it quickly, clearing his throat and turning to face her as he drawled, "Apologies. I see lots of trainees come through and then go off to die. It can be tiresome to remember all their names."

She scuffed at the mud with a booted foot, her stomach turning as she asked, "What happened to Yella?"

Vane stood, stalking towards her with a stealth only a seasoned warrior could achieve. He stopped in front of her, crossing his arms over his chest. He held a dagger in one of his large hands, the blade curved and wicked.

"I think you're smart enough to know the answer to that question."

Her gaze dropped. "She's dead."

"Regrettably."

A disbelieving laugh escaped her before she could stop it. "You don't care?"

He cocked his head at her, raising a brow. "Do you? She tried to kill your precious princess."

"She—" Soren cut herself off, remembering whose side Vane was on. She lowered her head, a familiar submission settling over her. Her shoulders curved in, the ache there a welcome home to the last decade and a half of her life.

"Of course. I am glad the princess is safe."

Vane didn't reply, and she didn't look at him, not until cold, sharp metal prodded at her chin. She tensed, lifting her head. He had the tip of the dagger nearly at her throat, forcing her to meet his eyes as he said in a low voice, "Don't."

"I don't know what you mean," she said, swallowing against the tightness in her esophagus.

His nostrils flared in time with his jaw tensing. "You hold power over them now, Soren. You must know that. Don't let it go to waste by letting them mold you any further than they already have."

"The king controls us all," she said, her voice barely above a whisper. "Anything beyond that reality is a dream."

He paused. "A good dream?"

"Depends on who you're asking. Aren't you loyal to Aren? To King Johannas?"

His smile was like a wolf. "Naturally. Aren't you?"

She opened her mouth, but he shushed her with the edge of the blade to her lips. "Don't answer that. We need to start your training for the day."

A small ember of hope flared in her chest, but she smothered it quickly. It didn't matter if Vane was loyal or a rebel sympathizer. They were both quite obviously trapped under King Johannas' hand. Besides, it was entirely likely Vane was simply trying to feel her out, perhaps for the commander. Something inherent told her she could trust him, but she could not rely on her instincts. She couldn't trust anyone.

They began with the strengthening circuit, which wasn't becoming any easier. If anything, her muscles were so sore from the days prior, it hurt even more. She ignored the pain, turning off her mind to it as she ran through the exercises. Before they began their run, Vane slapped a bar of mashed grain and seeds into her hand, brow raised.

"So you don't faint in my arms again," he said dryly.

She scowled at him but scarfed down the bar anyway.

After the run, she nearly threw it back up, and Vane barked at her to breathe through her nose and out her mouth. Begrudgingly, she obeyed, and, annoyingly, it helped.

"See?" he said as she straightened from where she had been kneeling. "I'm not entirely useless to you."

"Thought it was the other way around, sir," she gritted out.

He smirked. "Ah, there she is."

There was something that caught her eye about his half smile. She had the urge to see what a full-fledged grin or even a laugh looked like on him, but he hadn't done either, not since they had met. The wish was stupid anyways.

"Soren," he ordered. "Focus."

She blinked, her face flushing crimson when she realized she had been staring at him. Clearing her throat, she asked, "Are you finally going to teach me how to fight?"

He snorted. "Commander Eton wants you out there on the battlefield in two weeks' time. Our time here is better spent getting you well-acquainted with Thessilnn and your magic."

"And how are you going to help me on either of those fronts?"

"In another life, I was a scribe's apprentice," he replied smoothly. "My master specialized in the history of the gods as well as magic manifesting in mortals."

"I see," she said slowly. His words felt like a lie, and she entirely wasn't sure why. "And what about Thessa?"

He raised a brow. "She lets you call her that?"

Soren frowned. "I think she prefers it."

"She most definitely does not," Vane said, his brow creased. "She must... Well, she must really like you."

Soren shrugged. "I can already speak with her, which isn't normal, evidently."

"Mm." Vane wasn't looking at her anymore. He was flipping the dagger around in his hand, his eyes wandering to the horizon where the mountains met the sky. The strong column of his throat worked, and he almost seemed to be collecting himself.

"It's time for the midday meal," she said, chewing on her lip.

His chest expanded under the leather armor. "You won't be joining the other riders, not for the rest of your training."

"For my safety or theirs?"

Vane swept past her, and with little choice, she followed him. She caught him muttering, "Can it not be both?"

She did not reply, instead falling silent as he led her away from camp to the edge of the field, where Thessa awaited them.

Soren glanced at the dragon. "What about the meal—"

Vane threw another bar at her, and she shut her mouth as she took it, sighing internally. The bars were bland at best, if not bitter.

"Enjoy it," Vane said, walking towards Thessa and undoubtedly catching on to her disappointment. "Your rations out there in the true war camps will be few and far between and not always as hearty as this."

Soren resisted the childish urge to scream at the sky. She had not asked for any of this, had not even wanted to go with Princess Cion to the Choosing ceremony in the first place.

I weep for you.

Soren looked up at Thessa—the dragon would be

raising her eyebrows if she had them, though her attention quickly shifted to Vane.

Please don't burn him to a crisp, Soren thought. *Or do, but then I might be killed too.*

Thessa made a chuffing sound, and Vane reached out a hand.

"I wouldn't—"

But Soren shut her mouth as Thessa nuzzled against Vane's hand, her eyes shutting.

"Unfortunately for you and your plans, Thessilnn and I are previously acquainted. It would take a lot for her to kill me," Vane said.

His mouth was curved into a small smile, but there was no humor or joy on his face.

Only pain.

How do you know him?

Thessa opened her eyes and looked straight at Soren but did not reply. She opened her mouth to try asking Vane too, but—

Wind whipped through her hair, her palms pressed against smooth scales. Ahead, someone laughed, the sound nearly lost to the currents of the sky.

"Don't fall off!"

Another laugh. "You'd catch me," he called.

"Not up to me!"

"Thessilnn wouldn't dare."

He turned to look at the pale dragon beneath her and—

Soren gasped softly. She was on the ground, her head in someone's lap. Blinking rapidly, she tried to hold on to what she had just seen. The dreams always faded quickly, but perhaps this close to waking, she could finally see his face…

"Soren."

She jolted as Vane's form blocked out the weak beam of sunlight peeking through the cloud cover. Strands of his dark hair fell forward, his mouth pinched with worry. She met his eyes, and a shudder ran up her spine.

But she merely sat up, scooting away from him and saying in a voice that was too bright, "Guess your gruel bars aren't enough to keep me from passing out."

Standing, she ignored the lightness in her head, turning away from him as she collected herself and rationalized her thoughts.

She had finally seen the man's face. The rest of the vision had faded away at the edges, too blurry for her to grasp anymore, but she couldn't forget him.

He stood just behind her.

CHAPTER 16

Vane spent the afternoon showing her how to mount and dismount Thessa quickly before and after flight. She avoided his eyes, and he hardly spoke to her aside from orders or instruction. Thessa was quiet too, though as Soren dismounted for the final time and walked from the field, she could feel the dragon's knowing gaze on her.

Had Thessa somehow sent her the vision? She was nearly certain she was seeing through the same eyes—that nameless goddess from her dreams. Perhaps she was the rider Thessa had once spoken of, but how could Vane have been there? She didn't know his age, but he appeared perhaps only a few seasons older than Soren herself. Maybe the man she'd seen was a blood relative of his.

That had to be it. It was the only plausible explanation.

"Do we eat dinner together too?" she forced herself to ask as they reached the edge of camp.

Vane didn't look at her as he replied flatly, "No. I have a meeting with the commander."

"Right. I'll see you in the morning—"

"And after, we'll meet back in the field for more training."

She stiffened. "At night?"

"Yes."

"Why?"

But he didn't reply, stalking towards the center of camp. She ground her teeth and headed back to the field. There was no way she was showing her face around the other riders again. It was bad enough she had to sleep in Cion's tent.

When she arrived back in the field, there was a small pack sitting next to Thessa, who was curled up in a ball, asleep—or at least Soren thought she was until she spoke.

He left that for you.

Soren eyed the pack. *When?*

You were busy sulking and avoiding him. He brought it while we were airborne.

Soren didn't reply, peeking inside the pack. Her stomach rumbled rebelliously as she saw three portions of dried meat, a half loaf of bread, and a plum. Thessa closed her eyes and went back to 'sleep,' though Soren was fairly certain she was still watching.

With a loud sigh, she muttered, "Why does he have to be a *nice* asshole?" then pulled the food out and promptly devoured it before she could let herself think too much about where he'd gotten it or why he had given it to her.

A slow hour passed. She finished the food as the sun dipped below the horizon, trading places with the waxing moon. Her eyes grew heavy, but she fought the prospect of sleep. That meant more dreams, and she was growing afraid of what she would remember when she awoke. She had a bad feeling that just because the goddess had sent Vane's lookalike away, it would not be the last time she saw him in the visions.

Vane didn't return until what had to be nearly midnight. He looked tired, and his hair was wet, as if he had just freshly washed. She stood as he approached, but she let him speak first.

"Have you considered the commander's offer?" he asked, his voice hoarse.

She bit her cheek, tasting copper. The commander must have told him about it during their 'meeting.'

"I can't really refuse it."

"Your life is yours."

She let out a puff of air. "It won't be anything at all for much longer if I refuse."

Vane's expression sharpened. "What *exactly* did he say to you?"

"I thought you knew." She felt empty as she spoke. She was sure he knew, had to be toying with her, but she was too tired to play.

Except he lowered his chin and said roughly, "Soren. What exactly did the commander say to you?"

She paused, considering her next words. If the commander hadn't told Vane everything, it had to be for a reason. She didn't trust either of them, but she had to decide now which of them she wanted to trust more.

"It doesn't matter," she finally told him after a few tense moments, deciding not to put her faith in either man. "What exactly are we doing out here in the dark?"

"He threatened you."

"As he tends to do."

"Don't be so damn stubborn and just tell me what he——"

"*Vane.*"

She meant to snap at him, but his name on her tongue came out much softer than she had meant. He stilled, and his eyes widened incrementally as he gazed back at her. He took a step closer to her, inclining his head down—not to touch her, but almost as if to just be closer to her. The air suddenly felt cloistered and warm, despite the cold of the season settling around them. Her chest felt tight, but neither of them moved further, locked in some understanding as they stared at each other.

Something was beginning to shift between them, and she knew she needed to resist it. If they remained as they were, simply a soldier and her trainer, they could pretend they were safe. *She* could be safe. Still, Soren felt the shimmer there, a threat just as great as any army or tyrant king. Caring for someone in a world such as this was a dangerous game to play.

He broke the spell first. "You ate."

"Yes… Thank you."

"You'll need your strength for tonight."

She pressed her lips together, unease twisting her stomach. "How exactly am I supposed to practice my magic? It just kills people."

Vane lowered his chin, circling her. The heated moment had still not dissipated, and his eyes were dark even as he asked her, "How many people have you killed at once?"

She looked down, shame heating her face as she twisted her hands. He would be disgusted if she told him. Anyone would be, though maybe that was for the best. Perhaps if he knew exactly what she could do, he would stay away from her. Maybe it would stop him looking at her like he wanted something from her.

She forced herself to look up, to look at *him*. "Five."

"Were they armed?"

"I… No."

"Fighting you?"

"No, but—"

"Were you emotional?"

She huffed out a breath. "Yes. They made fun of my hair."

"Children?" His expression was flat, void of disgust, or really any emotion at all.

She tightened her jaw. She just needed to say it. "Yes. Children from my village in Mise. I didn't understand what I was doing. It just happened."

He nodded. "Just like yesterday, you were angry, out of control and unfocused. We need to ensure you are none of those things on the battlefield, or instead of being a killer, you will be killed."

"I don't understand," she whispered.

The words were about more than just what he had said. She didn't know why he was still looking at her the same way, why he wasn't suddenly disgusted or afraid. Anyone with sense would be.

But Vane just stopped circling her and explained, "Your magic needs to be second nature to you, not something that erupts from you when you're angry or afraid. You need to *be* afraid and still be able to access it."

"And how in the gods' names am I going to achieve all that in two weeks?"

His answer was brutally stark. "Practice. Right now, there are three traitors to the crown waiting in an unmarked tent not far from here. You're going to kill them."

CHAPTER 17

Soren stood outside the tent, her heart pounding in her chest. Her fingertips tingled and her head felt light. Next to her, Vane stood, his features impassive.

"This isn't right," she whispered. "You know it isn't."

He glanced sidelong at her. "This is survival."

"For me, yes."

"That's all that matters."

She didn't push as to why he seemed to care about her survival. In the end, he was right. For her, choosing to do this or not was ultimately life or death. If she defied orders, she was sure she would be silenced, no matter how useful she was.

Taking a deep breath, she stepped inside the tent. As promised, three people, one woman and two men, sat, chained to wooden chairs. Two of them appeared to have been beaten brutally, and the other couldn't have been older than Soren herself.

Vane stared at them for a moment before declaring, "All three of you confessed to aiding Misean forces, as well as conspiring to kill several high-ranking Arenean generals. Your violence will be met with such. If you have any last words, say them now."

They all remained silent, their eyes on Soren as she took a step forward. The youngest had blue Misean eyes, though they were slanted up at the edges, signaling one of their parents was from Aren. Soren could only imagine life as a bastard during the war, forced to betray one of their families at every turn.

She knew all three rebels could see her slave anklet and her features clear as day. She only hoped they didn't hate her for not being as brave as them.

"Now, Soren," Vane said, standing just behind her. "Live."

Kill to live. Kill or die.

She shut her eyes and reached for that well of darkness inside her, a tear tracking down her cheek. But as soon as she let some of it leak out, she reared back. It was so cold, a kind of deep night that never ended. *That* was what she was dooming these people to. She tried to take it back and shove it into the prison again, but it was too late. The darkness was already overwhelming her, taking hold and clawing its way out of the cells she kept it in.

She opened her eyes, and as she did, an unnatural darkness settled over the tent, blowing out the gas lamps. Shadows swirled around the chained ankles of the rebels, and the youngest drew in a sharp breath. One of the others gasped, "Gods help us."

"I'm sorry," Soren whispered, though she felt nothing.

The temperature plummeted abruptly, and one of the

rebels took a quivering breath before all three of them went limp in their chairs, eyes wide in empty terror as they died.

The darkness retreated, sated for now as it slunk back inside her. She faced Vane, her mind blank and her hands numb and tingling.

"Now what?" she said, her voice flat.

He looked vaguely pained, and she did not know why. She had done what he asked.

"You're going to hate me for this before you thank me," he muttered before stepping forward and crushing her body to his chest.

She didn't realize how cold she was until she was pressed up against the blazing heat of his skin. It started to melt the numbness overtaking her body and mind. Her psyche had frozen emotion out of necessity, but now that the task was done and heat was flooding her once more, she let out a choked gasp as it all came crashing back down and she realized what she had done.

"There it is," he muttered.

"I killed them," she rasped. "Just like that."

Vane nodded, his chin brushing the top of her head. "Just like that."

"I hate you," she choked out, still held in his tight embrace.

"You should get some rest," he said, lips moving against the top of her head.

He didn't let go of her immediately, but when he did, he moved slowly. For a fraction of a second, their faces were close enough to touch, and Vane's hands tightened on her back. Time grew sluggish, the moments sticky between them as she stared into his eyes. But then, he looked away, giving her just enough clarity to step back.

"I suppose this doesn't earn me a break in the morning?" she said wearily, knowing the answer already.

He flexed his left hand, running his gloved thumb over his pointer finger. The movement almost seemed like a reflex.

"No. We need to make sure you're ready. There isn't time for breaks."

She sighed. "Right. My 'survival.'" She brushed past him and added, "Next time, just say the truth. I need to live for the king, and I'm only allowed to do so because of my usefulness."

"We all have a place in this war, Soren," was the last thing he said before she left.

Princess Cion was thankfully asleep again by the time Soren returned to the tent. As she laid down, exhaustion overcame her before she could even think to worry about the coming dreams.

～

"This was a bad idea."

A few paces away, the man stood. She had returned to the field in a blind panic nearly an hour ago now, blood in her eyes and sobs catching in her throat. He had been there, just as he had promised, catching her and murmuring soft comforts.

He hadn't demanded retribution as soon as he had seen the blood, even if she was entirely sure he had wanted to. It was what any god would have done—become hell-bent on revenge—but he had been more concerned about her. Bloodlust came second. The way that made her feel was dangerous, as dangerous as the fact that he had lived in her head all the days she was gone.

"We both know how dangerous this is," he finally said, pulling back just slightly to look at her. "Are you going to keep returning and regretting it, or will you just walk away again?"

She sighed sharply and stepped back. "You make me sound cold."

"You are anything but, goddess."

"You wouldn't think so if you knew who I really was."

His worn leather boots crunched on the ground as he moved closer to her. She looked around at the field, the crop surviving surprisingly well in Aren's climate. She wondered if the man knew it was because of him. Magic had a presence living things tended to flock to.

"I know enough," he said firmly, lifting her chin to look up at him.

A single, silver-hued tear ran down her cheek before he brushed it away. She felt shaky, whispering her confession. "I wouldn't be able to forgive myself if something happened to you."

His small smile was infuriating. "So you did miss me."

"Is that all you're worried about?"

He dipped his head, and the next words were spoken brushed against her lips. "No. What I worry about each day is whether I'll find this field empty, or if I'll find you here, bleeding from the inside out because of whatever that bastard is doing to you. I know, little goddess. There is much you don't tell me, but you don't need to keep trying to protect me."

She didn't know what to say. Half of her wanted to argue with him, to call him an idiot for not fearing what could happen to him if they were caught. But another part of her, a softer part, won out. She curled her fingers in the coarse fabric of his shirt and pulled him even closer. His eyes flared, and he threaded his hand in the hair at the nape of her neck, tilting her head back, taking some control. She liked that, *especially from him, because she knew he would never use that control to hurt her, only to please her.*

"I want to show you something," he murmured just before he kissed her.

She sighed softly, melting against his touch as he dipped his head and sucked on the sensitive skin just above her collarbone.

"Fine," she said, her eyes fluttering shut.

He pulled away, and a whimper slipped past her lips before she could stop it. He chuckled darkly but took her hand, leading her through the field. She tried to focus on her surroundings, but her eyes kept wandering to the strong muscles in his back and ass as he moved, to what his body might look like without the clothes, moving above hers—

"Patience, goddess," he said, looking back at her with a smirk. "You're burning up."

She realized they were by a small creek bed now. Here, without the tall grasses of the crop obscuring her vision, she could more clearly see the towering peaks of the Ellys Mountains caging the valley.

"Swim?"

She swallowed. "Fine."

He grinned again, and she cursed the fluttering in her chest.

"Don't act as if you weren't already trying to get me to take my clothes off."

She swatted at him as he pulled his shirt off, displaying a torso taut with muscles that spoke of all the years of his work. Her focus shifted as she looked at him, and he took advantage, picking her up easily and pulling her into the icy mountain water.

She gasped at the cold but relaxed in his arms wrapping around her from behind. He nibbled on her earlobe, and she arched into him. Her breasts heaved, nipples hard and visible in the thin, wet fabric of her dress. He slid his hand up her torso, eliciting a moan from her as he cupped one.

"Tell me your name," he rasped.

She moaned again as he played with her nipple but managed a broken, "No."

"You'll need mine, though, little goddess. Fair is only fair."

"Why?"

Slowly, he turned her so she was facing him. She shuddered as he leaned in close and whispered, "Because I want it on your lips when you come for me. And when you make me come, I need to be able to say yours."

She should turn away now, protect him and herself, but she was so lost in him, she feared it was far too late. She opened her mouth to finally tell him—

Soren opened her eyes. Her core was pounding, and her breasts felt heavy. The dream had felt so real. Seeing the man again only reminded her how much he resembled Vane.

Vane, who she hated for making her kill. Vanc, who had held her afterwards, as if he knew she would need it. Vane, who she was suddenly imagining with his fingers between her legs.

She sighed sharply in the quiet of the tent. The princess was asleep, or at least pretending to still be, so Soren quickly dressed and crept out of the tent. The air was even colder this season, and she shivered, wrapping her arms around herself as she walked through the quiet camp.

Vane wasn't there yet when she arrived in their usual spot, so she started her strengthening circuit, eager to get it over with. She was nearly finished when Vane's voice caused her to jump.

"You're still weak."

She looked up. He was towering over her, wearing the

same leather armor he always did, his hair carelessly tucked back and held by a slim dagger, of all things. But there was something off about him. Shadows circled his eyes, and he was favoring his right leg.

"Did you sleep at all?" she blurted before she could think too much about what she was saying.

His pierced brow raised, and slowly, he tilted his head. She swore the irises of his dark eyes lightened in strange fractures, but she was probably just imagining it.

"You're too observant for your own good," he said, crouching beside her. "It's going to get you in trouble. I'm surprised it already hasn't."

She looked away. "You're injured. Is that why you showed up late today?"

"Miss me? It was only an hour."

"*Vane.*"

He froze as she said it, and her lips parted as their gazes clashed. The heavy way he was looking at her didn't make any sense. Beyond her bond with Thessa, she was nothing and no one. There were probably thousands of displaced Misean slaves just like her within Aren's borders. Wasn't he the one who had just said she was weak?

"Finish the exercises." His voice felt like a caress. "You need to be as strong as possible before you face what's out there."

She searched his features, trying to find an explanation for what she had remembered, perhaps even an explanation for the way he was acting around her now. There was no mistaking it now, the agony in his dark eyes as they drank her in.

Perhaps pushing him was a mistake, but…

"And what *is* out there on the front? That's where you were, wasn't it?"

His jaw tightened. Their faces were still inches apart. "And how would I get all the way to the border and back in a matter of hours?"

"Dragonback would be a good way," she whispered.

"I'm not a rider—"

"And I thought *I* was bad at lying."

His gaze dipped to her mouth, and her mind chose to remind her of this morning, when she had woken up aching for him. But was it him, or some long ago near-copy from his bloodline? The mix of desire and confusion was dizzying.

"Stop thinking so hard, Soren," he commanded softly. "And pay attention."

She narrowed her eyes, forcing herself to put some distance between them. "To what? And are you going to answer my question?"

Vane rolled up to his feet and chuckled, though the laugh sounded strained. "I wasn't aware you asked me one, darling."

She shot up to her feet, and before she could think twice, reared her hand back. Before she could strike him, he caught her wrist, the strength of his grip vice-like. She fought him, straining her arm, but it didn't budge in his hold.

"Some personality," he said, lip curling. "How refreshing."

"Stop lying."

"Start moving," he ordered instead, dropping her wrist. "Then maybe you'll earn some answers."

She let out a puff of air. Around him, it felt like she was unfurling slowly. It was as if there was another person entirely beneath the bowing servant she had been forced to become. Vane stripped her of that. She needed to be anything but weak if she was going to survive this, but around him, she was both vulnerable and vicious.

Frustration fueled the rest of her exercises and the following run around camp, during which he was always a few paces behind her. Eyes trailed them as they wove between tents and around the perimeter. Soren avoided their eyes, trying to ignore the obvious judgement.

"Does it bother you?" Vane asked, easily catching up with her. "The staring?"

She swallowed, her throat dry and raw. "I'm not used to being seen."

"A secret for you," he said, slowing as they approached the field where Thessa waited. "Don't ever let them see you. Not truly."

Her voice was quiet as she replied, "I never have. Now, will you tell me where you're hiding your dragon?"

He clicked his tongue. "As I said. Observant."

"Stop avoiding the question."

"You want answers I cannot give."

He turned and approached Thessa, who was 'sleeping,' though Soren could practically feel her listening. The damned dragon had heard every word of their conversation.

He lifted a hand, and the corner of his mouth twitched as he brushed his fingers over the dragon's side. For the breath of a moment, he looked lighter, almost happy, but the small hint of a smile on his face fell quickly, and he turned back to Soren.

His expression shifted almost immediately when he looked at her. She hadn't noticed the mask he slipped over his features when with her, not until now, after seeing it fall so fully for a few seconds. She wondered if he was aware how many cracks were in it.

"Get on the saddle," he said, looking at Thessa.

"Then what?"

This time, his smirk was mirthless. "I want you to try and kill me, Soren."

CHAPTER 18

Soren reared back as if struck. The words were a harsh reminder of what she was capable of. She was a fool to think she could forget the souls she had taken last night, and this was just proof of that. But she *couldn't* touch that part of herself, not again, and certainly not now with him.

"Did you think last night was the end of our training?" Vane asked, as if it were a casual, simple question. "You did well, but we need to make sure you can wield atop Thessilnn too."

"I will end up killing you, you——" She cut herself off before the insult could lift from her tongue.

Vane didn't let it slip, though. "You 'what?' What were you going to call me, Soren?"

She crossed her arms over her chest. "I was just going to..." She shook her head. "It doesn't matter."

"Yes, it does. You're afraid of what I'm going to do if you insult me, aren't you?"

"Fine!" She threw her hands up in the air. "Fine, yes. But you don't have the right to call me weak for that. I had to survive in that palace for over a decade, and that included learning to hold my tongue."

Fury she did not understand darkened his eyes and tightened his jaw. An unusually warm breeze disturbed the strands of her hair as she balled her hands into fists at her sides.

"I don't begrudge your survival," he said in a low voice. "Quite the contrary, Soren, which is why I am telling you now to let go of your fear. Insult me however you wish if it helps. I might even enjoy it."

She hated the sudden flush of heat she felt as he tacked on those last words. He had made her kill 'rebels' last night, and she *knew* he was keeping secrets, and yet…

She wanted him.

It was an odd feeling, the desire. She wasn't necessarily a stranger to the sensation, but not like this, not so sudden and raging like summer floodwaters swelling in a river, threatening to sweep her away at any moment. It was so much worse since the dream last night. In the days before, she had felt a draw to him, but now, the pull was taking shape. The vague feelings were becoming emotions she could not afford to have, not for him.

She turned away from him, striding towards Thessa, just to get some space and clarity.

"Don't hold back," he called.

She bit her lip until she tasted blood. This was infuriating, and he was more stupid than she had thought if he was so sure she couldn't hurt him. She didn't *want* to, but the power inside her was so strong, so overwhelming now that she had finally let it out. Stopping it would be a feat itself.

You do not give yourself enough credit.

Soren settled on the saddle. *Let's hope so. I think the commander will kill me if I kill my trainer.*

You won't.

Soren sucked in a breath as Thessa flapped her wings once, then again until they were airborne, circling the field. And Vane…

He merely stood there.

"What in the name of the gods," Soren muttered, wind whipping her hair and stinging her face.

I believe he is waiting for you to begin. I will continue to circle, as dull as it is.

Soren shut her eyes, half of her trying to push the power down and half attempting to drag it out of the cages she kept it in. In the end, the power won out.

Thessa dove, as if sensing it, and Soren splayed her hands wide. Shadow, dark as ichor, surrounded Vane as they shot past him, low to the ground. Soren felt his life in her hands, bright and hot as a blazing fire.

She knew she could extinguish it whenever she wanted.

Thessa landed, the force of it pulling Soren from the hazy lull of the magic just as Vane fell to his knees. She gasped and tugged on Death's hands, forcing him back before he could consume Vane any further.

Frantically, she slid of Thessa's back, ignoring the pain that shot up her legs as she hit the ground and sprinted over to Vane. He was *laughing* as she approached.

"Good," he said, voice rasping. "You're already stronger than I thought."

This time, he did not catch her wrist as she bent down and slapped him hard across the face.

"I could have killed you!" she shouted. "I almost did!"

Vane's hand rose to his face, his fingertips brushing across the reddening skin. When his gaze met hers, she froze.

"Don't say it."

She swallowed hard. "Say what?"

"Sorry. I know you want to."

Shifting her gaze to the horizon, she blinked back a sudden burning in her eyes. "Earlier, before I stopped myself, I wanted to call you an idiot. Which you are."

"Mm, perhaps. But now, we know you can do it."

She flicked her gaze back to his. "What? Stop myself?"

"No, Soren. Kill someone you care for. You may have to someday, given what side of the war you are currently on."

She bristled. "First of all, I didn't kill you, and second, you are my trainer, nothing more. We both know that."

Humor disappeared from his face. His jaw flexed, and he said, "Perhaps you're right."

"I am. We can't be friends. Friends do not keep so many secrets between them."

Vane said nothing, instead rising and offering her a hand. She ignored him, standing on her own and avoiding his eyes.

She practiced with Thessa for the rest of the day, Vane giving instructions that the dragon seemed to understand before they took to the air. Soren didn't speak to him beyond nods and vague acknowledgments. Still, even as she tried to rebuild a wall between them, the tension did not dissipate, and her emotions only continued to run wild. It all grew worse when she looked at him, so she tried to avoid doing so.

When evening darkened the sky and they landed for the

last time, she found Vane had gone, leaving another gener-
ously filled pack of food in his place. She tried to continue
being angry with him. It was a task that proved more difficult than it should have been.

She waited until camp was quiet to return to the tent,
curling up on the sleeping mat and trying not to cry until
sleep claimed her.

*A dagger whizzed past her ear, nearly nicking it before it embedded
itself in the tree behind her. The air was cooler now, the foliage around
them shades of tan and brown.*

"Not bad," she mused before sauntering over to him.

*She kissed him, slow and thorough, letting her fingers twine through
the dark strands of his hair. He groaned into her mouth, and she arched
against him.*

*"Show me," he said on her lips. "I want to see you try to kill me,
darling."*

She grinned and pulled back. "Try? You underestimate me."

"I'm sure I do."

*She drew her blade first, tossing him the other. He caught it easily,
and as they began to circle one another, she asked, "How did you learn
to fight? I don't assume many farmhands have use for killing?"*

*"My mother," he replied, dipping his chin. "She didn't want me to
be defenseless, I suppose."*

"And who taught her?"

*He made the first move, and she sidestepped him easily before
swinging out her foot. He stumbled but managed to steady himself.*

"I'm not sure. She never told me."

She lowered her arm. "You don't talk about her much."

He smiled sadly. "She was strong but afraid. My entire life...I remember her always with fear in her eyes."

"What did she fear?"

He moved like the wind, tripping her but catching her with a hand to the small of her back as they hit the ground. His mouth hovered above hers, his blade to her throat as he said, "You."

"The gods," she whispered. "She feared the gods."

He planted a quick, hard kiss to her mouth, lifting the sword and pulling them both up. "Yes, though I never learned exactly why. Something to do with me, I think."

"She wanted to keep you safe," she said softly. "I understand. Our world is a dangerous one for mortals."

He grabbed her hand. "Don't. You don't need to protect me, remember? Besides, I just handed you your ass in a duel."

Her lips twitched. She could have beat him easily, and she was sure he knew that. She just couldn't stand hurting him.

CHAPTER 19

Vane was late again. She ground her teeth, irritated it was making her so anxious. She didn't care about him—or at least, that was what she repeated in her head as she waited. But as soon as she heard footfalls crunching on the frost-covered grass, she whirled, eyes wide.

"You haven't begun," he said.

He sounded tired, and the circles under his eyes had darkened into deep shades of violet.

She shrugged, trying to brush off how worried she was. "Why aren't you sleeping?"

"I thought we agreed yesterday we are not friends."

"We're not."

He strode towards her. "Finish your strengthening circuit quickly. We're going to go through the basics of hand to hand combat today, in case you ever get caught on the ground during battle."

"I hardly think one day will help," she muttered, lowering to the cold, hard ground.

"Perhaps not. Or maybe it will save your life."

She put her hands behind her head and began to lift her torso. Her muscles burned, but she thought they had begun to finally get stronger.

"What's with you and saving my life?" she said between puffs of air. "Like you said, we aren't friends."

Vane loomed over her. "Your words, not mine. But if you need the truth, King Johannas assigned me to you for a reason."

She grunted, lowering into a pushup. "Because of my dragon and my—magic."

"Amongst others, but yes."

"Others?"

He nudged her with his booted foot and ordered, "Up. We'll run our lap and then begin."

She clenched her jaw at his cold demeanor. He was hiding something beneath it, but she had yet to see him crack today.

As they ran, she noticed his limp was already gone—or maybe he was just exceptionally good at hiding it. Despite how exhausted he appeared, he was still faster than her and hardly out of breath by the time they finished.

"Let's go." He waved his hand and began to jog over to the dragon field, ignoring the fact that she was still doubled over and breathing hard.

She caught up to him just in time to see him stroking Thessa's scales again. Confusion felt oddly cold as it washed over her. Why, of all people, did Thessa let him touch her? Vane had mentioned it would take a lot for Thessa to kill him. Perhaps he had some previous connection to her. There was no other explanation for the way she closed her eyes and chuffed softly as he patted the side of her enormous head.

"She's…agreeable," Soren commented as casually as she could manage.

Vane tilted his head, eyes still on the dragon. "Hm, I'd be careful if I were you. You don't want to offend her honor."

"She's just oddly—" But before Soren could finish, Vane was in front of her, tripping her and catching her arm as she futilely tried to swing at him.

She yelped as they both plummeted back, the dagger that had been in his hair suddenly in his hand and at her throat as they fell to the ground. He caught the small of her back with his other hand, pulling her up just before she hit the hard ground.

The air knocked out of her, completely at his mercy, she blinked slowly at him. This felt…familiar, and it took a few seconds to remember why.

Last night, in the dream, the goddess and the man had been in a similar position.

"You don't need to protect me, remember?" she muttered before thinking.

Vane went still, his muscles locking up around her. "What did you just say?"

His dagger was still at her throat, their faces inches apart. She tried to shove him away, but he held firm.

"Let me go!" she snarled, squirming in his hold.

His eyes flashed, and there it was—the first crack in his armor of the day. What she had said bothered him. She had an inkling as to why but was still pushing away the truth because it was simply impossible. He couldn't be the same person as the man in the dreams.

"Make me," he ordered, his voice rough with tension.

She wanted to scream. He knew very well he had her trapped, and there was no getting out of it through force.

But maybe there were other ways to escape. Perhaps she could even use this tension between them to her advantage.

One of her hands was pinned beneath her, the other on the hilt of his dagger, keeping it where it was. She shifted her fingers, slowly caressing the rough skin of his calloused palm. His breath caught, just barely, just enough for her to hear it. But there was no way for him to hide the way his pupils spread, making his eyes nearly black.

His grip on the handle loosened, and she slowly guided it away from her neck, keeping her gaze locked on his. He still had her pinned to the ground, so she leaned in, brushing her lips against the shell of his ear and whispering, "If I stab you now, will I be punished or praised?"

A low sound, almost a groan, escaped him, and she took the opportunity, rolling and flipping their positions so she straddled him, the dagger that had loosened in his grip now held to *his* throat.

For a moment, they just stared at each other, both breathing heavily. Vane broke the silence first, his voice a phantom caress as he said, "Very good, Soren."

She was trembling with an aching feeling she did not want to admit to. It made her voice waver as she demanded, "You goaded me, didn't you?"

His lips lifted. "You won't learn to fight in a few days, not well enough to stand against soldiers trained their whole lives. But I can teach you ways to cheat that system."

She was still on top of him, but as she tried to move away, his broad hands caught the swell of her hips. The distracting heat swelled, and she froze. He did too, before rolling his jaw and releasing her. Quickly, she moved off him, and they both sat a few feet away from each other, neither deigning to speak about what had just occurred.

Eventually, when she couldn't take the silence anymore, she said, "So, what else?"

He didn't look at her, not at first, his chest rising and falling in a slow breath. When he did finally meet her eyes, his expression was closed off, the mask firmly in place again.

"Let's throw some daggers."

Her brows lifted. "You mean…at people?"

His lips twitched, just barely. "No, Soren, at a target. I won't ask you to kill, not today."

He stood and tilted his head, a silent request for her to follow. She scrambled to her feet, trailing after him as he strode towards camp. Vane's face was impassive as they wove through the tents, passing groups of soldiers training or taking breaks.

As they passed a group of three men eating around a low, burning fire, Soren heard one of them mutter, "Bet she'd spread her legs for me if I asked. Never fucked a Misean cunt before, but I wouldn't be against trying."

Just ahead of her, Vane stopped walking abruptly. He turned towards the soldier, and a shiver raced down her spine at the dark look on his face.

"Can we help you, Vane?" the soldier asked, his eyes darting to his companions.

Vane let out a low laugh, tilting his head at the man.

"What makes you think you can speak to me like that? And more importantly, why do you think you can speak about *her* in the way you just did?"

The man paled. "I'm sorry about the lack of formality, sir, but the girl… Well, she's Misean, isn't she?"

Vane stepped forward, his smile humorless. Her heart beat rapidly in her throat, and she almost told him to stop, but a twisted part of her wanted to see exactly what he would do.

"She is worth an innumerable number of you spineless bastards," Vane snarled. "And if you even *think* of fucking touching her, I will make sure it's the last thought you have. Understand?"

The man shared a look with his companions but nodded, muttering, "Yes, sir."

Vane turned, meeting her eyes, but as he did, one of the men muttered, "Fucking gods," and Vane whirled.

His fist made contact with one of their noses, and Soren flinched as she heard the resounding *crack*. Someone shouted, and there was a flash of silver. Innate instincts had her magic rising to protect Vane, but before she could strike at any of the men, he had already snatched the dagger away, the blade now pressed to its owner's throat.

"Trying to kill your superior?" Vane murmured. "And threatening one of the king's most valuable riders? I might just have to report you to Commander Eton."

"Please," the man squeaked, a droplet of blood trailing down his neck.

Soren took a single step forward. "Vane." Her voice sounded wrong, shallow and breathless. "We should continue training."

His jaw tightened. "Perhaps." He released the man and spat, "Fortunately for you, I have better things to do at the moment than dole out punishments. You'd better hope I forget about this before I meet with the commander again."

And with that, he stalked away. She hurried after him, not wanting to hear what the men had to say next.

He didn't speak to her, didn't look at her until they were standing in another small field on the other side of camp. There were several targets riddled with divots and holes, a few soldiers sparring with each other just beyond.

Vane gathered a handful of throwing daggers and wordlessly handed one to her. She glanced sidelong at him. "Vane."

"Throw."

"Are we not going to talk about—"

"Throw the dagger, Soren."

She eyed the small blade in her hand. "I don't know how."

His gloved left hand curled into a fist at his side, the other daggers grasped in his right. She caught his thumb sliding over his pointer finger, just as it had the other night in the tent.

"Try," he said gruffly.

She took a deep breath and reared her hand back, the handle of the blade between her digits. Her eyes were on the target, but she heard Vane sigh and drop the other daggers. She stiffened as his hand pressed to her bicep, and he murmured, "Lower your arm a bit. You're too tense."

She obeyed, not trusting herself to speak. He moved to her hand next, adjusting her fingers on the handle.

"Keep your grip nice and loose as you release it."

"Can I throw it now?"

She turned her head to find his lips tilted up in as much of a smile as he seemed capable of. "Go ahead."

She cocked her hand back a bit more and let the blade loose. It flew through the air, caught a breeze, and hit the side of the target before ricocheting off onto the grass. She frowned and found Vane wearing a similar expression, his eyes far away.

"Apologies," she muttered. "For not meeting your expectations. I did tell you I've never done this before."

He cleared his throat. "I know. Let me show you."

Leaning down, he plucked one of the other daggers out of the yellowing grass. Fluidly, he brought his arm back and released it. It spun through the air, landing in the direct center of the target. Gods, was he bad at anything?

She didn't think she said it out loud, but he replied, "More things than you would think."

"So humble too."

He sighed heavily. "Try again."

She did, again and again, until she finally hit one of the rings around the center, and the blade stuck to the wooden board. He cleared his throat. "Good, Soren."

"It's not moving. People will be."

Vane nodded once before picking up a handle of blades, and then, in a stream of motion, he began to throw them at the target, one after another. A muscle in his jaw flickered as she watched him line the daggers around the center of the target in a perfect ring. She would have called him a showoff, but this didn't seem to be about that. He appeared to be funneling his anger right into the target board.

But why?

The questions surrounding him were endless. She had no idea who he was, why he looked so much like the man in her dreams and visions, why he seemed to have any amount of care for her.

By the time he lowered his arm, she had worked up the courage to say, "Why did you bother earlier, with the men by the fire?"

He went still, though he didn't look at her. "You said we're not friends."

"I did."

She wasn't going to back away from her words now, especially not with so many secrets still between them.

"Then it doesn't matter."

"That's not true."

He narrowed his eyes as he finally looked at her. "They threatened you."

"They're not the first to do so, and they certainly won't be the last," she replied softly. "I still don't understand why you cared enough to say anything."

"Who else will?"

Now, it was her turn to narrow her eyes. "I don't need your pity, Vane. I've gotten this far without it, and though it hasn't been easy, I know how to take care of myself."

"I know." His voice was a fraction softer now. "And it's not about pity."

"Then what—"

"Evva!"

Vane shut his eyes briefly before turning to face the approaching commander. "Commander?"

Commander Eton squared his jaw. "You're needed."

"We're in the middle of training."

"And you can continue come morning. Go. King's orders."

Vane stiffened, his breath catching, just loud enough for her to hear it. He gritted his teeth and said, "Fine then."

She wanted to say something to him, but she was not sure what. Goodbye? Good luck? She had no idea where he was going, or why he was on orders from King Johannas. In the end, she kept her mouth shut.

But just before he strode away, he caught her gaze, and she swore she heard him whisper, *"Tomorrow, Soren,"* though the commander didn't appear to hear it. His fingers brushed her hand as he walked past her, back towards the camp.

The commander snorted softly, but all he said was, "Continue training for the rest of the night, Mise."

She did not lower her gaze as she replied, "Yes, commander."

CHAPTER 20

SOREN WOKE with a jolt the next morning. She couldn't remember any details of her dream for the first time in many seasons; instead, she just felt panicked.

It was still dark out, the princess asleep next to her, and she dressed quickly before hurrying to the field. Thessa stirred as she approached, opening her enormous maw in what appeared to be a yawn.

He is not back yet.

Soren blew out a breath, trying to calm her racing pulse. *Back from where?*

Thessa feigned sleep after that, and Soren resisted the urge to slap her scales. Instead, she paced back and forth, her mind running over every possible scenario or explanation.

Vane had to be someone's descendant. An ancestor of his must have lived when the gods had, *loved* one of the immortal beings. And as for Vane's odd behavior now…

She could not find a reason. He was cold enough to her most of the time, but she was beginning to see it was mostly just a part of that mask he tried so hard to keep in place. Every time they got close for a moment, he became distant again, as if he was trying to hide whatever he felt. And as for her feelings, she could admit now that they felt oddly strong for knowing him for so little time. It was likely just the influence of the dreams.

"Soren."

She whirled, finding Vane a few paces away. His arms were crossed over his chest, and gods, he looked so exhausted. Whatever the king was having him do was wearing him thin.

"Where were you? Or am I not allowed to know that?"

He took an audibly shaky breath and took a step forward, but his foot caught on the grass, and he faltered. She rushed forward as he all but collapsed onto the dew covered ground. Panic surged, and before she could think about what she was doing, she cupped his cheeks and demanded, "What's wrong with you?"

He froze, his dark gaze flicking to hers. Then, slowly, he lifted a hand and wrapped his fingers around her wrist. "I'm fine."

"You're not. Are you injured?"

He took a shallow breath. "I thought we weren't friends."

"We aren't," she whispered. "But I…"

His gloved finger slid along her skin. "You what, Soren?"

"I just want to make sure you're okay."

She said the words in barely a whisper, and his eyes fluttered shut, his forehead falling against hers. Her breath shuddered in and out, and he nodded against her.

"I don't sleep much," he murmured. "Makes healing injuries a bit difficult sometimes."

The sun was cresting over the horizon, the field bathed in golden light. He opened his eyes, and she found they were a liquid hazel in the early morning sun. They were so close, and the feeling was frightening. She had not been this close to someone in a long time, and with Vane especially, it incurred confusing thoughts and emotions.

"Where are you hurt?" she asked.

His nose was brushing hers, the tip of it cold and his eyes were half-lidded. "It's nothing. Just a flesh wound."

"Let me see."

"So stubborn, Soren."

She couldn't stop the shiver that raced up her spine as he said her name like that, soft and rough around the edges at the same time. His hand still rested on her forearm, and she was still touching his face. The moment felt fragile, fledgling in the clouded breath of early morning.

"Please," she whispered. "Maybe I can help."

He sighed and pulled back. She didn't want to admit that, for a split second, she chased him as he moved away, not wanting to lose his presence this near to her. It was impossible and nonsensical, but Vane was beginning to feel safe, like a home she had long ago lost.

He was still close, kneeling on the grass. As he untied the leather armor and pulled up his shirt, she was suddenly overwhelmed by a number of things.

He was covered in scars as well as barely healed bruises —a shallow but long slice cut from his ribs to low on his stomach, the 'flesh wound' he must have been talking of. She was ashamed to admit to the sudden rush of looping heat in her belly at the sight of the small strip of his exposed skin.

Shoving aside the distracting rush of lust, she drew closer and examined the wound, running her fingers along the side of it. The defined muscles of his abdomen flexed under her touch, and his hand curled in the grass beside him.

"Does that hurt?"

His throat bobbed. "No."

"Has it been cleaned?"

"Not thoroughly, no. I didn't have time."

She pulled her hand back and stood. "Where is your tent? It will get infected if you don't take care of it."

He stared at her, still on his knees. "You don't need to do this."

It was hard to look at him. He carried so much pain, even if she did not know what it was, and now, he was barely keeping a damper on it. The mask was falling.

"I do. You can't train me if you're dead from a blood infection."

Finally, he relented, and with a sharp sigh, he stood, dragging her back towards camp. Thessa huffed behind them.

What?

Treat his wounds carefully.

I was planning on it, though it isn't that bad.

The dragon paused. *I think you know well enough now that not all his wounds are visible.*

The dragon fell quiet after that. The camp was still sleepy, most of the soldiers in their tents as Vane pulled her through it. He stopped in front of a tent a little bigger than her and Cion's, dropping her hand. She took a deep breath as he ducked inside before following him, but she froze in the entrance as he tossed his armor to the side. He didn't fully remove his shirt, though, thank the gods. It wasn't that she didn't want to see him, but perhaps she wanted it too much.

He sat down on a small, roughly hewn wooden stool in the center of the tent. "There's a basin of water and a bottle of clear liquor over there."

He inclined his head to the left. Slowly, she walked to the materials. The bottle of liquor was half-gone, and she wondered if it had been used for previous wounds or if he'd drunk it. Somehow, she doubted he indulged much.

She wet a small cloth with water then pressed the head of the bottle to it, soaking it with some of the alcohol. When she approached Vane, he looked half-asleep again. But as soon as she said his name, he stiffened and opened his eyes before lifting his shirt again. She knelt in front of him and pressed the cloth to his skin.

He barely flinched as she cleaned the wound. Instead, his gaze was heavy on her as she gently skirted her fingers over his skin.

She didn't look at him, instead focusing on cleaning as she asked, "Does it help?"

"Does what help?"

She pressed the cloth to the center of the wound. "Having me do this? You seem distracted at the very least."

His abdomen tensed under her hands, and she peered up at him. He hadn't looked away from her, but his features had clouded slightly. Silence stretched between them, and she lowered her gaze.

"Sorry, I shouldn't assume. Besides, it's an overstep on my part—" But the rest of the words fell away as he brushed her chin with his calloused fingertips.

"It does help."

She swallowed. "Good, then. Any other injuries I can help with?"

One of her hands was still on his stomach, and she didn't want to move it. He was so warm and solid—perhaps the first stable thing in her life in many years.

"No," he said after a moment.

She shoved away her disappointment and stood, turning swiftly. But he caught her wrist before she could go far, tugging her back. She stumbled, pressing her palm to one of his broad thighs to keep from toppling the ground. They were both breathing heavily as she went still, meeting his gaze. There was a catch of silvery light in the dark depths of his eyes.

"I wish…" he began, voice uneven. But then he took a deep breath and shut his mouth.

There was so much anguish in his eyes, it was disarming. She wanted to do something for him to ease it but didn't know what. How did you save someone who was drowning in sorrow?

In the end, she simply leaned in and wrapped her arms around his neck, pulling him tight against her, her head resting on his shoulder. It took a moment, but his broad hands eventually slid up her back, holding her too. He tucked his face in the curve of her neck and shoulder. When she threaded her hand through his hair, gently stroking the soft strands, he shuddered.

Slowly, the sounds of soldiers waking and leaving their

tents filtered in, but they remained holding each other. She prayed to gods she did not believe in that her touch provided Vane some semblance of comfort.

When the passing of time became too heavy to ignore and the sounds of shouting and rustling about outside grew louder, she finally started to pull back. When she saw Vane's face, a stone dropped in her belly.

His cheeks were damp with tears.

"Vane?" she whispered, slowly lifting a hand and brushing her fingers against his face.

He leaned into her touch for a moment before he said, "Don't worry yourself with it, Soren. But…thank you."

But there was something wrong.

Inside her…

A pain that mirrored his.

His brow creased, and she wondered if he saw it on her face. He seemed on the verge of saying something, but he remained silent. Her breath shook, and she pressed the heel of her palm to her chest.

He followed the movement, and his jaw tightened. "We should get you started with training for the day. We don't have much more time."

She gave a single nod. "I know."

Her hand was still against her chest, as if the answer could be found in the alien pain she felt there.

Vane stood and brushed past her, re-securing his armor. She finally lowered her hand, and they slipped out of the tent. Her breath clouded in the air, the cold shocking her out of the haze that had settled over them. But the feeling… the unyielding *pain*…

It remained.

The next morning, they were interrupted just as she was finishing up her strengthening circuit.

"Evva!"

Soren jumped at the sound of the commander's harsh voice. She twisted to see him striding across the field. Thessa, who had been laying not far from her, rumbled, the sound low and aggressive.

Commander Eton glanced at the dragon warily before he said to Vane, who was now on his feet, "You're needed. Mise, you'll train by yourself for the next two days."

"She isn't ready," Vane argued, holding the commander's hard gaze. "Taking away two days of training right now isn't wise, not when we have so little time."

"Do I look like I care?" the commander snarked. "You're needed."

"You wanted me to make sure she was ready to fly to Alesia in less than a moon cycle," Vane said, stepping closer to the commander. "We need more *time*."

Soren's stomach dipped. Alesia was a small town in Mise, right on the border. If they wanted her to fight there, it meant Aren was pushing the front ahead, and she was going to help them do it.

The commander's flat expression held. "It's an order from the king. Go, Evva. Now."

Vane tightened his jaw and gave a short nod, Soren staring at him in disbelief.

He was right—she was nowhere near ready, and he was just going to leave her now? Logically, she knew he couldn't disobey an order directly from King Johannas, but she didn't understand why the order had been given in the first place. It negated the point of Vane training her personally, if he was going to be constantly pulled away for other duties.

"Keep up with your strength circuit and laps," Vane told her, leaning in. "And practice the same maneuvers with Thessilnn. She'll remember if you don't."

"I'm supposed to leave in less than a week," she hissed, her gaze flicking to Commander Eton, who was watching their interaction closely.

Vane grimaced. "I know. I should be back before you go… I'm sorry."

And with that, he turned and strode away.

Once he was gone, Commander Eton snorted. "I suppose I should congratulate you on your quick work."

Soren narrowed her eyes. "I don't know what you mean."

The commander raised a brow. "I think you do. I commend you. Snaring a captain, especially one like him, isn't easy."

She bristled, taking a step back. "He's not a captain."

"And how would you know that? Has he ever revealed his rank to you? Do you think just because he wants to fuck you now, you know anything about him?"

She felt sick. Commander Eton was absolutely right, but she wasn't going to admit that to him, not when he obviously wanted to disarm her. Instead, she raised her chin. "I should continue with my training as requested, commander."

His lip curled. "So the wolf finally sheds her sheep skin. I knew you were dangerous from the moment I saw you."

"Why?" she said softly. "Because of what I can do or the

system I challenge by simply holding any amount of power?"

The commander's left eye twitched, but he ignored her words, barking, "Back to your training, soldier."

He left, and she turned to Thessa. *Shall we?*

Ignore the commander. He only has as much power as you give him. But yes, we should begin.

Soren mulled over the dragon's words as they practiced dismounts and dives until her body felt like it was one bruise away from breaking apart completely.

The next morning, she completed the circuit alone then ran, ignoring the pain and exhaustion. She slipped some bread and dried meat before anyone arrived for midday meal, ate, then jogged back to the field where Thessa waited.

The next two and half days were similar, and for two nights, she had no dreams of the goddess. She chalked it up to being so exhausted each night when she laid down.

The break didn't last long, though. They never did.

CHAPTER 21

"ARE you sure we can trust her?"

Ana's breaths were shallow in the cool air of the cavern as she whispered, "I would trust her with my life. She practically raised me."

Ahead, torchlight illuminated the hollowed out space, and a woman came into view. The goddess eyed the three of them, handing the torch to Ana. "You are both sure of this?"

"We're aware of the risks." Her voice was firm, Ana giving her a small nod and a nervous smile.

The goddess drew closer, her gaze landing on him. "And you, son of Vulcan, are you quite sure? You risk the wrath of someone who would bring upon you far worse fates than death."

"Vulcan?" Ana whispered. "You didn't say he was his father!"

She stared at the goddess, shocked. "I didn't know."

The goddess' smile was cold. "You are still untrained in the world, daughter of Nyx. I sensed it the moment I walked into this chamber, the way the flames flickered and bowed to him."

"I don't really give a damn who my father is. All I care about is that you don't breathe a word of this to a soul."

The goddess shook her head slowly. "It's a shame. You could have *been many things, Vane Evva, had you not met her, but the fates have had their way. We should begin. The ceremony is rather lengthy."*

Soren rolled over on the sleeping mat, her heart beating so fast, she thought she might pass out while lying down.

The man in the field, the one who had kissed the goddess and ridden dragons with her through the sky…

It *was* Vane.

She felt as if she was going insane, her mind whirring and her palms sweating under the thin blanket, despite the cold.

There was more too. The woman in the dream, the one named Ana—Soren had recognized her. She didn't know why or how, but her features had been familiar enough that she couldn't dismiss it. Plus, the timeline of the dreams was becoming confusing. One moment, the goddess had been leaving Vane behind in that farm field, seemingly forever, and then the next she was riding with him. Then…

The cave.

A 'ceremony.'

Soren tried to remember what they had been wearing. She could not see the goddess herself, had never been able to, but Vane and the others…

Gods, she couldn't remember. And besides, Arenean weddings might be different to whatever the gods did.

But if she was right—

Wait.

She forced her whirring thoughts to slow, clouded by the

usual haze that set in when she awoke. The goddess, the one with Ana, had said that 'Vulcan' was Vane's *father*.

Vulcan. The god of fire.

Which meant Vane wasn't even fully mortal, and if he had come from a time when the borders to Arcadia were still passable by mortals, he was over a century old.

The knowledge was too much, and she shut her eyes tight, wishing for the haze to take with it the realization. But the knowing remained, and with it, a decision to be made.

Did she confront Vane about it?

She couldn't, not without raising suspicion as to how she knew. Perhaps he would be angry with her, or even kill her. Others must be unaware, for if the King of Aren knew he had a demi-god in his army, he surely wouldn't be wasting his time training her.

In the end, the answer was clear.

She had to pretend she had no idea.

Soren was awake the rest of the night, rising as soon as dawn was a whisper outside. But when she slipped out of the tent, she heard running and whooping. She lingered near the tent entrance as a few soldiers rushed past her, shouting something about '*those Misean bastards*.' Her throat tightened. Something must have happened.

Arenean flags waved as more emerged from their tents, drawn by the noise. Behind, she heard Cion rasp, "What's going on?"

Soren took a deep breath and turned to face the

princess, who was looking at her with narrowed eyes. "I don't know. Some victory, I think."

Cion nodded slowly. "Interesting. Last I heard, Misean forces had pushed us back towards the border, despite Meesling's recent betrayal."

Soren shut her eyes briefly then looked at Cion and said, "Princess, I didn't know… What I mean to say is, I didn't intentionally hide what I could do. It was out of fear. I never intended to use it. I had vowed to myself I wouldn't a long time ago, but I was afraid for you—"

"It's alright," Cion said tersely. "And…thank you. I would be dead if it weren't for you."

Soren looked down. "Right. You're welcome, princess."

Cion laughed softly. "It's odd to see you become yourself after all these years. It's happening slowly, but I think I'm finally meeting you for the first time."

Soren wasn't sure how to reply, or if she even should. Cion sighed and grabbed her arm. "C'mon, let's see what all the fuss is about."

She followed Cion through the camp, soldiers eyeing Soren as they went. When they ran into Ilav halfway through shouting something that sounded a lot like 'Fuck Mise,' Cion tugged on his arm roughly and shouted in his face, "What happened?"

He grinned, his gaze landing on Soren as he replied, "The Miseans may have spirit, but we have something even more powerful. *Mòr Maslach.*"

Cion stiffened. "They sent him to push them back away from the border?"

Ilav gave an enthusiastic nod. "He burned hundreds of them. They had no choice. Now, we have our foothold back in Misean lands. Without the aid of the wyverns, it's only a matter of time before they all burn."

Soren took a step back. The entire morning had been too much, more than she could handle or bear.

The dream.

Vane.

The demise of so many Miseans in one fell swoop by that *monster*…

Turning away sharply, she ran, ignoring Cion's shouts behind her. Her lungs burned and her legs felt limp from the training the day before, but she ignored the pain. She ignored everything, letting the rush of the air past her ears sweep away any thought that tried to overwhelm her.

She didn't stop when she reached the edge of camp, skirting the dragon field and sprinting towards the creek where she had bathed several nights before. Sloshing into the water, she collapsed in the middle of it and hung her head. Her entire body convulsed as a sob tore its way up her throat. For the first time in over a decade, she wept. The necessary layer of ice around her heart broke apart under the pressure of it all, her howling cries an outlet for the pain ravaging everything that made her.

She did not stop weeping when she heard someone in the brush behind the creek, unable to bring herself to care what happened or who saw her. Only when she heard the splash of someone stepping into the creek did she finally raise her head.

Vane stood a few paces away from her. His hair was pulled back with a dagger, his jaw tense. She resisted the urge to leap at him and demand answers. Instead, she merely rasped, "Did you hear the news of our *victory*?"

He nodded once but said, "You care for them. Your people."

She looked down at her hands, the pale of her palms red now in the icy cold water. "It doesn't matter if I care or not. I'm betraying them."

"You're surviving, Soren."

Shaking her head, she whispered, "Don't say my name like you know me. We barely do, and I…" She took a sharp breath. "I know you hide things too."

She waited, expecting him to become defensive or to threaten her. Instead, he sat down next to her in the water. The tips of his cheeks and nose were tinged pink from the cold, and she hated she found that endearing.

"No more secrets between us," he said quietly. "What do you think you know?"

She inhaled sharply, looking straight ahead. "You would say I was crazy."

"Are you?"

Her gaze flicked his way, finding the intensity of his gaze almost unbearable. "I don't know anymore," she admitted quietly.

"Tell me, even if it doesn't make sense."

She shook her head. "I…I have dreams. I have since I was a child."

Vane looked tense, but he nodded. "What are they about, the dreams?"

"It sounds insane, but—"

"Stop thinking so much," he ordered, his breath clouding the air. "Leave sense behind for a moment and tell me what you see."

There had always been a trace of pain in his eyes when

he looked at her. But now, as the water ran past them and he stared at her, she wondered if his mask was finally slipping away. She had no idea why she was the one to shatter through his defenses.

"Fine," she rasped. "I see... There is a girl. I see things through her eyes. Pieces of her life, from before Arcadia was closed off."

"And?" he pushed.

Their fingertips under the water were inches away. She glanced down, and a shimmer of gold caught her eye. Normally, he wore gloves, but now that his hands were bare, she saw the thin gold band on the pointer finger of his left hand.

"You didn't tell me you were married," she said, eyes on the ring, her chest caving in with a surge of foolish disappointment.

She had suspected what the goddess in her dreams was to him, but seeing it now, in her waking hours, was a sharp punch to the gut.

Vane blew out a breath. "Yes."

She swallowed, but her throat felt tight. Gods, her people were burning, and suddenly, she was not only crying for them, but for this stupidity with a man who had likely killed them too.

"What happened to her?" The words came out sharper than she had intended.

Next to her, he took another audible breath. "Tell me more about your dreams."

She had begun to shiver, both from the cold and the confusing emotions sweeping through her. Rising from the water, she trudged back to the rocky shore. Vane followed her, and when she tried to look away, he brushed his fingers over her chin, forcing her to see the anguish so clearly written across his features.

"You saw something," he said roughly. "Something that bothered you."

She blinked away the burning in her eyes and finally blurted out, "I saw *you!* Whatever goddess' life I'm cursed to relive, you loved her."

He didn't move his hand from her face as he said, "I never stopped."

Breath caught in her throat. "Then—why? What… You–you aren't even mortal, Vane! Does anyone even know that?"

"Very few."

She ripped herself away from his touch, as difficult as it was. Something was happening to her and to them—except there *was* no them. He was in love with this goddess who was now somehow gone from his life.

"You never said what happened to her."

She watched from a few paces away as his jaw hardened in an effort to keep his composure. It was mostly in vain, though, because his eyes betrayed every emotion he was trying to hide.

"She died," he said.

Soren felt a flood of shame. Just seconds ago, she had felt jealousy for this goddess he loved.

"I didn't know a goddess could even—" But she cut herself off. It was too harsh to say aloud as he stood in front of her, hands balled into fists.

He smiled, though, even as a single tear tracked down his cheek. "Be killed? They cannot, Soren. Not truly."

"So…she's not dead?"

Soren.

She looked past Vane to see Thessa just behind the brush line, her eyes shining with a silvery substance. It took a moment for Soren to realize they were tears, slowly falling to the hard ground and creating small, luminescent pools.

This truth may be too much too soon.

Vane looked at Thessa, eyes narrowing, almost as if he was speaking to her. Gods, could he? It had to all come back to this goddess who haunted their lives.

"Why can't I hear what you're saying to her?" she said, stubbornly wiping away the cold tears tracking down her cheeks now too.

Vane's shoulders rose and fell heavily, his eyes fluttering shut. "Perhaps Thessilnn is right. Maybe this isn't the time."

"The time for what?" Soren shouted in his face, pounding her hands against his chest in frustration. "Gods, I don't understand!"

They were both breathing heavily as she stilled, her hands still splayed across his front. His eyes met hers, and he whispered hoarsely, "I thought revenge could keep me sane, and it did for a time, but I was near the brink by the time I saw you."

"I still don't—"

"You are my *salvation*, Sora. You were then, and you are now."

She froze as she realized just what he was saying. Shock felt cold before confusion and disbelief replaced it, the emotions like a raging inferno.

She lowered her hands, numbly whispering, "That can't be," as she stumbled away from him. "You're mistaken."

He shook his head. "I did doubt it for a moment at first. After all I watched… He made me *watch* what they did to you. Someday, I will tear him apart piece by piece for it, but pure born gods and goddesses cannot truly die. I knew it was only a matter of time and chance that your soul was reborn into this world."

A memory like a knife sliced clean through her: a vision of Vane on his knees, begging and screaming as they held him with glowing chains, and—

She smiled, her eyes on her husband, a single silver tear tracking down her cheek as Kronos approached. "Don't look, my love."

"Sora! Please. Please, kill me. No, not her, you bastard. Don't fucking touch her—"

She gasped softly. Kronos looked down on her, his face too calm for what was occurring. It was a curtain pulled back on his madness, that he could be so serene as his hand reached directly into her chest cavity.

She was blinded by pain. Vane's hoarse screams ricocheted off the palace walls. There was a pull and a tear, and then—

Warmth. The void was ablaze as it welcomed Death's daughter.

CHAPTER 22

Soren sank to her knees as the memory faded, the cruel vision disappearing like smoke in her hands, but the damage was done.

Now, she knew the truth.

She wanted nothing to do with it. There was enough chaos, enough heartbreak in her life without the knowledge of what her soul had already endured. Vane was a tether to that pain, and she could not give him what he wanted.

Her.

Sora, the only daughter of Nyx and Thanatos. A brave young goddess—his *wife*.

She was none of those things. She was simply Soren, a slave-servant from Mise who had been thrust into a mortal war.

"I'm sorry," she whispered. "I can't do this. You…I think you should go. Tell the commander I need someone else to train me. *Please.*"

Vane, who was on his knees too now, ran a hand over his face. "I wish it were that simple, that I could give you what you ask. Because I would go, if that's what you truly wanted and I had the freedom to do so. But we are both bound to this war, down to its very core."

"How—"

She was interrupted by the sound of a gong ringing through the camp. Vane swore softly next to her, his eyes on the horizon.

"What is that?"

He stood, scanning the area. "It's a warning. They're coming."

"Here? But they all said Mise was pushed back to their border—"

"Could be rebels from within our forces," he said, throat working. He crouched, hands on her shoulders as he said quickly, "The commander will require you to fight now. I know we haven't had much time to prepare, but Soren…" He put a hand to her cheek. "Despite what I've just told you, despite the fear you might feel or the allegiances you might want to uphold—do not hesitate. Your enemies will see it right away and take advantage of it."

"They're not my enemies—"

"It doesn't matter what you think. They see you as such and will be after you. This camp was likely targeted because word of you and Thessilnn reached them."

She shoved him off. "I don't care."

He shut his eyes briefly then pulled the dagger from his hair, letting it fall in his face as he handed it to her. She set her jaw, even as he said in a raw voice, "I can't lose you again, but I cannot protect you alone. I am bound to other roles. Please, Sora."

She snatched the dagger from his hand, its weight unfa-

miliar in her hand. "That's not my name," she snapped
before turning and running to where Thessa waited.

He is right, you know.

Soren glared at her before mounting the saddle. *How
could you not tell me?*

*It was not my place and you were not ready. Clearly, you are still
not ready. The timing of this attack is unfortunate.*

Really?

Thessa shuffled her wings, readying to take off. *You may
not want to, but listen to Vane. You cannot hesitate today. These
attackers have wyverns.*

How do you—

But Soren didn't need further clarification as she heard a
shrill cry in the distance. Thessa took to the air, and Soren
gasped as she saw the forces approaching the camp. There
were more than enough to overtake everyone here, as well as
five wyverns now circling the camp.

Soren stiffened as they noticed her, their riders shouting
and pointing as Thessa dove to avoid a volley of arrows
from the ground.

You have weapons. Use them.

Soren looked at the small dagger in her hand. *I don't think
this will do much.*

Not that one.

A well of darkness called on her, coaxing her closer.
Death sensed the closeness of so many lives in peril, and his
call was a siren's song. Soren felt the ichor of the magic
trying to leak from her fingertips, and she almost let go
before she saw the face of the rider ahead.

Oh gods.

Kelshie.

Her long-lost sister cried out to her companions, but over the wind and the chaos of the battle ensuing down below, Soren could not hear what she said.

"Kelshie!" Soren screamed. "Kelshie, it's me!"

Her sister whipped her head towards her, but there was no softness or mercy on her face, only resolve.

"Traitor!" Kelshie called out shrilly, her wyvern circling Thessa.

Archers from atop two of the other wyverns let loose a wave of arrows. Soren's gaze snagged on one of them, his face familiar. It took her a moment, but she realized who he was as he cried out to one of his companions.

It was Lanor, the knight who had been so kind to her when they had journeyed to the temple. Now, she knew why. He was a Misean sympathizer—

Soren screamed as one of his arrows tore through her arm, and Thessa all but shouted, *Focus, Soren!*

But she couldn't, not with everything Vane had just told her and Kelshie staring at her with hate. She was done. There wasn't a point anymore, there couldn't be. She had thought her hope had died long ago, but now she knew: today was the day it would truly fade into nothing.

Soren!

She ignored Thessa and closed her eyes. Blood ran down her arm to her fingertips as she waited for the final strike. But then, a shadow passed over her, and the blow never came.

Opening her eyes, she gasped softly as she saw the enormous, black-scaled dragon above her. Kelshie's companions were waving frantically to her, all of them shouting as they were dwarfed by the second Vemon dragon, the shadow to Thessa's moon.

It could only be one rider.

Mòr Maslach.

The rebel riders scrambled into some formation, and Soren ripped the arrow from her arm, screaming between her teeth. She had to try and save Kelshie. The masked rider above would likely kill her for it, but at least she would die saving her sister.

Thessa. Go after him.

Beneath her, Thessa rumbled, her scales vibrating. *You do not know what you're doing.*

I'm saving my sister.

The dragon didn't argue further, soaring up into the air as the masked rider and his dragon dove for one of the wyverns. As they shot past Soren and Thessa, she got a better look at the mask. It was made of some dark, almost obsidian-like material. The shape was hard to decipher, the material molded to the rider's face in jagged pieces.

She didn't have time to think further on it, though, because the screech of a wyvern split through the air as the masked rider's dragon tore through its neck below her.

Dive, Thessa.

She didn't argue further, angling down as the other wyverns circled the masked rider. Flames shot through the air all around Soren, but Thessa kept a straight course, her mouth opening, revealing her dagger-like teeth as she pummeled towards the black Vemon dragon.

Then, in slow motion, everything changed.

Soren doubled over on Thessa's back as something slammed into her torso—a blade thrown her way. Thessa

196

screeched and reared back from the black dragon as spots filled Soren's vision. Vaguely, she saw Kelshie readying to throw another dagger and deliver the killing blow.

"Stop," Soren rasped.

But only hate burned in her sister's eyes. Years as a soldier had taken her kindness or mercy. The stern, sweet sister Soren remembered from childhood was gone, and now, she was met with a choice.

Live or die.

Kill or be killed.

She reached out a hand, as if to try and touch Kelshie one more time. Her sister threw the dagger at the same moment Death and Night descended in a cloud of fury, darkening the sky. Soren's vision blurred as the wyverns cried out, their riders limp as they fell from the sky. Below, screams cut through the air, ringing in her ears.

She realized she did want to die today, not again. There was a sweeter song beckoning her now.

Revenge.

She wanted to kill both the kings who had caused the gaping hole in her heart. They had turned her into what she was now.

A monster.

She hoped they enjoyed what they created. It was her last thought before she slipped limply off Thessa's back.

CHAPTER 23

Rain had come with the dark clouds—Nyx's tears, crying for her lost child. He could feel the sorrow in each drop, but he had no sorrow left for the goddess. She had doomed her daughter to this fate as much as anyone else.

Night and Death stirred in his arms, whimpering softly as Heles landed, Thessilnn just behind them. Beyond, in the camp, Aren's forces gathered prisoners and ran blades through those too injured to be useful. He ignored them, his eyes on the blood steadily leaking from her arm and abdomen. Her lips were pale as the silvery strands of her hair stuck to her forehead. He brushed the hair aside—she hated having it in her face—then slid off Heles and hurried for camp.

Through his mask, soldiers stared at him warily, some of them shrinking back despite the way they had praised him mere hours ago.

Good.

They should be afraid of what would happen to them, to the world, should she not survive.

CHAPTER 24

A VAGUELY FAMILIAR voice pulled Soren from the depths. She blinked heavily, wincing as consciousness brought with it pain. Her belly was on fire, aching and sore, and her arm didn't feel much better.

"Vane. She's awake."

The soft voice paired itself with an unexpected face. "Anabeth?" she croaked.

The scribe's daughter smiled. "Glad to see you're awake."

But as Soren's vision became clearer and her mind caught up, she realized Lady Anabeth was familiar for more than one reason. She had been in the cavern that night, hovering next to the other woman, the goddess who had performed the ceremony.

Now, Soren remembered the truth. 'Lady' Anabeth was not real. She was truly the demi-god daughter of the goddess Juno, and one of the only souls who had known about her and Vane before they had been betrayed.

It was all becoming so clear now.

Soren jolted and Anabeth gently caught her shoulder. "Soren, it's okay," she said in a hushed voice.

"Was it you?" Soren asked, ignoring the near-agonizing pain as she sat up.

Anabeths's brow creased, and she glanced back. Soren followed her eyes to the entrance of the tent, where Vane lingered, his stance tense and his arms crossed over his chest.

"You didn't tell me she remembered," Anabeth said, brow raised as she looked at him.

His jaw rippled. "I said she remembers some. I didn't realize she would recognize you yet, beyond the way she knows you in this lifetime."

Soren slapped away Anabeth's hand, biting back a gasp of pain, gritting out, "Stop talking about me as if I'm not in the room."

Vane said nothing, his expression flat.

Soren scoffed at him. "Right. Tell me the worst of everything then go and leave me during an attack and expect everything to be just fine. And now *you're* the one acting like I did something wrong."

Anabeth's brows rose, but Vane bit out, "You nearly died. Do you know that? If you were mortal, you would be gone."

"I am mortal," she snapped. "I was born in Mise twenty-two years ago, and I had a family. I don't need another one."

"They are no more your family than the royals in Aren."

"How *dare* you—"

"She knew. Your mother in Mise."

Soren's breath caught. "You can't know that."

He laughed coldly. "Wake up. Look at what she named

you. Besides, Cavell is an old surname, one I know well. I don't know how the fuck Nyx did it, but she made sure you were brought into this world again by the granddaughter of one of her mortal spies from the old days."

"It doesn't matter," Soren shot back, even as her stomach twisted.

Vane's nostrils flared. "Regardless, you cannot go back to pretending you're anything but what you are now."

"What do you mean?"

Anabeth shifted, muttering, "Vane, not now."

But he ignored the demi-god. "We crushed the rebel attack despite the fact that they overran us. Do you know why?"

"No," Soren whispered hoarsely, remembering the screams that had surrounded her when she let her magic loose. "I wouldn't have killed them all. I would have at least protected the rebels."

"You didn't protect anyone, Soren. Magic doesn't have morals, and yours took enough on both sides. But it gave those in the camp the edge they needed."

She felt faint. The torches flickering in the tent were too warm and bright, the air cloistered and stale. She had to go, had to get away from this.

"Vane," Anabeth cut in sternly. "You need to calm down or shut up. She needs rest."

The demi-god lifted her hand and gently put pressure on Soren's torso, blood seeping through the bandages.

"I'm sorry, Sora," she said softly. "For pretending all those years and watching what they did to you in silence. I don't expect forgiveness, but this might be my last chance to say that to you."

"Not my name," Soren slurred.

Her vision crossed and blurred, but she swore she saw Vane in the corner, head on his knees. Anabeth said something softly to him, but the words sounded slow and echoed to Soren. The torches in the tent flared just before Soren lost consciousness again.

When she came to again, the pain was gone. A soreness remained in her torso as she sat up in the dark, but she could move without feeling faint. Anabeth was gone, but in the dark, she saw someone curled on the ground next to her under what appeared to be a few overcoats.

"Vane?" she rasped, her voice hoarse and wobbly.

He stirred, and the torches flared to life around them. Now fully awake, she glanced around. The tent was large but nearly empty besides the sleeping cot she rested on, a basin for washing, and a menagerie of weapons on a small rack near the entrance.

"How are you feeling?" he asked, sitting up and knotting back his hair, his brow creased.

She shrugged, swinging her legs over the side of the cot, but he stopped her with a hand to her knee.

"Take it slow," he ordered.

She ignored the heat from even his subtle touch and muttered, "Says the man who reopened all my stitches with just an argument."

He paled. "I'm sorry. I shouldn't have acted the way I did." He still hadn't moved his hand from her leg, and his grip tightened slightly as he added, a shade quieter, "You scared me."

Looking away from him, she said, "I need you to tell me. My sister, Kelshie—she's dead, isn't she?"

"Yes," he said without wasting a moment to let her guess or wonder.

"I killed her, didn't I?"

His thumb slipped down her inner knee in gentle motions. "You saved her from a far worse fate. Death by dragonfire is not a kind way to go."

"Who is he? *Mòr Maslach*?"

Vane's thumb stilled. "A monster in a mask," he said in a low voice, adding bitterly, "a pet for King Johannas."

"Have you met him before?"

"We have bigger problems to worry about," he said, shaking his head.

She narrowed her eyes. His hate for the masked rider seemed personal, so she didn't understand why he wouldn't reveal who he was. He had already told her most everything, and she didn't like the secret between them.

But she let his bait work for now and asked, "Like what?"

"Anabeth still has connections to Arcadia," he said, lowering his voice. "That's why she was here. She came to warn us."

"Who and…how?" Soren asked.

Outside, someone was walking past the tent.

Vane let the footsteps fade, eyes on the canvas flap, before he said, "You saw the Three Sisters, didn't you? Not long ago?"

"I don't know…" she said, trailing off as she remembered those voices in the mountain on the journey to the Sisters of Arcane's temple.

Vane caught her hesitation, nodding. "Anabeth thought so. The Sisters are under Juno's jurisdiction, so when they appeared on this side of the barrier, Ana said she felt it."

Soren wrung her hands. Vane slipped his fingers away from her leg, leaving coldness in his wake. Resisting the urge to ask him to touch her again, if only to chase away the cold, she said, "What do they have to do with Arcadia? I thought no one could cross the barrier."

"No mortals."

She stared at him, shocked. "Then why are you still here? Why did Anabeth stay in Aren, for that matter?"

Vane grimaced. "I was raised here. And after…everything, neither of us were welcomed back to Arcadia."

"She wasn't the one who sold us out?"

"No."

Soren paused. "What about her father? The scrollkeeper in Aren?"

"Her brother. A godling. He decided to stay with her in mortal lands, to protect her should Kronos send anyone to try and hurt her."

"And Kronos just…let you go?" she asked quietly. "Once I was dead?"

Vane flinched, and for a split second, she saw it—not from her eyes but from his…

The white marble was slick as he crawled to Sora's still body. Above, Kronos grunted and brought down the barbed whip again. His body convulsed, but the pain was nothing compared to the ripping in his soul. He just kept crawling, even as tears and blood obscured his vision.

When he reached her, Kronos just stood there, watching, as if his pain was a show.

Her bright blue eyes were wide open, but the familiar silver hue that had always lit them up was gone. A gasp turned into a heaving sob, clawing its way up from his chest. His body shook violently as he pulled her into his lap, her blood staining his hands, his legs… There was so much of it.

His punishment was setting in now. All he wanted to do was lie down and die with her, but Kronos wouldn't allow that. He was going to force him to endure an empty world, one void of her.

Eventually, once Sora's body was cold and the blood was beginning to dry on the marble, Kronos kicked him and barked, "Burn her body."

He looked up at the Kronos and snarled, "No."

Kronos barked out a cold laugh. "I thought you might say that. Burn her body, or I will chain you up again and make you watch as my guards chop it into tiny pieces to feed to the dogs."

He wanted to scream, to tear out his own heart and the king's, but Kronos had always been true to his word. This was no mere taunt.

He was so weak after hours of torture, he couldn't even stand, much less fight the king of the gods.

He finally released her, pressing trembling lips to her brow and whispering again and again, "I'm sorry, my love. I'm sorry. I'm sorry."

"Any day now, demi-god."

He crawled half a pace back and shut his eyes. He barely had the strength to access his magic, but when he felt it flare, when he felt the heat of the flames and smelled burning flesh, his body finally gave in.

He welcomed the darkness as it consumed him, praying he would never wake.

"How…long ago?" Her words were strangled, each an effort after what she had just seen. She had no idea how he had shown her the memory, but she had to know the answer first.

Vane's hands were clenched at his sides. "One hundred and three years. In less than one moon cycle, it will be one hundred and four. I..." His voice shook slightly. "I didn't mean for you to see that."

"How *did* I see it?"

He cleared her throat. "Thessilnn connects us. She must have been tuned in and ferried the memory to your mind."

You needed to see it. There is a price for everything.

Soren ignored Thessa's faraway voice, her eyes still on Vane. "You said Anabeth had a warning for us."

Vane shut his eyes. "Yes. Kronos knows. That was all she could gather, but—"

"He knows what?" she cut in. "That I'm alive? I'm not. Sora is gone. She died that day in his palace, and I know you want me to be her, but I'm *not*. Her memories don't feel like mine, and I don't think they ever will. You want me to be the wife you lost that day, but I don't feel the same emotions Sora felt. I'm sorry."

She almost expected Vane to get angry, but instead, he opened his eyes again and looked at her, his gaze searing. The faintest hue of silver swirled in his dark irises as he closed the distance, crawling towards her. He traced his hand up her leg, his touch featherlight as he paused at her knee. Her throat was dry, and the memory of what he and Sora had done in that creek bed flashed through her mind.

"You say you don't remember how you felt," he murmured, leaning in and replacing his fingers with his mouth. "But I've seen the way you look at me, Soren. You remember more than you say. You *feel* more than you admit."

Her lips parted, but she managed to say, "Even if that was true, didn't you learn your lesson? Loving Sora, loving me… It's a death sentence. Worse. How is that worth it?"

"You are worth everything," he said, sucking on the soft skin of her thigh, his hands sliding up to the bottom of her oversized tunic. "Anything."

Her legs widened on instinct before she could stop them, and triumph flashed in his eyes. She bit her cheek, fumbling as she asked, "Did we—I didn't see if we had ever…" She trailed off. As Soren, she had never been with a man in that way, but had Sora?

Vane's lips curved, and his pointer finger, the one he wore his marriage band on, slid down her leg, caressing sensitive skin just shy of her undergarments. She gasped softly, heat pooling low in her belly.

"We're married, my love."

"We're not. Sora was your—"

He nipped at her thigh, and she had to swallow the moan before it could surface as he scolded, "Your soul is the same. Fate even decided to mirror your faces. But do not think I am in love with some mere figment of a memory and placing it on you. I know you've lived a life and have had hardships of your own. It doesn't change how I feel. You will always own my heart."

Her chest rose and fell quickly. They were walking a dangerous line, and it had grown razor thin between them. One misstep, and she was terrified she would fall for him again.

Thessa was right. There was a price for everything. Love

did not come free—not for them, not in this world where kings like Kronos and Johannas reigned.

But she was tired.

Tired of fighting herself, of fighting Vane and this feeling between them. She didn't want to admit it, but she had lied. She had always felt the shimmer. Fate had brought them together for a reason. She wasn't naive enough to believe fate would save them, but fighting against its current was more than she could handle right now.

It was weak to give in, but maybe she was just that.

Slowly, she touched Vane's face, tracing down the curve of his cheekbone and lifting his chin to look at her. He froze, a kind of predatory stillness a mortal could not achieve. His shock did not last long, though, and he rose up fully onto his knees. He was so tall and her so short, they were nearly eye level like this, with her sitting on the cot.

His hand cupped the back of her head, fingers splayed across her cheek. He leaned his forehead to hers, his breath shuddering as the tips of their noses brushed. Her lips parted, the rush of exhaled air that escaped her audible in the quiet of night. She threaded her fingers in his dark hair, pulling the strands free so it fell loose around his face. He groaned softly, his other hand coming up to grip her thigh.

She wanted to kiss him, but even now, they were still on the edge of a barrier, and if she did that, it would finally shatter.

Her resolve was pointless in the end, as it always had been when it came to him.

"Please, Soren," he whispered, their lips nearly touching.

He was on his knees, begging, but he couldn't know she

was just as desperate. He was fire, and for so long, she had felt so achingly cold. She hadn't realized it was not merely of her own choice that her heart was coated in ice—it was the absence of him.

She closed the final distance between them, both gasping as their lips met. There was no soft build-up, only a collision of two powerful forces. He parted her lips, and she moaned in his mouth as she tasted him finally—*finally*.

Fire and Night.

Death, burning and ablaze.

"Gods," she breathed between kisses.

He paused, pulling back, his eyes nearly black as he traced her swollen lips with his thumb and said in a low voice, "You and I are the only gods here, my love."

A strange, heady sensation spread through her at his words—the feeling of power. She nipped at his bottom lip, and he hissed, but as she looked at him again, his eyes widened.

"There she is," he murmured, his gaze locked on hers.

She blinked. "What is it?"

His mouth curved. "Ether, in your eyes. I can see it again."

Ether…something only a powerful god possessed. Silver-hued magic, imbued into their bodies, into *her* body, and he had finally pulled it to the surface.

She curled a hand in his tunic and tugged him closer, kissing him desperately now. Need coursed through her, a current she could not—*did not*—want to fight. Not now, not anymore. But Vane hesitated. She could feel him holding back.

"You're still healing," he murmured.

She pressed her lips together. In the minutes that passed, the ache in her abdomen had faded even further. Something was happening to her, some change, perhaps brought on by the ether. Maybe she was becoming more of Sora than of the mortal she had been born as.

Carefully, she lifted her shirt up to find there was still a raised red scar where Kelshie's dagger had embedded itself in her stomach, but the wound was closed, and it didn't hurt any longer.

"I think I'm alright," she said, tracing her fingers over the scar.

Vane put his hand over hers and nodded once. His eyes were dark and heavy-lidded as he said in a rough voice, "Scoot to the edge."

Heat flooded her everywhere as she realized what he was intending to do, half from desire and half from embarrassment. No one had ever seen her, not even in the state she was now, and he wanted to see *all* of her.

"Now, Soren," he ordered, flicking his gaze up to hers.

She bit her lip, and before thinking, she replied in a sharp voice, "Yes, sir."

He smiled darkly as the power play began. It had been like this between them, or at least it felt familiar enough that she thought it must have. She would submit, and he would bring her to the edge, but in the end, she always won. She was a god, after all, and he was *hers*.

His calloused hands slid up her thighs, widening them. "You'll need to stay quiet," he said against her skin, his mouth migrating further and further up. "Do you think you can do that?"

She opened her mouth to reply, but then he pressed his

mouth to her center, over her thin underclothes, wetting the fabric. She had to bite her lip hard enough, she tasted copper to stop herself from moaning.

He chuckled, the feel of the vibration against her core driving her mad. "Good, darling. You're doing very well."

She fisted her fingers in his hair—a silent demand. A low noise rumbled from his chest, and he murmured, "So impatient. Hips up."

She obeyed, and he slid the undergarment off, tossing it to the side. Heat burned her cheeks. She was ready for him, almost too ready, swollen and already soaking wet. But he merely rasped, "Fuck, Sora," laid a hand flat against her stomach, and licked across her center in one long swipe.

Her hips bucked and her legs closed, but he held them firmly open, sucking on her clit. Pleasure lit her up, every inch of her sensitive and aching. He groaned against her, and then… *Oh gods,* she thought she might actually die as he tongue-fucked her.

When he replaced his tongue with his fingers, he rasped, "Touch yourself, wife."

She didn't even remember to argue with him about the logistics of their marriage, instead lifting her hand to her breast. He pumped his fingers inside her, knowing just how to work her. He knew her body, even now, even after all these years.

"Wait," he ordered, sensing her near the edge.

Her chest rose and fell in heavy breaths, the game coming to a peak between them. They had reached the deciding moment, and perhaps as Soren, she would have submitted. But there was another piece locked inside her, and it was coming out to play. Perhaps it was Sora, or maybe both of them together. It had always been there inside her, and it had taken Vane to obliterate the lock and throw away the key.

Her words were broken, but her voice was firm as she told him, "Come—with me. Now."

She had no doubt he was close, even just doing this to her, even without her touching him. And from the way his breath caught just before he went down on her again like a man starved, she knew she had won.

She barely had the wherewithal to cover her mouth with her hand as release barreled through her, arching her back and filling her vision with stars. The torches in the tent extinguished, and a touch of that dark ichor seeped from the prison she kept it in. Her breath caught as she felt it, panic flooding her.

But Vane gripped her hand, breathing hard against the curve of her hip, looking up as he assured her, "It's alright… it's alright. I give you a part of me. You give me a piece of you."

"But the magic is Death. It's—"

"I'm fine, my love. This is how it's always been. You didn't hurt me."

She relaxed slightly, and the torches lit around them again, bringing her back to the room. She felt dizzy as he kissed her stomach, gentle over the scar. But as her mind began to work again, catching up to the conversation they had been having, unease prickled at her skin.

"Vane?"

"Mhmm?"

"King Johannas knows what I did during the battle, doesn't he?"

Vane stiffened then lifted his head and said quietly, "Can we just have a few minutes?"

"Vane, it's almost dawn—"

"Then we wait."

She pressed her lips together, understanding his request. They'd had so little time, even when she had been Sora, daughter of Nyx and Thanatos, and him just a half-mortal man in a farm field. Fate did not smile kindly upon them, even though she was sure it had plans for both of them.

He wanted just a few minutes. She could at least give him that before she tried to let him go completely.

So, she whispered, "Alright. Until dawn."

"Thank you." His breath fanned across her skin, a featherlight touch that made her shiver.

"Do you need to…wash?" she asked, scolding herself internally for her embarrassment, especially after what they had just done.

He smirked, his expression full of smug, male satisfaction. "Yeah, I do."

She bit her lip and turned her head, averting her eyes as he stood to his full height. But he touched her face, forcing her to look at him again. Her cheeks were aflame, and yet she was curious, because some reckless part of her wanted to know everything about him…*see* everything.

He dropped his hand and walked towards the small basin in the corner. She didn't look away when he pulled off his shirt, though she nearly gasped when she saw it. His back was a mess of scars, overlapping and long.

The whip in the memory. Kronos had done this.

Rage made her feel cold, and the torches flickered. Vane must have sensed it, because he turned his head back, anger mirrored in his eyes. Not for himself, she knew, but for her, especially as he said, "It was nothing, that pain. I *deserved* that pain for not stopping what he did to you."

Her rage quieted, replaced by a heavy sorrow. "There was nothing you could have done," she whispered. "He would have killed us both."

Vane laughed bitterly, shirking off his pants. Now, she did look away. Not because she didn't want to see him like this, but because, for a moment, looking at him at all was too heavy, too painful. There was a deep wound between them, the knife still buried in both their chests where Kronos had ripped out her heart. And for it, for all Vane had suffered, for Kelshie, she would rip out his.

The cot bowed as Vane sat next to her, wearing his usual leather breeches, his chest still bare.

"It's almost morning," she said, and he nodded.

She sighed heavily. Outside, a dragon screeched, and dim light filtered in through the tent. She glanced at Vane. "King Johannas—"

But Vane cut her off, kissing her hard. She gasped against his mouth, though it was over by the time it had really started. He pulled away, still cradling his face with one hand as he said, "He'll likely send someone to investigate. You were quite high up when it happened, so there's no telling what they all saw."

"That I was going to try and kill him," she confirmed sharply. "The masked rider."

Vane took a quick breath. "Yes."

"And the rest of it? The others in Aren's army who I…" She trailed off, not quite able to say it.

Death was a whispered beat inside her. It always had been, but that didn't stop her from being afraid of it.

Vane's expression grew hard. "Johannas likes his weapons, and he prefers to be on the winning side. If you can provide him both of those things, he won't touch you, at least not personally."

"Vane…does he know about you?"

His gaze dropped as he opened his mouth, but then a horn sounded from somewhere in the camp. Vane shot to his feet, grabbing a shirt and leather chest armor, tugging them both on.

"More rebels?"

He shook his head. "I don't know, just—" He cut himself off, swearing softly under his breath. His hand twitched at his side, and he muttered, "Damn it."

"What?"

"The king is here."

CHAPTER 25

SOREN DRESSED QUICKLY while Vane paced silently near the entrance of the tent. When she had finished, he ran a hand over his face and spoke again.

"He'll want to see you."

She swallowed hard. "I know. It's fine. I've dealt with him before. I lived in his palace for nearly all my life."

Vane didn't look comforted at the thought. She finished tying up her boots and stood, a little wobbly on her feet after recovering and all they had done in the past hours. He was at her side instantly, brow creased and a hand on her arm.

"I'm fine."

He took a deep breath. "Alright. We should go."

"How did you know it was him?" she asked as he turned away from her.

His shoulders tensed, but he merely replied, "The horn call is different from an alarm."

She hadn't heard the difference, and she had a hunch he was lying, but she ignored the feeling, following him out of the tent. The camp was bustling, the soldiers' breaths clouding in the cold morning air as they sat around fires or started training. The winter season had truly reached Aren, even this far south.

Stares trailed both her and Vane as they walked the short distance through the camp to meet the king. Some looked at her with disgust and fear, others with awe. She didn't blame those who despised her now. She had no idea who she might have taken from them.

A sudden thought sent a spike of fear through her.

"The princess—"

"Is fine," Vane replied curtly. "She was on dragonback when you cast, and from what I heard, managed to burn some rebels before it was all over."

Half relief and half anger overcame her. Of course, Cion would fight for Aren, and naturally, that meant killing both Miseans and any rebels who might push back. But the reality still hurt: Princess Cion was not her friend and never had been.

Vane stopped in front of the Commander's tent, his features tense. She slowed with him, balling her hands into fists.

"Enter, Vane."

Soren flinched at King Johannas' voice. She had not been expecting him right away.

When they emerged into the tent, the king was wind-blown and taking off his riding gloves, appearing to have just arrived. He wore leather riding breeches and a ridicu-lous azure cape, latched with a gold brooch at his throat.

She wanted to take his precious gold and shove it down his throat.

One of the torches still lit in the corner flickered subtly, but Vane caught the small crack in her control. Discreetly, he brushed his fingers against hers in warning. She took a quick breath and swallowed her rage, kneeling on the ground with Vane.

Still, she must have not hid her defiance well enough, because the king laughed softly. "I would have never guessed that of all my slaves, *you*, Soren Cavell, would be the one to turn against me."

Vane's breath grew slightly uneven, not loud enough for the king to hear but enough that she caught the shift, kneeling next to him.

She kept her head bowed as she said quietly, "No, my king. I only—"

But cold fingers on her chin killed the words in her throat. She lifted her head to find the king staring down at her, smirking coldly. "Do not worry, Soren. I don't plan on killing you, not as long as we can come to an agreement about your uses. Rise."

Vane remained kneeling as she stood, and she glanced back at him while the king led her to the table at the edge of the room.

King Johannas flicked his gaze from her to Vane and snorted. "Ah. I'm not planning on killing him either. He is far too useful to me."

Soren furrowed her brow at the statement. She knew Vane was strong and a good fighter, but exactly what did the king want with him? She had to be missing something here about his part in all this, and it made her deeply uneasy.

"At the edge of Aren's border, there is still an encampment of Misean forces," King Johannas said, pulling her back to the room. "We had pushed them back nearly a week ago, but a recent resurgence of rebels—defectives from our own armies—aided them in the last battle. You are going to help me smother the spark the rebels have lit. We have Meesling and their wyverns now, save a few beasts the rebels managed to steal, so winning the war now should be a closer reality. I want you to ensure we don't have any further missteps in that goal."

"And if I refuse?" she dared.

King Johannas met her eyes. He had the same green eyes as the princess, though his were a shade duller. "I don't think you even need to ask me that. You're smart. I suppose," he laughed, "my daughter's tales of her young, bright servant should have tuned me into your danger in the first place, but I will admit, you played the role well."

Soren tightened her jaw. She didn't like him mentioning Cion. It made him feel too human, even as he threatened her.

"It was no role," she said in a low voice.

The king's eyes flashed. "So you thought."

She went still at the words. The king could simply be referring to her magic, or…

He knew what she was.

Before she could push him further, he said firmly, "You are dismissed. If you decide to take my offer, ready your beast. I will send you off by midday to the border."

She did not bow before turning, and that alone was a testament to all that had changed since she left the quiet prison of the palace walls. Vane remained, still on the ground, his head low in submission, not meeting her eyes as she ducked out of the tent. It unnerved her to see him like that, and once she had left, she lingered a moment outside.

"Apologies, but you know I cannot pass on such a useful weapon," she heard the king say, adding dryly, "I know she is yours."

"She is no one's."

"Hm. Kronos seems to think otherwise."

Soren froze. How did King Johannas know anything of what Kronos wanted? It was impossible to speak to him, with the borders to Arcadia barred to mortals. Unless Kronos had crossed it himself…

Cold fear rushed through her, drowning her like the current of an icy river. She backed away from the tent and ran, away from camp and to the dragon field. Thessa waited for her there, her head resting on the ground.

Soren was breathless as she said aloud, "Do you know anything?"

Thessa huffed, the warm air from her nostrils hitting Soren in the face. *No more than you. You need to prepare for flight.*

"If I decide to take his offer," Soren muttered, sitting heavily next to her.

You will. You want to live, and his threat is not empty.

"I know."

Vane had disappeared without a word by the time she returned to camp. As she craned her neck, searching for him through the throng of wary soldiers, Commander Eton said from behind, "Evva is gone. It's time for you to depart."

She whirled. "Gone?"

"Yes. He was sent on a mission for the crown."

"Where?"

The Commander narrowed his eyes. "Careful, Mise. It is unwise to reveal too many of your emotions to your enemy."

"And is that you?"

He raised a brow. "That is up to you. The king awaits with your dragon to send you off."

The words were an added threat—King Johannas was with Thessa, and her dragon was right: Soren did not want to die, not yet.

She hurried past a grim-faced Commander Eton and jogged back to the dragon field, dressed in leather riding gear, equipped with extra straps to stay secure, as well as several holsters for daggers she still did not know how to use. Her boots hit just above her knees, also secured.

King Johannas smiled when he saw her approach, but his next words stung a long-open wound.

"If you complete this mission successfully, I'll allow them to remove the shackle hiding under your boots."

She wanted to spit at his feet but instead bowed her head slightly, playing the part he wanted. "Yes, my king."

"Good. And Sora, dear, when you arrive, do not hesitate. He will be ready for you, as will the others."

He strode to the edge of the field to watch her go, and it was not until she was on Thessa's back and about to take to the air that she realized what he had just called her, what he had promised.

Her stomach dropped as Thessa lifted off the ground, her enormous wings flapping on either side of Soren, cold currents disturbing her hair. The king knew who she was, and not only that—someone waited for her at the border, to lead the battle.

It had to be *Mòr Maslach*.

Perhaps finally, she would learn who he was. After all, he had been the one to save her when she had fallen from Thessa, her dead sister's dagger in her belly. Perhaps she could return the favor by shoving a dagger in him too.

The journey to the border wasn't a particularly long one, and as time crawled by and the landscape below began to change, she wished for more. It was obvious they were nearing Misean territory. The temperature rose slightly, even at their elevation, and below, more and more green began to dot the landscape. She even thought she saw a tiny farm.

Wheat brushed against her palm as she walked away.

"I can't leave you to him again."

She turned, finding his beautiful face full of anguish. Her smile was sad. "This is what you get for loving a god."

Pain.

Powerlessness.

Ruin.

Shouts rang out, and Thessa rumbled beneath her. *We're nearly there.*

Soren took a shaky breath. She hadn't dreamt of Sora's memories since she had been injured, and seeing another now was unsettling. Below, the ground was covered in Aren's vast army. The fight was well underway as they held the border against Mise, ready to push it back and end this war. Just above her, a shadow passed over. She turned, looking up to see an enormous, black Vemon dragon forging ahead, leading them to destruction and death. Her hands grew white-knuckled against the saddle, and she tried to ball up the rage stewing inside her. From all she knew, the masked rider was responsible for this war as much as King Johannas. Aren was a reigning power, but *Mòr Maslach* was the blade that wielded that control.

Thessa pushed ahead, soaring past the masked rider atop his dragon. It roared, the sound resonating to Soren's core, but she didn't look back, not until she felt a sharp sting at her ear.

A dagger whizzed past her, just nicking her ear, and she whirled. The masked rider was kneeling atop his saddle, pointing up at where the thick cloud cover hid the sky. She followed the trajectory of his gloved hand.

Something was up there.

Mise had no dragons or even wyverns any longer, so it had to be more rebels. Except that when the first wyvern emerged from the darkening clouds, its rider carried Meesling's flag and wore a crown.

Soren's stomach sank. Could the rider be Prince Kellmere? His younger brother was barely out of childhood, and his father was rumored to be too old and injured to ride. Perhaps the prince had defected from the marriage agreement with Aren on his own.

In the end, it didn't matter. Soren was going to have to kill him, and if she didn't, *Mòr Maslach* surely would.

Thessa roared, a battle cry, as the prince's small legion of wyverns descended from the clouds. Rain started to fall, and Soren froze as the icy droplets hit her face. She couldn't do this, couldn't kill them so brutally and efficiently as the king wanted.

The masked rider took the lead when she did not, his dragon shrieking shrilly. She was not born a monster, but perhaps she was not strong enough to stop them from making her one. Because in the end, survival won out, and she cried, "Forward, Thessa!"

Tears streamed down her face with the rain as she reached for the prison inside her. The darkness shook the bars greedily, ready and always waiting. Thessa roared, letting loose a stream of white fire that swallowed up three wyverns and their riders in one fell swoop. To her left, the masked rider *stood* atop his saddle, throwing daggers as his dragon let loose red-hot flames, roaring as it did.

Your magic, Thessa ordered. *It's time, Soren.*

She opened her palms, and shadows melted into the darkened sky as she released a wave of Death. Wyverns screeched in agony, their riders falling limp off their backs to the battleground beneath them.

Prince Kellmere was bellowing something to the riders left in his fleet, and they changed course, diving for the ground. Thessa dove after them, *Mòr Maslach* and his dragon hot at their heels. They pulled up just before the muddy ground swallowed them whole, but Prince Kellmere and his riders were sliding *off* their wyverns and joining the battle by foot.

He's giving the wyverns a chance to live. He sees defeat as clearly as you can see victory.

Clarity sliced through the ice surrounding her. The prince had been foolish to think he could take on two Vemon dragons, double the size of most of their wyverns, but he was *good*. He had been brave when no one else from his kingdom would be.

He was going to die today, but he didn't deserve dragon-fire. She could give him nothing but a painless sleep.

Let me dismount.

Thessa snarled, her roar cutting through the screams around them. *Do not be a fool. You are not trained with a blade.*

Let me, or I'll jump off now. Follow the other Vemon dragon and its rider.

Rearing her neck, Thessa roared again but flew low enough that Soren could roll off her back like they had practiced. She landed hard, the force of it rushing painfully up her legs and back. A sword swung down, and she cried out, moving just in time and shooting to her feet.

All around her, there was Death.

Through the sheets of rain, she saw blades run straight through flesh, saw blood and insides making puddles with the water, heard men screaming for their mothers. In the chaos, she found Prince Kellmere fighting three Arenean soldiers at once, blood running down his forehead, a harsh cry escaping his lips.

She ran towards him and made it halfway there, her magic felling soldiers as they rushed at her. But she was untrained in this body, and even the magic began to tire her. She screamed and doubled over as someone swiped a blade against her upper thigh. On her knees, in the mud and bloody water, she wondered if she deserved to go like this, a nameless face in the thick of the war she had begun.

She knew that now—remembered Kronos' taunts as magic had ravaged her body, moments before her death.

"I will chain him and his world. Know, my beloved betrothed, that as you die, this punishment on mortals will outlast your end."

This was a resource war, begun by the loss of magic that started a famine in Aren nearly three decades ago. For love, for *him*, she had cursed this world, and now, she would die as no one, just as she deserved.

Instead, blood rained down on her as her attacker's head flew from her body and landed with a squelching thud. Breathing heavily, Soren turned her head to see the masked rider towering over her, holding a curved sword dripping with gore. He held out a gloved hand, slick with rain and blood, and she shoved it away. But as she struggled to her feet, swallowing a scream of pain, the rider caught her arm before she could fall.

"Stay the fuck away from me," she hissed, shoving him off.

He said nothing, but as she looked at him, a strange feeling pulsed inside her. She had a strange hunch that, like before in the tent with Vane, ether was rising in her. Ignoring it, she limped towards Prince Kellmere, a dagger held in her hand.

"Prince!" she screamed over the thunder booming overhead.

Prince Kellmere whirled. He had been cornered at an outcropping of rock but had still managed to kill all who had come for him. Obviously, he was trained, probably since birth. She needed to do this quickly before he killed her.

"*You,*" he snarled. "I've heard of you. A Misean slave girl turned weapon for King Johannas."

She took a shaky breath. "I want to help you, Kellmere."

He smiled, and there was blood on his teeth. "You want to kill me. I've seen what you can do. Do you think it a mercy?"

"Do you not?"

He pushed off the rock and circled her, heavy sword in hand. "It would be a dishonor. I will die by a blade today, fighting to the end, not put to sleep like a dog by a monster."

She backed up a step, then another, until she could retreat any further. She had to do it *now*. But even looking at the prince with murder in his hazel eyes, she could not make herself pull the magic out. Even weapons had their breaking points, it seemed, and perhaps it was a good thing that her morals finally won out, even if it meant her death.

"Goodbye, traitor," he said in a low voice, raising his blade.

But before Kellmere could make the final blow, he whirled moving aside, just before the masked rider shoved his blade in his back. Soren sucked in deep breaths as they dueled. Her leg was on fire and her head felt light.

She knew she was about to watch the prince die. Even if he was a strong fighter, *Mòr Maslach* moved like the wind. He caught the prince's belly, Kellmere rearing back just before the blow could become fatal.

"Coward!" he bellowed. "Reveal yourself!"

The rider only tilted his head at the prince, as if to say, *make me.*

Prince Kellmere lowered his chin. His gaze flicked to Soren, and then he reared back his hand. Silver flew through the air, and she swerved just before the dagger struck her in the chest. When she looked back, Kellmere was holding the rider's mask, and the rider—

Her lips parted, her chest squeezing so tight, she could barely take another breath as she saw Vane standing in the rain. His eyes were black with rage as he swung at Kellmere again.

The prince laughed, unhinged in the face of death. "I thought so," he shouted, glancing at Soren. "The beast has a weakness. They always do."

She wanted to die, wanted to kill Vane and scream at the sky. He was the leashed pet to King Johannas, the one he had spoken of with such bitterness. Now, she knew why. But he had lied to her, was responsible for the death of so many of her people. *Her* people, because Mise was where she, Soren, had been born to a mortal mother.

He had touched her with a killer's hands.

Still, as he fought Kellmere, she flinched when the prince caught his leg with his sword. Vane hardly slowed, ignoring the wound as if it were a mere nuisance. When it became obvious Kellmere was going to lose, the prince reared back, breathing heavily. Vane paused—his only mistake, because the prince was bluffing.

It all happened so fast.

Prince Kellmere bolted towards Soren, and she gripped her dagger tightly, freezing in panic. Vane sprinted towards them, his eyes wild as Kellmere lifted his sword. He reached them, wedging his blade between her and Kellmere's sword.

"Soren," he said, eyes wide. "Do it. If not for me, then for yourself."

"I will not be what they made me," she snarled, "even if you will."

Vane's breath shuddered, clouding in the air. His blade slipped under the pressure of Kellmere's, and in a blur, the two men turned. Vane's sword fell to the muddy earth as Kellmere sliced into his palm, and then the prince angled it for Soren's heart. She closed her eyes, waiting, anticipating the final blow.

But death never came.

Instead, Vane's arms caged her, his forehead pressing to hers. "You," he rasped. "You are my every…reason."

He grunted, and she looked down to see Kellmere's blade inches from her chest. Her eyes widened in shock, and as Kellmere pulled his sword from Vane's body, she no longer hesitated to reach inside herself and deny the prince any semblance of honor in death. Seeing Vane injured like this unlocked an innate instinct to protect him, despite his betrayal.

The prince collapsed just as Vane fell to his knees before her. Above, two dragons screeched in the air, letting loose streams of fire aimed at the retreating Misean troops. Soren stared, wide-eyed, as Vane coughed, specks of blood staining his lips.

"Go," he choked out. "Run, Soren."

This was… He was…

He was Vane Evva, the demi-god she had fallen in love with over a century ago, the trainer she had fallen for again in a matter of weeks, and *Mòr Maslach*, a killer she hated.

"Can you stand?" Her voice shook.

His fingers were covered in crimson, pressed to his abdomen. "We've won," he rasped, "but there are still Misean soldiers afoot. You need—find Thessilnn. Fly back to camp. Tell the king I have a message for him: *fuck you*."

His words were broken, becoming fainter and fainter as he spoke, his face pale. She sucked in a breath and caught him, pulling his near-limp body against hers.

Thessa. I need you. Now.

Heat filled the air as white fire cleared the area. *I know you do.* The dragon sounded enraged.

Please, Thessa, I don't what to—

I know. We need to hurry. He is dying.

Tears of rage, at both herself and Vane, ran down her face as she choked out, "I can't get him onto the saddle."

Thessa didn't move, but Soren jumped as Vane's dragon landed with a thud, picking him up gently with her mouth. For a few seconds, Soren stared, shocked, but it broke quickly, replaced by fear.

She scrambled onto Thessa's back clumsily, ignoring the blazing pain in her leg.

You are injured.

"Just go!" she shouted.

Thessa huffed but took off into the rain. Both dragons kept low, as if searching for something. The downpour began to slow as they landed by a small stream.

Here should do.

Soren jerked her head, scanning the area. *How is this helpful?*

You need water to wash the blood and dirt.

"Water will not heal him!"

No. Nothing will heal these wounds. He is nearly gone, but you have a place inside you where you keep Death, where you can coax him and cage him until it is time.

Soren watched as Vane's dragon carefully set him down by the stream. She felt numb as she slid off Thessa and walked towards him, so still and so pale. She had no idea if she could truly do what Thessa spoke of, and if she failed, if Vane—

Part of her still hated him for all he'd done, but she had to try. He couldn't die now.

Collapsing to the ground next to him, she hovered her hands over the gaping wound and shut her eyes. At first, she felt nothing, but as the moments slipped by, she heard the whisper. It was not a word, but a presence. The shadow of Death hovered over Vane, waiting for the moment he could finally take him. Inside her, she opened all the cells. Death chuckled, smiling at her, his daughter, as if to say, *You cannot trick me.*

But she was Night's daughter too, the very power that had seduced Death in the first place. She threw a cover of impenetrable darkness over Death, the valley around her plunging into a thick, unnatural night. Quickly, she struck in the dark, ripping him away from Vane, shoving him into her prison and slamming each barred door.

Clever, my child, he whispered.

Night faded away, Death with her.

CHAPTER 26

Time felt odd, slogging along too fast, and at the same time, moving oddly slow. The world was hazy, and he only caught pieces of it.

Bloody hands, small, braiding back silver hair.

Blue eyes ringed with exhaustion.

"I thought he would be awake by now."

He tried to claw his way up through the heavy water he was floating in. Her voice was a tether, but he couldn't quite break the surface. Heles lingered with him, the dragon's presence a small comfort.

One-hundred and five years ago, Heles and Thessilnn's eggs had been given to Sora. A betrothal gift—two female Vemon dragons from the same azure mother. When they had hatched dark and light in front of him, Sora, and Anabeth, Ana had declared it an omen. Something was on the horizon, a force both full of light and matched with a powerful darkness. At the time, he remembered brushing the words off, but now, Ana's words floated with him in the strange stasis where he slept.

Soren held the power to end this. He knew that, and as Sora, she had known she could prevent it. Kronos was a mad king who had only ever wanted one thing.

Absolute control.

He didn't care about her, nor did he think he owned her. He simply wanted to use her as Johannas had used him. When Nyx refused to be his consort, signing away a daughter she did not yet have, his rage had been tucked away.

But Sora was more than Nyx. If anything, she was more her father. Kronos held the embers of the world, chosen by Sol after the world had been born. But with Sora, he had the flip of the coin: not just the life and light Sol had gifted him with, but the darkness of Sol's twin and the destruction of Thanatos all in one soul. One weapon.

Kronos could not be killed, not without the backing of other powerful gods. Even then, it was a mere chance. Though, as Nyx had learned, his crazed nature could be sated.

But Soren was no weapon. She was powerful and wild, but she was also kind-hearted. Kronos would break her in order to use her.

Just like Vane himself had been broken.

Used.

Beaten.

Orders were orders, and he was bound to Johannas' mortal line by Kronos' eternal curse. Perhaps it would be better to let go, to let himself sink into the still waters around him. Maybe then, she could finally be free.

"Vane."

The water shimmered.

"Damn it." Hands shook his face somewhere far above him. "You can't lie to me and then just go and die."

He was selfish. He reached for her.

Silver shimmered in her blue eyes, just above the surface. He fought against the current that tried to sweep him back to the depths. Tears fell down her cheeks, imbued with ether and sparkling like liquid moonlight in the dull sun.

He gasped as he broke free.

CHAPTER 27

VANE ROLLED onto his side as he finally opened his eyes, coughing and sputtering. She gripped his shoulder, unsure of how bad his injuries still were. When she had brought him back from the brink of death two days ago, the largest wound, just below his ribs, had closed, leaving a tender, angry scar, but he was still covered in bruises and other, shallower slices and cuts.

When he stopped coughing, he sat up slightly, wincing. His fingers brushed over his stomach, and his eyes widened.

"How?" he said hoarsely.

She set her jaw. "Thessa reminded me who my father technically is."

"You scared him off." The words were half-question, half-statement. She wondered if she had done it before.

Not like this, Thessa rumbled, her head resting in the crook of Heles' wing.

She cleared her throat, trying not to look too long at Vane's face. She had stared at it enough over the last day, willing him to wake. But now that he was looking back at her, it was nearly too much to bear.

He had lied to her from the beginning. He was no swordmaster or even captain. The king had probably sent him specifically to spy on her once word of Thessa reached him. What she couldn't figure out was: why? Why, given everything he had told her about their past, would he betray her like this? And if it was a lie, why would he have risked his life to save her during the battle?

Calloused fingers brushed across her brow, and she flinched. Vane took a shaky, rasping breath. "You're confused."

Her laugh was as cold as she felt inside. "How could I not be?"

"I can explain, Soren. I promise."

Shifting, she looked away at the nearly setting sun. Night would fall again soon, and the blistering cold would return. They had no food, only water from the stream, and King Johannas was surely looking for them. It was only a matter of time before they were found.

"Your promises mean very little to me right now," she finally said, glancing back at him.

He blew out a breath, coughing again as he sat up fully. She sighed and moved towards him, positioning herself just behind him then ordering, "Lay your head in my lap."

"Soren—"

"You still need to rest. This way, you don't need to prop yourself up with your arm while I decide whether to gut you again myself or not."

He grimaced but obeyed. She resisted the urge to thread her fingers through the waves of his hair, instead placing her hand on either side of her head, her already-filthy fingers curling into the grass and dirt.

"One hundred and four years ago today, Kronos took your life because you would not let him have it for his own to control," he began quietly.

She sucked in a breath and almost asked him to stop right then and there, but ultimately, she let him continue. Deep down, she knew she needed to hear this.

"All I wanted was to die with you, and he knew that. So, he made sure I lived in agony, banished to the kingdom that hated me as a child and bound in service to a line of mortal kings. I was an anomaly to King Jonah, Johannas' father. Most demi-gods fled to Arcadia as soon as they felt the veil sealing. Others went into hiding when mortals became suspicious of those still in connection to the gods. But I had nowhere to go. I was trapped, and the mortal king knew it. At first, he merely used me and Heles for various…errands, dirty deeds the crown wanted to be doled out in the shadows. Jonah was just as cruel as his son, but he was not as wise. When he died and Johannas became the ruler of a starving kingdom, he called me into his council room and asked what I would do if I were him. I suggested asking Mise for aid, as its climate was the most amicable to crops, even without magic. Farming had really only ever been possible in Aren because of the assistance of mages. The field we met in is covered in stone and dust now."

She tried to ignore the feeling of tearing in her chest at the knowledge that the field was gone.

"How many times did you go back there?" she whispered, her eyes stinging as she focused on the horizon, away from him.

He paused. "Every year. It isn't far from the capitol. I watched it slowly die as the seasons came and went."

She clenched her jaw. "Continue."

"Johannas already had a plan in place when he asked me that, one that included taking rather than asking. But when he proposed his idea of becoming a conqueror to his council, he told them I had advised him in that direction. They all know what I am. Any who disagreed with the idea kept their mouths shut over fear of 'provoking' me."

Vane let out a bitter laugh. "I realized then that I was no longer just a pet with a blade. Johannas wanted me to become a figurehead in the coming war. I became not only the reason, but also the tool he used to win it."

"You couldn't go against his orders?" she asked, finally looking down to find him smiling sadly at her.

"I still can't, Soren. I was something that disturbed the order and control Kronos so desperately needs and depends on. He remedied that—he cursed me."

She blinked rapidly, her hands shaking even as she dug them into the earth. "What are we going to do?"

"You could leave me behind," he said softly. "Run now. Go somewhere Johannas cannot find you."

"And then what? He would send you to hunt me, wouldn't he? And what of Kronos?"

His throat worked, and his next words were careful. "With you…I've been able to bend some of my orders a bit. There's always room for error when Johannas hands them out, and he's grown careless over the years, but this…it's different. If the last order he gave me had held, I couldn't have stopped Kellmere."

"What was it, the order?"

"Lead the battle. Win at any cost, even if it was your life." He paused then added, "Johannas isn't stupid. He knew about us, and it didn't take him long to figure out who you were."

"I see. And Kronos?"

Vane's eyes grew hard. "I'll find a way to kill him."

The sun was nearly set now, the world in a hazy twilight. She imagined it for a moment, a life away from all this, on the run, always looking over her shoulder. A life where she walked away, knowing that, once again, she had sentenced Vane to a fate worse than death.

She couldn't leave him. She couldn't do that to someone she cared for like this.

Tears began to stream down her face as she let it fully hit her. She had known how she felt when he was dying, but even that had been in the heat of desperation. Now, in the cold, quiet air of the valley, with him looking at her like she was the reason the sun rose and set, a wave of sorrow crested in her.

Vane sat up, even as she half-heartedly tried to stop him. His arms wrapped around her, rocking her as she wept.

"You know how this ends," she gasped against his shoulder. "And this time, his punishments will only be worse."

Thessa and Heles both made low, sorrowful noises, their heads low on the ground. The four of them were bonded by fate, trapped in its cycle of tragedy.

Fire and Death.

Darkness and Light.

The end was once again nearing…

Tiny cracks appeared in the jewel-toned eggs as the full moon crested in the sky. Vane, who had been nursing the fire, eyes half-lidded, sat up. Next to her, Ana stood, clasping and unclasping her hands as the eggs broke. First came the pale dragon, then the night-dark one. Both looked to her and Vane and made tiny mewling sounds.

"They're claiming you two," Ana said, her breath clouding in the air. "Gods, both of them... Fates help us."

Sora knelt, Vane next to her. It had been nearly six seasons since he had found her crying in a farm field. Her wedding neared, and Kronos had only grown crueler. She had recently had to physically restrain Vane from going to the king's palace and getting himself killed. Bruises faded, but his life was precious to her.

The dragons spit sparks, and Sora felt the bond between all four of them settling as they crowed and hopped around the cavern. Vane's mouth curved, and he said to the black-scaled dragon, "Heles."

She met his eyes and nodded before brushing her fingers across the moon-pale hatchling. "Thessilnn."

Heles: Beginning.

Thessilnn: End.

Fitting names for dragons born on the last night of the moon cycle, at the cusp of the changing of the seasons.

"Thessa," Ana said, smiling, but she reared back as the dragon hissed, spitting more sparks.

"She doesn't seem to enjoy nicknames," Vane chuckled, stroking the dragon's snout as she calmed.

Ana sighed. "No. I need to go. Can you two handle them for a few hours? I'll be back to take them to the temple at sunrise."

"We'll be fine," she assured Ana.

Ana took one last, lingering look at the dragons and then hurried from the cavern, down one of the tunnels that connected back to the glen of trees that hid the entrance. Once she was gone, they watched the dragons for a while in silence until the hatchlings fell asleep, nestled in a pile of hay Ana had brought.

"Sora," Vane said softly, nuzzling her neck.

"Mhm?"

"Marry me."

Her breath halted. "We can't."

"You know I don't give a fuck what he thinks."

She touched his cheeks with both palms, trembling. "He would kill you."

"I want this. I want you. Forever."

She looked down at the golden band balanced between his fingers, and a short sob escaped her. He was all she wanted, but this was more dangerous than either of them could likely imagine.

But she was selfish. Perhaps they both were.

She kissed him as she cried, and he slid the ring onto her pointer finger, the direct line to her heart. Muttered between heavy breaths and soft, possessive nips to his lips, she vowed, "If he kills you, I will die too. Fate has bound us."

Vane bit her lip, and she moaned softly.

"Don't promise that," he murmured.

"You know this is damning us both. You know, Vane. Don't tell me you would want to exist in a world where I was gone."

He pressed their foreheads together, his hand fisted in her braid and his breath coming quickly. "Never. I would rather die a thousand deaths."

"You understand then."

He hesitated but finally promised, "Together, my love."

The memory cleared, but he was still there, holding her as tears slipped down her cheeks. She wiped them away with one hand, cupping his cheek with the other. Her mind was set. They had made mistakes before, but they knew Kronos better now. This had to end.

"Together," she breathed, her gaze locking on to his. "We do this together."

"Sora—"

Ether flooded her, and his lips parted as she cut in, "You promised me. Does that vow no longer hold?"

He let out a breath. "Things changed. I broke my end of the promise when I sat by and watched him do things to you that will never leave me, not until I draw my last breath."

"You didn't have a choice—"

"I was weak!" he said, voice on edge as it rose. A hot wind disturbed the loose leaves of a Balor tree and the surface of the stream. He tilted his head back and laughed hoarsely at the night sky. "I thought I was ready to face him, but you were right—I was powerless and pathetic."

"Vane," she whispered, her eyes burning with tears she no longer wanted to shed. The sorrow building in her was too much, overwhelming her like a raging summer storm in Mise. The kind that would flood entire villages, the kind that left destruction in its wake.

On his knees, Vane lowered his chin from the heavens. Faint streaks of ether, gifts from a father he had never met, swirled in his eyes, rising to the surface with his rage.

"I am not powerless any longer," he said, his voice a deadly timbre of softness. "This will end—on our terms."

The wind quieted, though Thessa and Heles were still restless.

Soren glanced back at them. *What is it?*

Then, for the first time in this lifetime, Heles' rasp filled her mind. *Riders. We can sense the dragons approaching.*

Vane must have heard the warning too, because he took Soren's face in both his hands and said firmly, "They will want to interrogate us—separately. Insist on the interrogation being done with us together."

"Why?" She could hear it now, the dragon's screeched calls echoing in the distance.

"Trust me," Vane said. "Threaten them if you must, give a show of your magic. I am sure Johannas suspects both of us now, but I've been questioned by him before. Leave this first step to me."

She hesitated. An hour ago, she was unsure if she could ever trust Vane again. But everything he had told her was true, she was sure of it, which meant he'd had as little choice in this life as she had.

"Alright," she said.

Vane searched her gaze for a moment then kissed her hard. Even now, even with the riders looming larger on the horizon, she melted under his touch, chasing him back when he pulled away.

"I know, my love," he whispered, reading her mind. "I want more time too."

Time had never been on their side. They both knew that.

The hand of fate was coming.

CHAPTER 28

PRINCESS CION WAS the first of the two riders. Soren stood just ahead of Vane as she slid off her dragon and strode towards them.

"Soren. Vane Evva." Cion spoke crisply, like the leader she had not yet become—like the master who would someday hold the key to Vane's chains.

"Princess," Vane answered flatly.

Soren glanced back at him to find his gaze hard. He was standing tall, despite the still-healing wounds.

Cion swallowed, her throat bobbing as he stared at her. "Who saw you without your mask?" she finally asked him. "If anyone in the training camp is aware, it would be prudent to keep you separate from Soren."

"No." Soren didn't let herself think before speaking, firmly and without any semblance of reverence or respect.

Cion reacted immediately to her tone, the princess' lips parting and her eyes hardening. "It isn't for you to decide. You are still under my father's jurisdiction—both of you are."

The second rider approached behind her, and Soren nearly groaned. Of course, they had sent Ilav with her, of all people.

"You should listen to your princess, Soren," Ilav said with a smile that stunk of his believed superiority.

Vane made a low sound in his throat. "Who gave you authority?"

Ilav barked a laugh. "And to think, I was afraid of you, *Mòr Maslach.* You're nothing but a dog for the king."

"Shut up," Soren hissed. She let shadows drift towards him, whispers of Night, and Ilav at least had the where-withal to look wary as they toyed with his ankles.

"Stand down, both of you. Evva, answer my question," Cion ordered, a hand on the dagger at her hip, adding, "truthfully."

"It was a battle," Vane said, voice dark and dripping with bitter disdain. "Do you think I had time to look around and take much note of my surroundings?" He stepped past Soren, tilting his head. She could sense the heat emanating from him—flames begging to reach the surface. "You wouldn't, though, would you? To you, battle is a game, with a parade afterwards where they shower you with roses."

Cion stiffened. "I said, stand down." But her voice was wavering now.

Vane only smiled. "Do you know what we are, *princess*? Or has your dear father not chosen to disclose that partic-ular detail yet?"

Soren felt a seed of pity for Cion, small as it was. She had been in the dark all these years, just as Soren herself had. But Vane wasn't wrong—she must know some of it now. A line was beginning to be drawn in the sand, and it was unclear who stood where.

Kronos.

King Johannas.

Princess Cion.

Rebels.

Aren.

Mise.

War.

Something far more terrible than a conflict over resources was coming. Perhaps killing Kronos was the key, but there were endless obstacles to that. She and Vane could not do it alone, and it was obvious that even her death had not sated Kronos' immeasurable need for power and control. Even if they did manage to kill him, who would lead the gods? Would the mortal side of the world fall into disarray? Only an organized force could take on a power that had reigned for so long. They needed more than hope now. They needed revolution.

Cion could be a part of that, should she choose it, but Soren only saw fear in the princess' eyes as she replied, "The gods granted you power."

Ilav was watching the whole exchange closely, his gaze flicking to Soren's momentarily. She shivered, unease creeping up her spine at the cruel curiosity in his eyes.

"That's what he told you," Soren stated, brow raising.

Cion's mouth tightened. "The gods are wise, but their decisions have always been difficult to understand—"

"Who told you that?" Soren had an inkling.

"Anabeth. She visited me at camp this past week, just

after my father explained things to me. She helped me understand."

Vane snorted softly. "She helped you to believe the lies he fed you, and she wasn't there for you at all. That she wasted time on you at all makes me think she actually does care for you in some way."

Cion's eyes shone, but her expression grew sharp with anger. "You're lying. Even Soren can tell you: Anabeth is just the scribe's daughter."

The second rider. Mind him, Thessa said.

"Also a lie," Vane said. *I have my eye on him.*

Soren's breath caught. Now that the four of them had an open pathway, it made sense that she could hear him too. A faint wisp of memory told her that had been the case before too.

Cion began to walk towards her, dagger in hand. "Soren, he's lying. I don't know what he's told you, but you know—"

She cut herself off on a yelp as Vane stepped in front of her, his hands engulfed in flame. He was on edge, Soren could feel it in the shimmering heat of his magic that thickened the air.

"No closer until you drop the dagger," he snarled, tiny sparks of ether flickering in his eyes. "Or I'll give you a true glimpse at the power the gods 'granted' me."

Cion's eyes widened, landing on Soren. "Are you *with* him?" she said, voice disbelieving.

Ilav snorted. "You're quite unobservant, princess, if it took you this long to pick up on that. Besides, does it really surprise you that a slave would try to gain favor by fucking her superior? Too bad he's just as chained as she is."

The darkness, sleeping in its prison, opened an eye.

"I would like to think it's not a crime to fuck my husband," Soren said, raising a brow. She was done denying the truth to herself, and the words were a release, letting go of all the uncertainty she had felt over the past few days while he had been asleep.

Glad to finally hear you say it, wife. I'll have to make sure you remember what it's like as soon as we're alone again.

Cion's eyes widened and her mouth dropped open, Ilav's brow rising nearly up to his hairline. The princess glanced at Vane, testing his reaction. He simply took a step closer to Soren and said, "The truth is far worse than you want to imagine, mortal princess. And given that I'm not under any specific order to keep you alive, killing you is quite possibly in the cards if you don't agree to help us. Your little friend, too."

Cion paled, retreating a step, then another. Her dragon growled, the low sound vibrating through the earth. Ilav inched closer to his own dragon.

"Cion..." Soren wanted to at least give her a chance. "You need to listen."

Cion let out a broken laugh. "Listen to what? You're both mad! *I* should be the one threatening you, not the other way around."

"We're more alike than you think," Soren said quietly.

Nyx was no queen, not after her refusal to marry Kronos. Still, all the principal gods held enough influence to be considered royalty. Soren had been raised as such in her life as Sora.

"Explain. Then, we go. My father, *your king*, is waiting on us."

Soren pulled on the ether that had slowly begun to finally show itself in her blood, watching as Cion and Ilav's attention went to her eyes.

"It's complicated," she told them. "But what you need to know is that Mise, or even the rebels in your own ranks—they're not the real enemy. Over a hundred years ago, a god didn't get what he wanted, and this world descended into chaos for it."

"Your eyes," Cion whispered.

"Ether," Vane supplied, lacing his bare left hand in Soren's. The cool metal of his wedding band slid against her skin as he squeezed hard. Behind them, Thessa and Heles rumbled.

Cion shook her head. "Ether only exists in Arcadia, in the gods."

"The border sealed off mortals from entering Arcadia, but it does not prevent gods from entering this world. Vane was born and then banished here."

"Holy gods," Cion whispered. "You're both demi-gods?"

"Vane is, but I—"

Vane's hand tightened on hers, and she looked up at him. "Soren," he said in a low voice. "This is Johannas' daughter."

"And he knows already anyways. Besides, we need her on our side."

Cion looked at Soren expectantly, her eyes still wide and shining. Soren checked that well, the prison of power inside her, one last time. There was no denying what she was, not anymore. She could feel the power humming through her.

"A long time ago," she said softly, "the only daughter of two powerful gods was betrothed to Kronos. But she fell in love with someone else, and he and his mortal kin paid the price for her selfishness."

"*Darkness rises, an ember of light to meet it,*" Cion said, shaking her head. She looked up at Vane. "I always wondered what that part meant. Now, it's becoming clear."

Soren met the princess' eyes, realizing what she meant. "The prophecy, the one that destined you to be a rider. There was more to it, wasn't there?"

Slowly, Cion nodded. She opened her mouth, but Ilav cut in, stepping forward, Vane tense next to Soren as he said, "Are you seriously saying *you* are a god? I thought you were born in a dirt pit in Mise."

Vane let go of her hand, closing in on Ilav so they were face to face. "Watch. Your. Mouth."

Ilav looked up at Vane and said tersely, "It's a simple question. How can she be your goddess wife and a slave from Mise?"

"Kronos didn't let me live after what I'd done." The words said aloud were a harsh reminder of Vane's screams echoing against the palace walls in Arcadia. Her skin raised, as if she was hearing them now, and both Heles and Thessa made low, keening noises behind them.

Vane didn't step away from Ilav as Cion said slowly, "So, you're not a goddess, or you are?"

"Gods cannot die," Soren replied simply. "Not their— our—souls. I am both Sora, daughter of Nyx and Thanatos, as well as Soren, a girl taken from her from her family in Mise."

A shocked silence filled the area, perhaps the whole valley. The mortal world held its breath as she willingly announced herself. But the terse air broke quickly as Ilav asked, "Goddess or mortal, why in all the world would you pick a demi-god over a king? I mean, your power could have been limitless with Kronos, right?"

Cion interrupted before either Soren or Vane could reply. "We need to go. We've already lingered too long, and my father will send more riders if we don't return soon. He will interrogate you both."

Soren reached for Cion's arm, but she shied away. "Cion," she said, lowering her voice. "Please. I can tell you more, but—"

"If you betrayed a king once, you obviously would do it again," the princess snapped. "And besides," she flicked her gaze to Vane, "I know about his binding to my bloodline. Why wouldn't you try to kill me and my family to break it?"

"I'm not a monster," Soren whispered.

"Love makes us all monsters," she said. "Follow us to camp, or the king will force your hand and tug on that one's leash."

She jogged over to her dragon, her dark hair a shadow behind her. Ilav gave Vane a lingering look before doing the same.

Vane feigned kissing her head, murmuring into her hair, "Something is wrong with the boy."

Soren furrowed her brow. *What—*

"Not there." They had reached Thessa, and Vane kissed her, whispering against her mouth, "He has too much power for a mortal."

He pulled back and held out a hand to help Soren climb on to Thessa's back. She remembered the first memory she had of Vane, when she had been able to sense his magic swirling under his skin, in the aura all around him. But Ilav was just a general's son. How could he be a god, or even half? Could he be reincarnated too?

Ready yourself, Soren, Thessa rumbled.

Soren braced against the saddle as Thessa took off into the air. The mountains swelled around them as they left the valley behind, bringing colder air. To her left, Vane rode on his knees as he had in battle, his eyes ahead on Ilav and his dragon.

A few short hours later, when they circled the training camp again, Soren's hands tightened on the saddle, unease a steady beat in her chest. *Thessa. Did you sense it? With Ilav?*

Vane is right. You need to be careful, even with your thoughts.

The unease grew, making Soren feel light in the head. It only got worse when Thessa dove downward, and Soren's vision grew dark and fuzzy around the edges. She gripped the saddle, trying to take deep breaths in the air rushing by. When they landed, they were immediately surrounded by guards, but Soren was suddenly too exhausted to care. She hadn't eaten, had barely slept in three days, and it was beginning to wear on her body.

"Dismount, now!" one of the guards shouted. "Both of you."

Thessa growled, sensing Soren's weakness. *You are not well, and they do not intend to do anything but harm you.*

"Now!" the guard barked.

Vane slid off Heles first, and two guards grabbed him before he could go to Soren. He easily fought them off as she struggled off Thessa's back, landing in a heap on the ground by the time she managed it.

More guards surrounded Vane. He gutted one of them,

but before he could reach Soren, a booming voice called, "Stop. Do not harm them."

Soren watched in horror as Vane's body locked and his face contorted in pain. Through gritted teeth, he growled at Johannas, "Fuck you."

The king merely laughed, striding towards them casually. "Good work, daughter," he said as Cion slid off her dragon. "And you, Ilav Thil, the general's son—you'll be rewarded, as I promised. Guards, take them."

Soren raised her head as the guards dragged her up. Delirious, she reached for her magic but found only whispers. Her vision crossed, and vaguely, she heard Vane shouting her name.

"Don't die," she said faintly. "We promised…together."

Darkness consumed her.

"Sora, wake up!"

Ana's face hovered over her, panic twisting her features in the near dark. She had no idea how her friend had gotten into the fortress her mother called a home. The high stone walls had always been a mockery to her—heavily warded, and though her mother had never said it, they were meant to keep someone as powerful as Kronos at bay. It was ironic, given the fact that she had willingly signed away her own blood to him.

"How are you here?" she asked Ana, sitting up and letting the carefully placed shadows fall away from her left hand, revealing the marriage band.

Ana took a shaky breath. "Your mother let me in."

"My mother? Why—"

"You've been summoned. I was chosen to escort you."

A pit dropped in Sora's stomach. There was only reason Kronos would call on her at this hour, and with no warning. But it couldn't be...not yet. Not so soon. She wouldn't let herself believe it until Ana said the words to her.

She swung her legs over the side of the bed and dressed quickly in a gown she knew Kronos liked. She would need any leverage she could get if the worst came to pass.

In the entryway, her parents waited. Her mother's beautiful face was tight with worry, and Sora could see strands of barely concealed ether running under her umber skin. The power was trying to escape, but, like a coward, she wouldn't let it.

Her father stood next to her, always a dog at her mother's beck and call. But even his black eyes were pinched, and she swore he looked paler than normal. His gaze flicked to her left hand, and his mouth tightened.

There was no way he could see past the concealment. If he could, he would have said something days ago.

"Be respectful," Nyx said. "And remember, he merely wants something. If you can find out what it is, you will be fine. It is always a game of need with Kronos."

Thanatos stepped forward, and Sora stiffened as he pulled her into an embrace. Her father almost never showed her affection, much less hugged her. But she found herself leaning into him, holding on tightly. These could be the last moments she shared with him.

Just before he released her, he murmured in her ear, "Death is merely a bridge for gods, daughter. You know how our souls are."

She hid the catching of her breath with a delicate cough. Ana glanced at her, but she kept her eyes ahead as they walked out into the waiting night air.

He knew.

Her father somehow knew he was sending his daughter to her death. Someone had betrayed them, but she was nearly certain it was not him. He probably just sensed it.

Imminent death had a taste, a scent, even a feeling. Thanatos knew them all intimately .

As soon as she and Ana reached the road, Ana hissed, "He has Vane, Sora. He knows."

She tamped down a violent wave of panic and kept walking, her arm in Ana's as she whispered, "Someone betrayed us."

"Yes. I don't know who yet, but—"

A portal blinked into existence, pure silver ether swirling in a giant oval in front of them. Arcadia was massive, and Kronos had never allowed her to 'spend herself' walking to his palace. Ana gripped her arm in a death grip, and Sora gave a short nod.

"I will try to protect you."

Ana shook her head. "Just find him and get him out before Kronos kills you both."

She didn't give her space to argue, pulling her into the portal. Warmth enveloped them, lasting for a few seconds before everything tunneled, and they stepped directly into Kronos' throne room.

He was sitting there, sprawled back in the golden seat she hated so much. He had made her sit in it once while he had kissed her neck and called her his queen, minutes after leaving her cheek bruised. The memory made her want to vomit, but it was nothing like the way she felt when she saw the pool of blood at the bottom of the dais.

"Where is he?" Sora snarled.

Kronos' features grew twisted. "Dropping the pretenses so soon, beloved?"

"What's the point?" she said softly. "We both know what I've done."

The king of the gods stood and slowly walked down the steps of the dais towards her. His bare feet dipped in the blood, and Sora's head grew light. She ignored the feeling, even as Kronos yanked her left hand up and stared at the wedding band, eyes glowing with pure power.

He had no single power as king. He was the culmination of all of them. Sora knew in her heart she had no chance.

"Disobedient," he spat, and she gasped in pain as he ripped the ring from her finger and hurled it across the room. "Bring him in!"

Sora braced herself, but nothing kept her from falling to her knees as Kronos' guards dragged Vane into the room. They dropped him to the floor, his eyes meeting hers, his split lips forming her name.

"Please," she gasped.

Kronos let out a crazed laugh and reared his foot back. She screamed as he kicked Vane's stomach, and he coughed up blood. She summoned Night and Death, but Kronos merely flicked his fingers to null it. Even her power could not reach him.

Ana held her as Kronos hit Vane again and again. Still, her husband reached for her. Through every blow, his steady gaze never left hers.

But only when Kronos turned to her did true fear enter Vane's eyes.

CHAPTER 29

Soren was strapped to a wooden chair when she came to, a gag in her mouth. She blinked a few times, finding herself in a nondescript tent, empty aside from the chair facing her. She screamed once into the gag, letting the sound echo down the pathway in her mind that connected to Vane, Thessa, and Heles.

You are breathing. She swore there was relief in Thessa's voice.

Soren tried to focus on taking slow inhales and exhales around the gag. *Where is Vane?*

We cannot reach him. Moments ago, you were dark too. We are being kept with the other dragons. They sense something is amiss.

Thessa's voice grew fainter until Soren could no longer hear her at all. She reached for the dragons, for Vane…

Only swirling, opaque shadows greeted her. There had been a space inside her that had always felt empty and lost. Finding Vane and the dragons after so many years had finally shown her what she had been searching for. But now, the space was empty again, or perhaps blocked somehow.

Even her magic felt faint, and she had an inkling that though she might still be able to weaken someone, she could not slip them into Death's grasp.

The flap to the tent opened, and King Johannas and Commander Eton entered, trailed by Cion. The princess looked freshly washed, dressed in clean flight wear, but her face was lined with uncertainty as the commander approached Soren, a tiny dagger in his hand.

"You should have followed orders," Commander Eton said, cocking his head at her, a slant to his brow. "We can still work together, you know. You and Evva just need to cooperate, and no one has to get hurt any more than they already have."

Soren struggled in the chair. What had they done to him? She had no idea how much time had passed since she had lost consciousness. Based on the lack of light beyond the tent, it could have been minutes or hours.

"Remove the gag," Johannas ordered.

The commander raised a brow but obeyed. Soren gasped, sucking down the air greedily. It hadn't exactly been easy to breathe around the cloth.

"Where is he?" she snarled.

"Alive."

Both men looked to the corner where Cion stood, hands folded in front of her.

Her expression didn't change, not even when her father narrowed his eyes on her. "Watch and observe, Cion. Do not speak to the prisoner."

"Ah, so I'm a spectacle now?" Soren challenged.

The king moved towards her, a slow smile spreading over his face. "You once tried so hard to blend in amongst the other slaves in my palace. You never succeeded, though, and not just because of your appearance. My wife sensed your power, though she did not understand it, and used it to her advantage. That should have been my first clue. But she has picked up many talented assassins over the years, so I chose to ignore it. The moment I let you taste what power could look like, though, I began to wonder. I may not have magic, but my father and his father before him did. That kind of power leaves an imprint…a feeling. And when yours rose, I sensed it."

"The day you told the princess she would marry Prince Kellmere." Soren met his hooded eyes. "You looked at me in the council chambers."

"Observant," the king mused. "I told you, Eton."

The commander bowed his head. "I picked up on as much over the past month."

Soren grasped inside herself for a hint of power strong enough to at least knock the three out. But whatever had a hold on her, blocking the magic and Vane, tightened its grip. It was as if a hand was wrapping around her neck, slowly squeezing.

"Missing something?"

She flashed her gaze to the king. "How?"

"With some help from a friend?"

"Anabeth can't do—"

The king laughed. "No, no, the 'scribe's' daughter has been detained. She was becoming difficult."

Soren glanced at the corner where Cion stood. "Father?" the princess whispered. "What are you talking about? What did you do to Anabeth?"

Johannas sighed. "Ah. I forgot about your little dalliance

with her. I would have assumed that would have run its course by now. She is not who you think she is."

"She would have told me."

Johannas rolled his eyes. "Because you think she loves you? Is that it? Gods and their kin are hardly capable of such an emotion. They may claim to be, but what they truly crave is power."

"Anabeth isn't…" But Cion trailed off when Johannas raised his hand to silence her.

"The proposal I offer still stands," the king said, looking squarely at Soren. "Serve me, win the war, and you go free."

Soren's smile was bitter. "There is no freedom for me, not while Kronos lives. And I think you know that. I won't waste time killing for you."

"So you can spend your time finding ways to end him?" Johannas murmured, leaning down to look directly at her.

When Soren didn't reply, he straightened. "Fine, then. Come inside, Vane."

Soren's breath caught as the tent flap turned back and Vane entered. He was armed to the teeth, wearing leather flight armor just like Cion. His eyes were red-rimmed and his jaw was tight. She met his gaze, but he didn't react, the pathway connecting them still dark.

"Vane," the king said in a light voice, "I want you to torture her. Ah—wait. Let's be more specific. Break her left pointer finger. We'll start there and go on if we need to."

Vane took a step closer to Soren. She held on to his dark eyes, even as he reached for her hand, his muscles so tense, it looked painful.

"It's okay," she whispered. "I know you said you could fight it around me, but if you can't…it's okay."

"Sora," he said through clenched teeth, closing his eyes. "Do you remember the first time we kissed?"

Commander Eton glanced at Johannas, but the king merely waved his hand and muttered, "He can't resist it, not now."

"The memory is hazy," Soren said quietly but quickly. "But yes."

Vane was holding her hand now, his grasp tight but not hurting, not yet. "Tell me."

She shut her eyes even as he put pressure on her finger. "It was warm, that's what I remember most. The color of the wheat, the late afternoon sun, and feeling in my chest. I remember thinking I hadn't felt that warm in all my life."

The pressure increased, and tears pricked at her eyes. "I knew it was wrong, what could happen to you if anyone found out, but I couldn't bring myself to stop."

"Why?" His entire body was shaking with restraint when she opened her eyes to look at him.

A tear ran down her cheek, and he shut his eyes tightly. "For the first time in my life, I was choosing something. It was reckless and dangerous, and yet, in that moment in the field, I had never felt safer."

Vane exhaled sharply, eyes flying open. "Together," he breathed. "Always."

"Together," she vowed, the promise resounding with every frantic beat of her heart as he released her and whirled.

Commander Eton stepped in front of Johannas and the princess, two swords in his hands. "I thought you said you had complete control over him!"

Johannas, for once, looked shocked. "I do. That shouldn't be possible."

Cion glanced between Soren and her father before ducking past Vane's raised blade and hissing, "Who is Anabeth?"

"Cion! Back away. Now."

But she ignored her father, dagger in hand just above Soren's wrists. "Tell me, and I'll let you go free."

"She cares for you, Cion. That part isn't an act."

"Who. Is. She?"

Soren curled her fingers as Vane swung at the commander, who sidestepped the blow. "Her father was a mortal man long dead, and her mother is Juno, the goddess of the fates. She was my best friend a long time ago. That's why she was punished too."

Cion's green eyes shone with tears, but she nodded once and made quick work of Soren's restraints. "Go. I'll try to hold my father off if Vane can take care of the commander."

Soren grabbed her hand, brow creased. "Why?"

"You could have hated me all your life," Cion whispered. "But I could see it in your eyes… You are kind, Soren. Anabeth and her father—or whoever they are— taught me that a world withers when ruled by corruption, no matter how powerful. I believe you, and if what you say is coming arrives, you'll have a mortal princess at your command."

"Soren!"

She let go of Cion's hand at the sound of Vane's voice. He was breathing heavily, poised above the commander, his sword pointed at his heart while King Johannas held a dagger to his throat. A bead of crimson dripped down his pale skin.

Death comes in many forms, goddess.

Heles' voice was faint, but the words were clear enough that Soren understood what she had to do. She just needed a moment of focused power; that was all it would take. Reaching inside herself, she ripped open a cell door and destroyed the key.

No more locks or barred doors.

She needed everything she had if this was going to cut through the invisible hands gripping her power like a vice.

Johannas pressed the dagger firmly to Vane's skin, and she screamed, opening her palm. A flash of razor-sharp shadow rushed from her, sliding past the king's throat. He choked on the blood that bubbled up, and Soren fell to her knees. Cion cried out behind her, and Vane shoved his blade into the commander's chest, his eyes ablaze with rage. But when he turned to face the princess with his bloody sword, Soren ordered, "Don't touch her."

Vane met Cion's eyes. In another life, they could have been related. Vane had always claimed to not know who his mother was, but perhaps there was some blood shared between them. And now, Cion, as heir apparent, held control of his life.

"Go," she choked out. "I meant what I said to Soren. You are both free of your duties."

Vane didn't wait a second, lacing his fingers in Soren's and tugging her past the bodies and out of the tent.

"Thessilnn and Heles are waiting," he said breathlessly. "But we need to hurry."

"Right," Soren said. The world was becoming hazy

again. It must be the hunger or dehydration. She could make it…

Vane caught her as she stumbled. "Soren! Gods, stay with me. It's just a little further—"

But laughter cut him off. Soren blinked heavily, her vision focusing just enough to see Ilav standing a few feet away.

"Impressive," he mused in a voice that was not quite right. "You both made it much further than I would have thought. And the game was rather fun to watch, I will admit. Arcadia has grown rather dull over the years without the idiocy of the mortals providing amusement."

The reality of who—*what*—Ilav really was came to her slowly. Too slowly, because he was already moving towards them.

"Stay the fuck away from her," Vane snarled. She could feel his body heating, but she was sure his magic was dimmed too.

There was only one powerful enough to do that.

"Kronos," she whispered as Ilav knelt. His eyes flickered silver as she said it, and he smiled.

"Hello, Sora. I'd say you look well…but it's nothing I can't fix."

Vane held her tightly against him, as if he could shield them both from what was coming. Kronos' gaze fell to his hand, his eyes flicking over the marriage band there, and amusement was quickly replaced by rage.

"Come, Sora, if you wish him to live."

She coughed weakly and rasped, "You're a fucking liar. You always have been. "

"Fine," Kronos said, rising to his full height. "We do this the hard way, then."

Ether sparked the ground around them, and Vane shielded her with his body. But the blow never came, and two wild roars filled the air. Dragonfire, blue and red, torched the ground, setting the camp ablaze in seconds, and she lost sight of Kronos in the sudden chaos.

Dragons were taking to the sky around them, adding to the blaze Thessa and Heles had begun. People screamed in the camp as flames engulfed them. Vane helped haul her onto Thessa's saddle before practically jumping onto Heles.

Prepare yourself.

Soren coughed as smoke filled her lungs. *The other riders—*

The mortal princess gathered them. They fly with us.

Thessa took off running, catching the air and vaulting up into the night sky. Heles let out a cry behind them before forging ahead, leading the way. Kneeling atop her, Vane called out, motioning to the riders who circled the camp.

Stay awake, Thessa ordered.

Soren forced her heavy eyes open. *Why do the other dragons follow us? Why not try to kill us? We killed Johannas.*

We do not bow to a mortal king. We were forged in fire by Vulcan. They only bent the knee to King Johannas' war because his heir is bound to it so closely.

Heir?

Heles roared, letting another stream of red-hot flame loose in the air, Vane pointing north atop her.

Vulcan, like Nyx, only ever gave his ember of life to one child. Why do you think we chose you both that night?

Does he know?

A rider screamed behind them, and Soren twisted in horror to see three dragons at the tail end of the group, snapping their jaws. Their riders were no friends.

"They must have seen the smoke!" Vane bellowed, turning Heles around, his fingertips glowing like hot coals. Soren could feel her magic returning to her now too, Kronos' hold loosening. She didn't know why and didn't trust it.

Vane called out the name of a flight formation Soren vaguely remembered from her first few days in camp, and Heles roared. As Soren watched, she thought she could see the truth of Thessa's words now. Vane was powerful, a born leader. That kind of intuition didn't come from nowhere.

No. We were instructed not to tell you until the right time arose. Heles informs me we are to flee. I am opening the connection back up to them both.

Soren had only half-realized Vane couldn't hear her conversation with Thessa, but until she could tell him properly, and not in the middle of an ambush, she shut her mind to the issue.

Vane whipped his head back and roared, "Go! Get her to safety!"

"No!" Soren bellowed over the wind currents. "Do not listen to him, Thessa."

Ahead, a dragon screeched in pain, their rider screaming as they fell, the dragon's neck partially severed. Cion was letting loose arrows from the back of Valhamnor, and dragonfire lit up the night air.

"Soren!"

She sucked in a breath as Thessa dove, narrowly avoiding the snapping jaws of a large gray dragon.

We are leaving.

"No!"

Kronos drained you, even if his hold on you is gone—for now.

Thessa turned from the battle, heading for the thick of the mountain range, and Soren whipped her head back as they gained altitude. Vane wielded a stream of fire, twisting it with Heles' and obliterating the last enemy dragon and their rider. As they fell, he shouted at the others, who began to follow her and Thessa.

I promise, if I wasn't sure we could make it, I wouldn't have told Thessilnn to go. Vane's voice was breathless but gentle in her mind. *But you could barely mount her, and I couldn't focus on getting us out of there while worrying about you falling off her back again.*

She didn't reply, not trusting herself to not accidentally reveal what Thessa had told her. Heles caught up to them quickly, though, flying next to her. Every few minutes, Soren saw Vane glance over at her in between scanning the horizon. She wanted to argue she was fine, but she didn't have the energy to do much but stay awake.

They landed on a large outcropping of stone just as dawn crested over the horizon. Ahead, the entrance to a cave loomed, but none of the dragons appeared uneasy. In fact, they seemed to relax as they saw it.

Thessa landed next to Heles, and Vane slid off her back, calling, "Let go. I'll catch you."

"I am fine," Soren muttered, though her voice was thin from exhaustion. He caught her as she stumbled to the ground, adding, "I just need food."

Vane's mouth curved. "We'll see to it. Stop trying to walk."

"You are not going to carry me into a dark, unmarked cave," she argued, but he was already sweeping her up.

"It's not unmarked, or at least not unknown. Not to us, and not to the dragons."

Cion approached, and Soren squirmed uselessly in Vane's arms. The princess' lips twitched, just barely. "I suppose it isn't too difficult to believe you two are actually married."

Vane didn't smile. "Does anyone know, besides the riders you gathered?"

She lifted her chin and said quietly, "I told them the commander turned traitor and killed my father. They all report to me now, given I am Queen of Aren."

"And why do they think they're here?"

Cion shifted, crossing her arms. "I told them there is a way to restore magic to the mortal world."

Soren sighed sharply. *Let me down.*

No. "This isn't some magical quest."

"Remember who you're talking to, *Mòr Maslach.* I don't plan on keeping some barbaric hold on you like my father, but I will protect myself and my people against any threats. That includes Kronos. Don't include yourself in that list."

"And Mise? The rebels?" Soren said.

Cion worried her lip. "All three kingdoms are in chaos. Kellmere is dead and so is my father. My plan is to call a meeting with the kings of Meesling and Mise and propose a truce, as long as they agree to aid us in a solution."

"And if they don't." Vane began walking to the cave entrance.

Cion followed and replied crossly, "I haven't gotten that far."

He turned down the first tunnel on the left, shifting Soren to one arm and using his other palm as a torch. Footsteps behind them told her the other riders were joining.

When Vane stopped again a few minutes later, the tunnel opened into a small cavern. He flicked his fingers, and a ring of torches lit up the space, revealing a few sleeping mats, an abandoned clay mug, and a dusty scroll directly in the middle of it all.

After setting Soren down gently on one of the mats, he looked Cion directly in the eye and said, "Figure it out. And deal with your riders, preferably away from here."

"Where do you suggest we—"

"In a second cavern, about a quarter of a mile down that tunnel," he said shortly, pointing to the corner. "There should be a store of supplies there. They're old but should do just fine."

"Right," Cion said flatly. Soren was surprised she didn't argue, instead just grabbing one of the torches from the wall and shouting, "Riders, with me!"

They filed into the tunnel, and Soren closed her eyes, mumbling, "You didn't lie, right? There is another cavern, not a gaping hole where they'll all fall to their deaths?"

Vane chuckled roughly, brushing her hair off her forehead. "I did not lie. I just needed them to not be here."

She opened her eyes. "Vane, there's something—"

"Later, my love," he said. "You need to rest."

She bit back a protest, knowing he was right, and shut her eyes, letting oblivion take her.

CHAPTER 30

When Soren woke up, it smelled like stew, the scent of herbs filling the cavern. Her stomach gurgled, her mouth paper dry. As if sensing her needs right away, Vane handed her a clay mug filled with water and ordered, "Slowly, or you'll make yourself sick."

She listened, and over the lip of the mug, she said, "You need to rest too. And drink and eat. You were mortally injured, not me."

He grimaced. "The king ensured I was fed and watered before he called me to that tent last night. And I just ate. Believe me, the last thing I want right now is to be weakened."

She sat up further, and he handed her a bowl of stew. Swirling the spoon, she furrowed her brow and asked, "Where did you get this?"

"I made it."

She leveled a look at him. "Not what I meant and you know it."

His small smile lit up her entire chest, despite her worry

and annoyance. "The root vegetables grow in the soil of these peaks, and the rabbit, I caught with a snare. The broth is unfortunately just water from a small pool not far from here in the cave systems. But I did have a small store of dried herbs to help remedy the taste."

She took a spoonful of the soup, nearly moaning. He was bluffing—it tasted excellent. But still, a bitter truth cut through the warmth.

"This was it, wasn't it?" she asked softly, looking around. "The place where we would go. Where we hatched Thessa and Heles."

Vane smiled, but his eyes were heavy with sorrow. "It was funny to me, the first time I heard you refer to Thessilnn by that nickname. We tried that kind of thing with her before, and she hated it. Would leave scorch marks on your mother's flower beds if you said it once. But now…I think she missed you so much, she doesn't even care."

"My parents knew about the dragons?"

Vane nodded. "They were both still adolescents then, but dragons aren't exactly an easy thing to hide. You never told them you bonded to Thessilnn, or that Heles bonded to me. They probably wouldn't have believed you even if you did tell them about the dragons bonding with me. Dragons bond with mortals now, and some did then, but Vemon are a notoriously particular breed. There's a reason you didn't see any but Heles and Thessilnn in Johannas' army. Gods and godlings have historically been the only riders they'll bond with."

"But she bonded with you," Soren said softly, setting down her now-empty bowl.

Vane lifted a shoulder. "I always figured it was because of you."

"And if it isn't?"

He lifted a pierced brow. "What do you mean?"

She bit her lip, reaching out to Thessa. *Is now the 'right' time?*

Thessa's reply was sleepy and grumbled. *You are stubborn. I will not waste my time trying to stop you.*

"Soren?"

"When we were in flight, Thessa told me something about you. Don't be angry with them; they were told not to say anything to us. I probably shouldn't even be telling you now, but—"

Vane took her hand, searching her gaze. "I won't be angry."

She let out a breath. "Alright. You once said your father had lots of children. Who told you that?"

Vane blinked, once, then twice, obviously surprised. "My mother. She said she was one of many mortal women he'd… Well, she wasn't the only one."

"She lied."

His lips parted, his head tilting. "I don't understand."

"I'm not sure why I didn't know that wasn't true at the time, being Nyx's daughter, but Vulcan must have somehow hidden the truth. He didn't have other children. No godlings, no demi-gods. Just you."

Vane's throat worked, and she saw him trying to mask his shock, even for her. She tightened her grip on his hand, and his chest expanded in a deep breath. "But that makes me…what, exactly?"

"Thessa called you Vulcan's heir."

A laugh broke out of him. "That's impossible. Heirs of principals need to be named."

"Was I named?" she asked before she could stop herself.

His face softened a fraction. "Yeah, when you were a youngling. You told me the dress you had to wear was scratchy, and that it was the first time you met Kronos."

"Oh." She rubbed at her face. "I hate that I can remember so little."

"It'll return in time," he assured her. "And if it doesn't, I'll remind you every day."

She swallowed the lump in her throat and blinked rapidly at the burning in her eyes. "Maybe Vulcan hasn't named you yet for a reason."

Vane snorted. "Even if there was a chance he would have before, he won't now. I'm an exiled traitor, remember? Kronos put me under a curse tied to a mortal bloodline and closed off Arcadia because of what I did."

"What we did," she reminded him quietly.

His gaze dropped to their hands resting on the dusty stone floor. "If you had never met me, none of this would have happened."

"You're right," she said. "And I would also be married to an abusive tyrant, probably popping out godlings and trying to find a way to keep them safe from him."

Vane's mouth tightened, but the look on his face turned distant, his eyes wandering somewhere behind her. She reached out, touching his face. "Vane?"

He cleared his throat. "I know. As far as Vulcan goes, I wouldn't expect anything from him. I never have, and I've never been disappointed because of that."

She tilted her head. He still wasn't really looking at her. "There's something else, isn't there?"

He was silent for a long moment, and she could practically see his mind working. Heat emanated from him, and she was about to push again when he said, "We had four days after we were wed. Two of them, we spent here, and two of them, we spent apart. But the day before Kronos came for me, Ana showed up in the field where I was working and punched me in the face—well, tried to. Once she'd calmed down and stopped cursing me, she told me she'd had a vision."

He paused, and Soren's stomach turned with unease. "What did she see?"

A short breath escaped him. "Ana punched me because she thought you were with child and we didn't tell her. She thought I was putting you in danger, that we needed to run..." He trailed off. "I knew that wasn't the case, or I thought I was sure it wasn't."

"Vane, what did she see?" Her heart was pounding so loud and fast, she wondered if he could hear it.

He finally looked at her as he said, "The future. You and I, with a youngling." Anguish pierced his terse expression as he added, "I've never been sure I was wrong to deny her anger that day."

Soren's eyes widened as she realized what he meant. But she shook her head slowly, cradling his cheek in her palm. Tears ran down his face, and she swiped them away.

"I wouldn't have kept something like that from you," she whispered.

"So you weren't—"

"No."

His entire body shuddered, curving in on itself as silent sobs wracked him. "All these years," he gasped. "I didn't know. *He made me burn your body.*"

He said the last six words, nearly void of breath as he struggled to take in air. She pulled him close to her, threading her hands in his hair and murmuring, again and again, "I'm sorry, I know."

When a few minutes had passed and he was breathing steadily again, she whispered, "What are we going to do?"

Vane lifted his head, looking around the cavern. "There is something. I thought of it once you'd begun remembering, but selfishly, I didn't even want to consider it."

She looked at him expectantly.

"Arcadia's borders are closed to mortals. Evidently, Ana and I can't cross the veil without consequence. But you could..." He shook his head, as if he didn't even want to consider it.

But she finished for him. "I could just walk right in, couldn't I?"

"Theoretically, yes. But there's no telling what it would be like. A hundred years ago, many gods in Arcadia were already divided on Kronos' ability to lead and hold so much of the realm's power. You could be walking into a war, for all we know."

She raised a brow. "I could never survive that."

He didn't laugh, though. "You would be alone, and you haven't tested your magic to its full extent yet. I can't send you on a suicide mission."

"Thessa could go with me," she said. "She would be a direct line to you and Heles should anything go wrong. She would protect me."

"Soren—"

"I'll go to Nyx. Surely after everything that happened, she doesn't support Kronos."

Vane looked doubtful. "She never did. She just bent the knee to him."

"Then I will *un*bend it for her."

She could do this—she had to. If she could gather enough gods in favor of ending Kronos' rule, maybe it could be enough. Perhaps no mortals needed to die in this. Vane, Ana, Cion, and the others could be safe.

"I'm going to Arcadia tomorrow," she said firmly, ether warming her insides and shadows dancing around the cavern chamber. "I'm going to kill him before he can kill me again."

CHAPTER 31

The field was dead and abandoned now. Twenty years ago, it had been one of the most flourishing high-altitude farms in Aren, thanks to the skilled mage who had owned and run it. He wondered now if his master had taken him on as an apprentice as a favor, as his ailing mother had said, or if he had sensed his power. Fire and plant magic didn't exactly mix, but they were both earth-bound, so perhaps the old man just hadn't been able to tell the difference.

His black boot crunched on the remnants of a weed. He glanced at the bank of the dried mountain creek and curled his gloved hand into a fist. Then, he sat down and, for the first time in two decades, he talked to his wife.

"You would hate me if you saw me now," he said to the howling wind. "I hate me."

He curled his fingers in the dirt. It felt like ash.

"I just don't know what to do, Sora." His voice broke; like a child, he curled his arms around his knees and rocked. "Sometimes, I wish to see your soul again, and sometimes—" He broke off, choking on a sob. "I wonder if this is what I deserve. But you know me; I've always been selfish when it comes to you."

Tears stained the lifeless earth beneath him, and he whispered a plea to the place that was now sacred to him alone.

"Please come back, my love. Please. I'll wait for you, I promise, just... Please."

No one answered him but the wind. Eventually, the tears grew cold on his face, and he forced himself to wipe them away. He stood, staring out across the barren land one last time.

It would be a year before he would return.

Over and over.

Decade by decade.

He started to pretend he could go there and end it all, just to have something to look forward to, but the bastard king would never allow that.

Over three years into the next decade, he was lying awake in his barrack, debating whether he could convince Heles to do it for him. Death by dragonfire wasn't pleasant, but then he could become ashes just as she had.

But everything changed the next morning, when Heles sensed her sister awaken from the slumber she had slipped into for nearly a century. He flew out to the temple grounds just to see for himself, because he wouldn't believe it if he didn't.

His world shifted when he saw Thessilnn approach her, clad in Arenean slave-wear and wearing a shackle. Suddenly, death wasn't an option anymore. Now, he only wanted two things.

Her...and revenge.

278

CHAPTER 32

"You can't. I never should have suggested it."

Soren glared at Vane, ignoring the fear in his eyes and the way his body still trembled slightly.

"I've made my choice. If you want to spend tonight arguing with me about it, that's yours. It won't change anything."

"Stop," he snarled. "I can see what you're already doing."

She scoffed. "And what is that?"

His next breath was harsh, the air rushing between his teeth. "You're already acting like this is our last night together. And gods, Soren, it very well could be if you do this."

"If I don't, who will?" Her voice echoed off the walls of the chamber. "Someone needs to end this."

"Not you."

She got to her feet and began to pace. Vane followed her, standing with his feet wide and his arms crossed.

He knew they were at an impasse. He had to; this was

no longer just about them. Kronos had appeared to them in a mortal's body, and gods knew what had truly happened to the real Ilav. Knowing Kronos, he was probably dead. The king of the gods was overstepping—perhaps he always had, since the moment Sol had declared him king and the power had slowly begun to go to his head.

Eventually, after she had paced herself to exhaustion, she faced Vane.

"Done?" he said.

She rolled her eyes. "Oh, fuck off, Vane."

His lip curled. "Say that again. Please."

Sudden heat flooded her at the wicked gleam in his eye and the low timbre of his words. She tried to push the feeling away, insisting, "Not now."

"*Yes*, now. If you're leaving tomorrow, this is my last chance to remind you what it's like when we fuck."

She narrowed her eyes. "That's all you can think about right now? Fucking me?"

"Oh, no, my love. I'm afraid it doesn't stop there." He pushed off the wall and stalked towards her. "I want to taste you in every way imaginable, and I want you to taste me too. I want to obliterate every thought from that pretty little head of yours with my cock, and then I want you to bring me to the edge so many times, I can only beg for you to let me come. But mostly, I want to show you what it's like when we make love—to remind you how it feels when the only thing that matters in this entire fucked up world is *you and me*."

He had backed her up against the opposite stone wall, his hands on either side of her, caging her in. Her breath came in heaving gasps as the sparking heat of his power surrounded her, warming the ice that was always inside her.

They were two sides of a coin—fire and ice. Both were capable of bringing death, but to each other…

She remembered why she had risked everything for this.

Together, they were perfect—completion.

Her anger and fear did not slip away as she looked at him towering over her. She refused to hide anything from him. But he didn't back away from her hurricane of emotions. He never had, not since the day she had first wept in that field. Instead, she let everything—every bit of rage and anguish and terror—fuel the next three words.

"I want you."

He leaned in, and her back arched off the stone as his teeth grazed the curve of her neck. He dragged his tongue over her skin, swirling it across her pulse point, and she nearly cried out.

She felt his mouth curve as he moved to her ear, nibbling before he whispered, "Be patient. We have all night, and I intend to use every second of it."

A soft whimper escaped her, and he groaned, fisting his hand in her hair and tilting her head back. He searched her gaze, his eyes black with desire. The moment felt distended in space, separate from the others before and those that would come after. Her core pounded with her heartbeat, and her chest felt like it was caving open for him.

This was not merely lust or infatuation. This felt beyond anything she knew to be possible. She had died for him, and she knew without a doubt she would do it again. But now, she wanted to feel everything he had to offer. She wanted to pour herself into him, to be as close as possible in every sense.

Their lips were inches apart, both breathing fast and heavy. There was a game in this heavy emotion too, one they had always played with each other. Who would break first, knowing they both wanted it just as much?

Bend the knee, relinquish all control.

Only for you. Always for you.

His voice filled her mind, touching every part of her like a caress, but even as she trembled, she remained a breath away. Emotion and lust swirled within her in a dance, and the clarity of what this all meant hit her hard enough to make her gasp.

It shouldn't have been a surprise, to know just what she felt. But knowing Sora had felt it a century ago and knowing *she* felt it now were two very different things.

"Please," Vane moaned, mouth just barely brushing hers, begging her to give in.

She was breaking, but he would catch her. Of that, she had no doubt.

"I love you," she said, each word hushed and deliberate in the miniscule space between them.

His eyes widened, his pupils expanding impossibly wider as he muttered, "Fuck it, game over," and captured her mouth with his.

She stood on her tiptoes to reach him, a broad hand on her back to support her, but soon, that wasn't enough. They both needed more. More. *More.* The desperate need was a beat between them, an undercurrent in every touch, each demanding press of his tongue against hers. She fisted her hand in the material of leather armor.

"Take it off," she ordered, half-dizzy.

He nipped at her lower lip, pulling it between his teeth, then asking, "Which part, my love?"

She bit his lip right back, dragging her hands through his hair. "All of it."

"Good," he praised. "I fucking love it when you're demanding."

"Clothes off, sir," she muttered, kissing up his neck.

He groaned, his hands going to the ties on his flight armor. "You know, you said that to me the first day at camp."

She nipped at his jaw. "I know. Did it turn you on?"

"Much more than was appropriate at the time."

He tore the leather material free of the ties, and she pulled it off. His undershirt came next, and she traced careful hands over the scars on his back, kissing his shoulder as she did. She was still fully clothed as she reached for the ties of his breeches.

He gently grabbed her wrist to stop her. "Wait. I want to see you."

"You have. It's my turn," she said, punctuating the words by sliding her hand up the hard outline of his cock.

He let out a rough moan, his hand bracing behind her on the stone wall. "*Fuck*," he hissed as she worked him through his pants.

"Do you still want me to wait? Or do you want me on my knees in front of you?"

He traced her swollen lips with his thumb, his eyes heavy with lust. "Knees. But not for too long, or they'll bruise on the stone."

"We'll see," she whispered, kissing her way down his muscled abdomen before he could argue further.

When she reached the dip just below his waistband, she finally undid the ties and unsheathed his cock from the leather, thick and beading with precum at the tip. She took it in her hand, flicking her gaze up to his as she swirled her tongue over the head, lapping up the salty liquid. He fisted a hand in her hair and ordered, "Tap my leg if it gets to be too much, understand?"

"Mhmm," she hummed, using her hand to pump the base.

He groaned, pushing his hips forward. She had no memory of doing this before, but instinct took over well enough as she took as much of him as she could. He thrust gently the first few times before his control began to fray. That was what she loved most.

When he started to tremble, his groans near-guttural, she pulled back and kissed his hip. Through heavy breaths, he managed to say, "You are cruel, my love."

"I want you inside me."

He shut his eyes briefly and then looked at her and said, "Not yet."

"But you want to, now don't you?"

"Yes," he said, wasting no time. "But you need to be ready."

It took her a moment to understand the meaning of his words. She had never been with a man, not in this life. She vaguely remembered that there had been some pain the first time with him, especially given his size.

"I'm right, aren't I?" he said as she rose, her head barely coming up to his chest. "You haven't touched anyone else."

She took a step closer to him, his cock brushing up against her belly. "No one. I never wanted to. Now, I know why."

His eyes flared, and this time, he dropped to his knees. She gasped softly as his hands slid up the curves of her thighs, making quick work of her pants. She stepped out of them, and before she could think or even take another breath, he parted her from her entrance to her clit with his tongue.

She cried out, bracing a hand on his broad shoulder for some semblance of stability as she lost all sense of the room around her. He curved a hand around her ass and squeezed as he circled her clit with his tongue, teasing her until she was panting and pleading.

He pulled away, a cold rush of air taking his place as he looked up at her, lips curved. "Do you want to come?"

She couldn't think beyond the want. "Please," she gasped.

"Good," he said darkly. "Don't hold back. I want to hear my darling wife scream my name so everyone in these tunnels knows just whose face she's riding."

"You—are...."

But she lost whatever she was going to say, along any hint of embarrassment or incredulity, as he slid his tongue inside her.

Her eyes rolled back and her legs shook with the effort to remain standing. He replaced his tongue with two broad fingers, sliding them in slowly and curling, tapping softly inside her. She was so close.

"Good," he murmured. "You're ready."

She shattered. A million stars rained down, scattering

across the cavern as shadows swept out from her in an impenetrable wave and Vane licked her until she had to push him away.

The torches relit, one by one, clearing the shadows. He pressed one last kiss to her throbbing center then held her gaze as he slid his fingers into his mouth, licking them clean.

"I love that you made a mess all over our wedding band," he murmured, still on his knees before her.

"Vane." His name was half order, half plea. She was already throbbing and wanting again, her breasts heavy underneath the leather of her torn flight jacket. She tore it off and threw it to the ground.

He nodded once, rising up and easily pulling her into his arms. She wrapped her legs around him, and when he kissed her, she tasted herself on his lips.

When he laid her against one of the sleeping mats, his gaze sinking into hers, she whispered, "I take it back. Love isn't the right word."

He nodded, searching her gaze. "There isn't one. Believe me, my darling, I've searched for over a hundred years to find one that encompasses what I feel for you."

She pulled him closer, kissing him deeply. Control slid away, their mouths sliding in a clash of tangling tongues, heavy breath, and nipping bites. He only pulled away when he positioned himself at her entrance.

"This might hurt a bit," he murmured. "Tell me if it's too much."

"I will," she promised, touching his face.

Gone was the game. All that remained now was him.

She gasped as he slid into her slick entrance. There was

pressure, then a sharp bite of pain. He paused, his jaw tight.

"Soren?"

"I'm alright. Keep going," she whispered. "Just don't look away."

He relaxed slightly. "*Never.*"

It took a moment for it to feel good again, and he took her through that part in slow, shallow strokes. But when her back arched and pleasure raced down her spine, he began to pump his hips faster, eyes never leaving hers. She slid her hands up his back, and he increased the pace.

When she began to whimper again, he slid a hand between them, working her swollen clit as he filled her again and again. The climax that hit her was so abrupt, she didn't see it coming until her back was off the mat, her cry echoing around them.

When the violent waves of pleasure finally ebbed, he slowed the pace again, dipping his head to kiss her mouth and then her neck. She didn't even realize she was crying until he licked at the tears running down her face.

"Let go," she whispered, feeling the tense control he was holding as he moved inside her.

He ignored her order, lowering his mouth to her breasts, worshiping them with soft swirls of his tongue that made her already-sensitive body light up with a near-unbearable heat. Then, his hands ran over her, carefully and meticulously, as if he was trying to tattoo every inch of her to memory.

When his breath started to shake, she touched his face. "Let go, my love," she said again. "I'll still be here when you do."

He kissed her desperately, his hips jerking against hers as

his movements grew less controlled and he gasped for each breath against her lips.

"Don't—leave me," he begged, his hands sliding behind her to hold her as close as possible as he destroyed her with each stroke. "Not again."

"Never." She pressed her forehead to his, closing her eyes as his body tensed and he slammed to the hilt one last time. "I'll come back for you."

He shuddered, and each torch in the room flared red-hot as he poured himself into her.

Minutes passed in a haze, and neither of them moved, not until he said against her hair, "You're not going alone tomorrow."

She lifted her head. "But you said you can't enter Arcadia without a summons or pardon?"

"Without consequence, apparently. I never tried. Johannas forbade it."

"Vane, it's too much risk. You have no idea what—"

He was still inside her, and her breath hitched when he tugged her to his chest with one arm, the other hand gently gripping her face.

"It's worth whatever the risk. You don't know… I cannot send you into danger alone, not knowing if you'll return."

She shut her eyes. For all they knew, stepping over the border could kill him. She wouldn't be surprised if that was the price, but she understood his need to follow her. She understood it as much as she *could* understand the pain of his past century.

"Together," she finally whispered. "I did promise that."

He relaxed, if only slightly, nodding and kissing her forehead.

"Vane?"

"Mhmm?"

"Should you…should we not stay like this?" He chuckled softly, and her breath caught, already feeling him harden again inside her. "Already?"

His lips curved up. "I will never stop wanting you. It will never be enough."

Her gaze dropped to his mouth. "I know. It must nearly be dawn, though."

"Probably."

"We should speak to the others."

"Yes."

"*Vane.*"

He grinned. "Alright. Just know this is my preferred way to exist."

"You are such a—" She gasped as he tilted his hips into her.

"Hmm, my love?"

Her head fell against his chest as she tried to focus, muttering, "I need to bathe."

"We can do that. There are a few pools in these caverns, but we have to walk there."

"I can *walk.*"

He finally pulled out, a soft whimper escaping her before she could stop it at the loss.

"We'll see," he quipped, nipping at her ear.

He wasn't entirely wrong. Her legs shook as she stood, her core sore enough that thoughts of continuing were regretfully out the window. Vane's eyes flicked to her thighs, where there was a small smear of blood, his jaw tightening.

"I hate that it has to hurt you. I hated it the first time, and I hate it now."

She smiled softly, kissing his cheek. "It only stung for a moment. I'm fine."

He leaned into her touch then took her hand and wordlessly led her down one of the tunnels that funneled into the cavern, both still naked, a flame flickering in his outstretched palm. When they reached the pool he had promised, there were hanging torches ready to be lit. She let her eyes slide over the walls shimmering with some sort of sparkling geode, the water tinged aqua from the minerals.

"We used to come here too, didn't we?" she said, her voice hushed as memories flashed in her mind.

Slick skin against hers. He laughed as she splashed him. She cut him off with a kiss.

"What kind of stone do you think this is?"

Vane was looking at her now in nearly the same way he had before. But she saw it: the faint undercurrent of pain in his eyes each time he saw her. It would take years for that to leave—if they even had that much time.

She doubted it.

He said nothing, just sliding into the pool and holding out a hand for her. She took it and found the water pleasantly cool, not icy as she'd expected. Reaching for him, she ran water-slick hands over his chest and back before she took his hands in hers and scrubbed away the last remnants of blood. He brushed his lip to her forehead then dipped his head under the surface. As he rose, the water streaming off him in rivulets, she didn't doubt for a second that he was Vulcan's heir.

Vane was untamed, beautiful power, raw in a way even

full-blooded godlings couldn't be, not without the influence of mortal blood.

"Your turn," he said, gaze heavy on her. "It feels nice."

She sucked in a breath and dipped under the surface. It was calm beneath the water, peaceful even. She stayed there for a few seconds, savoring the feeling, before standing again and wiping the droplets from her eyes.

"We should go," she said, a little breathless. "Cion and the others are waiting, I'm sure. We'll tell them to go back to the capitol. If things go wrong in Arcadia, they'll be ready."

Vane nodded once, jaw tense. It was really setting in, what they were about to do.

When they returned to the cavern, they dressed quickly, and Soren braided back her hair. Vane led her down the tunnel to the cavern where he'd sent Cion and the riders. They were all awake when they entered; he must have lit the torches for them from all the way down the tunnel.

"I have a plan," Cion said as soon as they entered.

Vane threaded his fingers with Soren's. "Drop it. We have a better one."

Cion narrowed her eyes, but to her credit, she only said, "Alright."

"We're going to Arcadia," Soren told her. "We told you: the border only keeps mortals from entering, not gods."

Cion looked doubtful. "And what exactly are you going to do when you arrive there?"

"Not sure," Vane said casually. "But there's a high chance of unrest, based on how Kronos has handled the last century. We'll try to garner support from the gods who are already against him."

Cion stared at them both then laughed harshly. "*That* is

your 'better' plan? You're going to walk into Arcadia, the land of the gods, and just hope there's a chance they don't kill you?"

Soren bristled. When it was put like that, it did sound a little foolish, but they were out of options.

"Nyx and her consort will be on our side at the least," Vane said, and Soren's throat tightened. "But what we need to do isn't your concern, not unless we fail."

Cion's brows rose. "I'm assuming you want us to just fly back to my palace and wait for either good news or our deaths?"

Soren's lips twitched. In another life, Cion and Vane truly could have been bickering siblings.

"You assume correctly," Vane said flatly.

"And if I refuse? Pull your leash?"

"Then I would go alone anyways," Soren said. "Not preferable, given the promise I made, but to save the mortal realm from Kronos, I will."

"Promise…" Cion muttered, looking between her and Vane, her sharp features softening a fraction. "Fine—but only because I need to find Ana. She has a lot of explaining to do."

"That's it?" one of the riders said from behind Cion. "We came here only to return to war."

"If we succeed," Vane said, "there will be no more war, not for long. And if we don't, you all need to prepare yourselves. There's no telling what Kronos will do should we fail to end his reign."

Fear and resolve alike flickered across the riders' faces, but none of them protested further.

Cion took a short breath. "Soren."

"Yes, princess?"

Cion's smile was tight, laced with bitterness. "You were bound to me by your life but…you were always the closest thing I had to a true sister."

She knelt, and Soren froze as she reached out and unlatched the thin iron anklet, letting it fall to the floor.

"There was no lock?" Soren whispered.

Cion shook her head, her expression sad. "My father always said none of you would ever try. Fear was enough to keep you chained."

Vane looked livid, and the air rippled with heat, but Soren merely looked at the princess who was on her knees before her. "In another life, perhaps we could have been sisters. But in this one, you were simply my captor."

Cion's eyes shone as she stood. "You should go. Take your dragons and end this. If not, we'll be ready to die."

The mortal princess is not a complete idiot, it seems.

Soren's lips twitched. *Are you ready to go home, Thessa?*

My home is where you are, silly godling. But fine. Let us fly to our deaths.

Vane glanced at Soren and nodded. "It's time."

CHAPTER 33

CION

VANE AND SOREN became specks on the horizon, finally disappearing beyond the peaks. Still, Cion stood on the outcropping of rock, watching the empty air. Behind her, the others lingered, waiting for her to make the next call.

Queen.

She swallowed hard, her throat dry and thick with emotion she could not quite place. Her father had not loved her as a child, always as a tool. It was how he had seen most people. If he didn't have a use for him, they had no place at all in his eyes. Now that he was gone, she didn't feel sadness or even anger.

She simply felt nothing.

"Princess?"

She turned, finding a girl had stepped forward. She looked even younger than Cion herself, but she wore armor rippling with scales, a single medal on her breast denoting some honor. If Cion looked closely, she could likely tell what the girl had done to receive it, but they didn't have time for it, nor did the achievement matter anymore.

"You may refer to me as 'my queen' or 'Your Majesty,'" Cion said, lifting her chin.

The girl bit her lip. "Apologies, my queen, but I must ask. Will the generals listen to us? We've committed treason and run with those who I presume were responsible for the late king's death. We just want to know if we aid a rebellion or the crown?"

Cion's mouth curved into a slow, cold smile. "Does the answer matter to you? Will it change what occurs?"

A boy stepped forward too—Jona, one of the riders who had been training Cion and Ilav. "We follow you, my queen, but there are few of us… If you do not control Aren's army, we want to know."

"You want to know if I am leading you to your deaths."

Heads nodded, though no one moved to run or strike her as she admitted, "I cannot tell you, not with certainty. I will do everything in my power to convince the generals to side with me against the threat that may be coming for us if Vane and Soren do not succeed. Is that a good enough answer for you?"

The girl glanced at Jona, and he nodded. "It is enough. You are a rider now, my queen. You'll learn we tend to stick to protecting our own."

As if in response, Valhamnor roared, crawling up the side of the mountain.

We should return to your camp, princess.

Cion's lips parted. *You're finally speaking to me?*

You made the right choice, trusting the godling and her demi-god consort. And besides, as 'queen', you're going to need me.

Cion shut her eyes briefly as the dragon's shadow fell over her. When she opened them, all ten of the riders who had followed her to what could be their deaths were kneeling on the stony ground, head bowed.

Something was coming for this world. Whether it was destruction from the hand of a god king or a great change brought on by the return of magic, she would have the heavy duty of keeping Aren from falling in the wake of it.

"Rise and call on your dragons, riders," she said quietly. "It's time to face what lies ahead."

CHAPTER 34

AIR WHISTLED past Soren's ears as Thessa soared into the cloud line. Ahead, where a dip in the mountains lay, there was a shimmer and a pull. Energy surrounded the veil between their realms, the place where Soren had been born of two gods and called home in her first lifetime.

Arcadia.

Vane and Heles soared above her, leaving a shadow in their wake as they pushed ahead. Soren sighed sharply. "Vane!"

He glanced back. *What is it, my love?*

Let me go first. Just in case.

The connection went quiet, and she shouted his name down it as he and Heles sped towards the barrier at breakneck speed. Thessa didn't even try to catch them as they hurtled into the space where the veil lay.

"*Vane!*" Soren screamed shrilly, but it was too late. He was already disappearing behind the shimmer, hazy clouds hiding what lay beyond.

Thessa.

The dragon caught a north wind, letting it carry them swiftly towards the barrier. *They're alive, but Heles tells me we must hurry.*

Why can't I hear them?

The veil was rapidly approaching, but Soren hardly cared, fear for Vane and Heles clouding all other senses or worries.

We're almost there. Brace yourself.

Soren ducked her head against Thessa's back as they passed through the veil. For a few seconds, the air felt sticky, vibrating heavily with strong currents of power. They were suspended, somewhere between here and there, until air that smelled like honeytwine trees hit her square in the face. She blinked rapidly against the wind as Thessa hurtled towards the ground and then banked.

Relief swept through her when she saw Vane kneeling atop Heles just ahead. They were on the top of a hillside covered in grass and wildflowers that looked down over a sweeping valley. The air was warmer than it had been moments before, the sun shining through the parting clouds to reveal a blue sky.

For a few breaths, everything felt calm.

But then, Heles roared, the sound echoing off the peaks around them. Fear was cold as it consumed her, but she tamped down the panic, instead sharpening terror into a blade. She still couldn't see beyond Heles, but something made her feel threatened. Someone was there, waiting for them.

She swung her legs over the saddle, intending to slide to

the ground. Thessa rumbled, the low growl vibrating up Soren's body. She ignored the dragon and dismounted, her feet hitting the ground with a thud.

"Soren," Vane warned, his eyes just beyond Heles. "Wait."

She ignored him, ducking under Heles' wing. But when she saw what lay before them, just beyond sight of the top of the hill, she froze.

Four of the eight principal gods stood before her, three Vemon dragons just behind them. Juno was in the front, atop a familiar dark-coated horse—*Sgàilsuil*, the creature that had taken Soren to the temple. Now, she knew for sure the beast was no mere animal but a spirit of fate.

Juno's azure robes flowed in the wind as she dismounted, and Soren was reminded how much Ana looked like her, though Juno was taller than her daughter. Ether swirled in the goddess' eyes as she dismounted and said smoothly, "Hello, Sora. It's been a long time."

Soren didn't move, didn't breathe, especially as Juno stepped aside and a wave of familiar shadows rushed forward.

The goddess of Night was crying silver as she looked at Soren. Just behind her, Thanatos stared like Soren was a phantom he had sent to its grave. She supposed that was not entirely untrue in some sense.

"Are you going to hand me over to him now?" Soren said calmly to Nyx, despite the terror making her feel ice-cold.

The mark on Thanatos' forehead, marking him as Nyx's, rippled with ether. Soren had seen it happen only once before as Sora, when she had been very small. The line between her parents was pulling taut, their emotions tangling, and the mark knew it. But when he took a step forward, Nyx put a hand on his broad arm.

When Nyx stepped forward towards her, Vane appeared so quietly and swiftly, Soren did not sense him. He angled himself in front of her, and though he did not lift his sword, Soren could feel his magic heating the air.

"No closer until you state your intentions," he said, his voice sharp.

From behind Thanatos, Soren saw someone shift. Vulcan.

Soren remembered the god of fire had always been elusive to a degree, at least in Sora's lifetime. But now, she saw him just a few paces from her. He was an inch or two taller than Vane, but beyond that, they were shockingly similar in appearance. She saw Vane's gaze flick to where he stood for just a moment before he focused on Nyx again.

"Vane Evva," Nyx stated. "The demi-god who we might call responsible for my daughter's death."

Vane didn't move, but Soren felt him stiffen. She sighed sharply. "My husband is no more responsible than I am, much less responsible than you. What do you want?"

Juno exchanged a look with Vulcan, though Soren could not read it. Thanatos nodded at Nyx and murmured, "They're ready."

"Contrary to what you might believe," Nyx said, "we are not here to deliver you to Kronos."

Vane's hands were still nearly aflame, and he hadn't moved. "Don't tell me you want us to play assassins for you?"

Vulcan laughed, a rough sound, and flame finally broke through, crackling between Vane's fingers.

"I told you he wasn't an idiot," Vulcan said, glancing at Thanatos.

"How the fuck would you know?" Vane snapped, eyes on his father.

Vulcan's eyes swirled with silver. "Don't think I wasn't watching you all these years. I must say, I have been impressed."

Nyx cleared her throat, and Vulcan held out a hand, as if to indicate, *Yes, yes, continue.*

Soren's mother appeared to be the leader amongst this group of…rebels? If they did not stand with the king of the gods, that was what they were.

The council of principals was divided.

This is what we hoped for, she reminded Vane silently.

He brushed heated fingers against hers. *Not if they want to use you as a weapon.*

That was our plan too.

Not necessarily.

Nyx was watching them closely now, her eyes moving to Vane's left hand, to the band there. She tilted her head. "You can speak to my daughter without words."

Vane hesitated but then nodded. Nyx took a step closer to him, now barely a foot away. "How?"

Vulcan chuckled. "Nyx, dear, look up. The answer is quite literally staring you in the face."

Nyx raised her gaze to where Thessa and Heles loomed above them all, watching closely with narrowed, blinking eyes. They were larger than the other three Vemon dragons gathered behind Vulcan, perhaps the biggest this realm had ever seen. But their allegiances were not to Vulcan, who had forged their kind from fire and the embers of life and light from Sol.

Thessa let out a roar. *My loyalty is to you both, from the moment I saw you.*

For we knew there had never been a greater power than the one forged between you, Heles rasped, shaking her head in an act of aggression towards the gods before them.

Nyx's eyes widened, and even Vulcan looked surprised. "*Diombach rìogna*," he murmured, and Vane looked at him sharply.

"Why would you say that?" Vane asked his father.

Soren's brow furrowed. *What did he say?*

Diombach rìogna… It means 'doomed reign.'

"You sense it, though, don't you?" Vulcan asked, his voice low. "You and Sora have always been destined for something greater. I suppose now, we know why."

Juno looked sadly at Nyx and said in a hurried, hushed tone, "I tried to tell you—"

"Enough!" Soren shouted, splaying her hands. A wave of dark ichor swept out from her palms, rushing past the gods' feet. Juno jumped, but Thanatos looked vaguely pleased. "Stop bickering amongst yourselves like children. We came here for a reason, and with or without your approval, we're going to carry it out."

"You want to end Kronos," Juno said softly.

The air grew tense. There was still the question of the gods' loyalties to Kronos. Soren was nearly sure they were all here because they were against him, or at least displeased with his reign. But for her and Vane to admit they wanted to kill him could still be dangerous until they knew for sure.

Juno waited, though, pushing Soren to say it first. Vane set a hand on Soren's arm, a gentle warning to wait.

She didn't listen. They couldn't afford to be cautious anymore.

"We want to destroy him," Soren whispered. "*I want to rip his body and soul apart into so many pieces, there is nothing left to come back. I want you to tell me how.*"

"Death," Thanatos said, his lips lifting. "I see you have finally found the merits of its uses."

A flash of a memory momentarily blinded Soren—her, arguing with her father.

"Death is too final a power!"

Thanatos laughed, the sound as cold as a grave. "Do you have any idea what you could be if you stopped being so afraid? You cannot change what I gifted you with."

"I don't want it."

"You will."

Soren blinked rapidly and whispered to herself, "That day in Mise, with the children. I had never killed anyone before then, had I?"

Nyx answered, her voice soft as midnight. "You always embraced my gifts as a youngling. You were my evening star, Sora, but I always knew that, truly, you had your father's dark heart."

"Fear is powerful," Thanatos added. "But Death always comes for us."

"As it will come for Kronos," Juno said, touching her forehead. "We know it is possible to damn him with your mother's mark, to end him with your father's power. Doing so would make him yours alone. You would hold his fate in your hands."

Soren bit her cheek, shaking her head. "I've never seen the mark, never used it on my own."

"Yes, you have," Thanatos said, a smile playing at his lips, as if he was enjoying this. "Do you really think we cared enough to dispose of that idiot prince? It was a smart move, though, I do admit. The princess is much more suited as heir."

It took a moment for Soren's mind to catch up. She grasped for Vane's hand as she realized the truth, and he squeezed tightly, steadying her.

"Nell," she whispered, eyes wide. "That was me?"

The gods all looked at her steadily, Juno nodding.

"There is one final problem," the goddess of fate said, lips pressing together. "Kronos has always known you had the power to displace him."

A pit dropped in Soren's belly. He had known… Of course he had. It was why he had beaten her into submission so many times.

"Fear was enough to keep you chained," Cion had said to her mere hours ago.

She had always held the power to fight back against Kronos, but he had taught her, again and again, that in the wake of his power, she had none.

"What is the price?" Vane asked, an edge to his tone.

Nyx looked around. "We should discuss this somewhere else."

Neither he nor Soren moved, though, waiting for this final piece of the puzzle. None of the gods spoke at first, not until Vulcan sighed and said, "Oh, just tell them. If you didn't want them to know, you never should have mentioned it in the first place. And my son will find a way to kill us all if he finds out after the fact."

Soren knew the moment Vulcan finished speaking, and from the way Thessa let out another shrill cry, she knew too.

Thanatos looked past Nyx, straight into his daughter's eyes. "Death always finds a way."

Vane retreated a step, pulling Soren with him, but she held firm, holding him next to her as she said the harsh truth aloud.

"Kronos tied his soul to mine, didn't he? I can die by his hand and come back a thousand times, a thousand lifetimes, a mere nuisance to him. But the second I destroy his soul, mine will be gone too."

Vane was shaking his head. He stepped in front of her, blocking out the gods and cupping her cheeks with trembling hands. "Soren, please. We can still walk away."

A single tear ran down her cheek. "I'm sorry."

His forehead bowed to hers, his voice hushed as he spoke quickly. "You promised me. *Together.* I will not walk away from you, not ever. But please, *please* don't leave me behind again, my love. I will walk into the dark of oblivion with you without fear, but I cannot remain without you."

She kissed him softly and whispered against his lips, "*Together.*"

All of us, Thessa agreed.

Heles' voice was final. *Into the dark.*

"Are you two done?" Vulcan called out dryly behind them. "We should go, lest we draw attention before it is time—"

Vane was out of her arms and at Vulcan's throat with a wicked, gleaming dagger before she could even blink.

"We are not your fucking sacrificial pets," he snarled at his father.

Vulcan was relaxed, his hands still casually in his pockets, even as blood dripped from his throat. "None of us would prefer it this way."

Vane pulled the dagger back swiftly, shoving it into his hip holster. "Well, I would *prefer* it if you shut your mouth, but you seem incapable."

Juno looked mildly amused, and Thanatos rolled his eyes at the display, but Nyx stepped forward to Soren finally, holding out her hands, marked palms up. Soren looked down at the mark she would be placing on Kronos' brow, at the mark that would end her too, and placed her hands atop it. For a moment, mother and daughter remained like that, not holding or even looking at each other; just touching, just barely.

It was all Soren would give her.

She stepped back, and Nyx lowered her hands. "We need to go. There is a place we can keep you both safe until midnight."

"Why midnight?" Soren asked, her throat thick with fear.

Juno replied, looping her arm with Soren's. "It is when Kronos is at his weakest and you at your strongest. Why do you think he killed you last time at sunrise?"

Soren opened her mouth, but the reply died in her throat as a shimmering portal opened in front of her and Juno tugged her through it. Vane shouted her name, but they had already disappeared by the time he reached for her.

When they reappeared, they were in a vaguely familiar sitting room. This was her mother's house, it had to be. She had a faded memory of shattering a vase here, long ago. She had fallen asleep more times than she could count on the stiff couch near the window, which was currently shielded by a dark drape.

Nyx came through the portal next, Thanatos always at her side. Vulcan and Vane pushed through last, and as soon as they hit the floor, the portal closed, and Vane swiftly punched Vulcan square in the face.

Soren froze, waiting for the fire god's anger to finally emerge, but he only laughed wetly and said, "Friends, would you spare me a moment with my son? *Alone.*"

Vane's hands were ablaze, strands of faint ether in his eyes as he looked down at his father, covered in blood and sprawled on the gleaming, dark wood floor.

"Fine," he snarled. "Let's *talk.*" Soren met his eyes, and he gave a short nod, warning the other gods, "Touch her and—"

"You'll set the house ablaze?" Juno mused. "Dismember us? We know, and we do not plan on harming her where she was born."

"I'll be fine," Soren assured him. "Find me after."

He still had flames in hand, but he replied, "I will. I love you."

Her throat tightened; she knew just why he was making sure to tell her. Each time now had the potential to be the last.

"I love you," she said softly before turning and following Juno and her parents into the other room.

Nyx led them past the second, more casual sitting room and down a long hallway. Streams of weak sunlight filtered in from the windows as they passed.

"He's very intense," Juno commented, brow raised.

Soren didn't laugh. "He watched me die and then lived a hundred years chained under a curse Kronos created while all of you did nothing. He's the only one who ever fought for me."

Juno was quiet for a while, but as they reached what appeared to be an airy kitchen, she spoke, her voice a shade softer. "I understand, then—why you fell in love with him."

Soren didn't reply, especially not as she saw a familiar figure sitting cross-legged in one of the wide rocking chairs in the corner.

"Ana?"

Anabeth muttered, "Thank all the idiot gods," and rose, racing for Soren and pulling her into a tight embrace.

Soren slowly wrapped her arms around her, but as Anabeth pulled away, she asked, "How are you here?"

Anabeth smiled tightly. "My mother came for me finally, my brother too. It's amazing what kind of tricks the gods can pull when they need something from you."

"Cion wanted to talk to you."

Soren wasn't sure why those were the first words out of her mouth, but as she said them, Anabeth lowered her gaze and said quietly, "I knew she would. I will offer my own explanation to her once this is over. She didn't deserve to be lied to, but I didn't... There were some truths I spoke to her."

"You do love her, don't you?"

Anabeth lifted a shoulder, her smile tight. "She is not blameless in the horrors her father inflicted upon so many, but neither are we."

"You don't need to apologize. We can't always choose who we love," Soren said. "Cion will make a good queen. You should be at her side if she still wants you to be."

Anabeth blinked rapidly. "I hope she does. But first…" She took a deep breath. "First, we need to kill a god."

Soren didn't let her fear show, didn't even let it surface enough to quicken her heartbeat. "Indeed."

Thanatos was in the kitchen, making what smelled like cocoa, and Juno and Nyx had settled at the worn breakfast table. For the kitchen of the night goddess, the room felt oddly open and airy, though sheer curtains were closed over the windows, obscuring the world outside.

As Juno spoke in low tones to her mother, Thanatos asked, "Do you still like cream on top of your cocoa?" Soren realized the whole thing felt oddly domestic.

"Was it…always like this?" she asked Anabeth quietly.

The demi-god smiled, just barely. "It's strange, isn't it? They created this entire realm, and then they just play house while they plot the murder of their king."

"Duality, dear," Thanatos said, setting two clay mugs of cocoa in front of them on the counter. "Everyone is capable of such a thing, even gods."

Soren eyed the cocoa warily but took a sip. It was rich, with a hint of warm, familiar spices. It tasted oddly like…

Home.

"My… The woman who raised me in Mise used to make a similar drink," she said to Thanatos.

He nodded slowly. "She was the granddaughter of a mortal woman who was in this house many times."

"Nyx's spy. I know."

Thanatos shrugged. "A friend too. She doted on you as a youngling."

"How did you manage it? Making sure I was born to her bloodline?"

His silver eyes wandered over to Nyx. "You forget, your mother and her twin created this world. We merely followed the path they forged, and that includes Kronos."

Soren was about to reply when Vulcan joined them, grim-faced and rubbing his crooked nose.

As soon as Nyx saw him, she stood. "What?"

Vulcan looked around the room, his gaze landing on Soren. "There's been a complication."

Her stomach dropped, and panic whooshed through her ears. "Where is he?"

"Gone," Vulcan said, snapping his nose back into place with a wince.

Juno's eyes flashed, and a tremor went through the room. "What did you tell him?" she demanded.

"He's my son, Jun. He deserved to know there might be a way—"

"A way that just might damn us all!" she bellowed, a wave of power throwing Vulcan back against the wall.

Soren pushed off the counter and slowly walked over to Vulcan, who was straightening and dusting off his dark tunic.

"What did you tell him?" she asked in a low voice.

He briefly looked behind her to where she knew Thanatos stood then met her eyes. "Juno saw something. I believe the demi-god girl, your friend, did too—a future, one in which you and my son live."

"Fate is fickle," Juno hissed. "You know that, you *eejja*."

"She means 'idiot,'" Vulcan supplied. "Which I might be, yes. But perhaps, if Kronos is weakened enough, the tether he created to your soul could be snapped. It might require some convincing, but Vane has grown stronger over these years—"

Soren looked back to see Nyx rising from her seat. "One cannot bargain with Kronos! And besides, even your heir is no match for him."

"Yes, you would know all about his bargains," Anabeth muttered, looking down at the cooling mug of cocoa she held between her pale hands.

Nyx shut her eyes. When she opened them, they were swimming with bright ether. "Do you think I *want* to have my only child torn from me forever? But this is the only way. We all know that."

"Where is he?" Soren repeated softly, turning her head back to Vulcan.

Vulcan hesitated. "I meant what I said," he told her. "I was always watching over him, waiting for the day he would be ready."

"You knew about us. You could have told anyone. I'm sure Kronos would have rewarded you greatly for it."

He shook his head. "But I didn't want power. Like you, I was only after one thing."

"I don't understand—"

"Love." He let out a soft, incredulous laugh. "Believe me, my dear, you are not the first god to fall for someone of mortal blood. My Thora was as strong as she was breakable, though. She ran with our child as soon as she realized what I really was, thinking she could protect him from the horrors and wonders of Arcadia. But sickness took her, and I was powerless to stop it. I wasn't going to waste her sacrifice by pulling our son into a conflict he was not ready for."

"But I did," she whispered.

Vulcan nodded, though he didn't look angry. "Fate will twist our hands, even when we do not want it to." He paused. "He went to the palace astride Heles to try and do the impossible—defeat the king. Thessilnn remains, waiting for you."

"Thank you," she whispered before bolting from the room.

They called after her, but only Anabeth followed, breathless by the time they emerged into the fading evening light. Thessa waited near a grove of trees, her tail whipping around her.

Took you long enough, godling. They are nearly there.

Soren glared at her. *Why didn't you call me so I could stop him?*

You had to learn why first. There may be a way yet through all this foolishness.

We are all foolish in love.

As Anabeth approached, she whirled to face her. "You can't do anything to stop me."

"I know that," Anabeth said, crossing her arms. "But I can't let you go alone."

"Ana—"

"Shut up. We're wasting time standing here arguing, and you know it."

Soren let out a slow breath. "Fine. But as soon as we land, you need to hide."

Anabeth muttered something in the language Soren realized now to be the old tongue of Arcadia—the original dialect of the gods. She ignored her and mounted Thessa quickly, throwing down the ladder for Anabeth, who climbed up shakily.

The second they were both secure on the saddle, Thessa took to the air, leaving the house and the gods in it behind.

CHAPTER 35

Just as the gleaming gold spires of Kronos' palace peeked through the clouds, Soren doubled over on Thessa's back.

"What's wrong?" Anabeth cried out over the roaring wind.

Soren smiled through the agony. "I think he managed to injure Kronos."

Thessa circled the gleaming structure. If she wasn't in so much pain, Soren would have rolled her eyes at the unnecessary exuberance. At least six towers spiraled into the sky, nearly reaching the clouds. The entire estate that the palace sat on was at least twice the size of the one in Aren. Gates surrounded it, lined at the top with spikes, patrolled by an innumerable number of demi-god guards.

Kronos had created a near-impenetrable fortress for himself—too bad she had been here enough to know the best way in. The pain had subsided; they needed to hurry.

"Flat against her back!" Soren shouted.

Anabeth obeyed and rasped in her ear, "How exactly are we getting in?"

"The quickest way: the ceiling of the throne room is made of glass."

Anabeth screamed as they dove, her voice lost as the glass neared. Just before they broke through, Thessa let out a roar, and a stream of white fire billowed from her open mouth. By the time they shattered the ceiling, most of it was already melted by dragonfire.

They landed, the force of it sending glass and debris flying. Thessa roared again, the sound echoing as Heles circled.

Take Anabeth to safety, Soren ordered Thessa, already sliding off her back.

Godling—

Now, before she tries to follow. Please, Thessa.

Thessa took off with one final, ear-splitting screech. Soren knew the sound was a mix of rage and sorrow. Her dragon knew what fate she could be leaving Soren too.

Soren coughed, the air thick with smoke and debris. But as it thinned, and she saw ahead to the raised dais where the throne sat, her spine went rigid.

Kronos held Vane in what almost looked like a lover's embrace, his broad, golden arms wrapped around Vane's waist. He was saying something in Vane's ear with a smile, and in his hand…

Kronos had embedded Vane's own dagger deep in his chest.

There was a spot of blood on Kronos' torso, but she knew, deep down, the wound was already healed. Kronos finally looked at her, his expression crazed as he grinned, showing every one of his gleaming white teeth. A strand of brick-red hair fell into his eyes, swirling with both silver ether and gold—the manifestation of life itself.

"You always knew how to make an entrance, Sora." His voice boomed through the throne room. "Vane, on the other hand, tried to sneak in. Foolish. No one enters my palace unseen or unnoticed. I do admit, his skill with a blade has much improved since I last saw him—ah, was it really a century ago now?"

"One hundred and four years." Vane's voice was strained, and Soren curled her hands into fists. As much as she wanted to act now, she must wait. Kronos was inches away from killing him, and he knew it.

"He kept count. How sweet," Kronos sneered. "It really is all coming back to me now. The way you both screamed. The sight of your blood on my gleaming marble floors. The smell of your burning flesh—"

Vane jerked, a low snarl escaping him. Kronos laughed and dragged a finger down his cheek. "Careful, there. One slip, and I might just kill you. Then, once she and I are gone forever, you'll be forced to live…again."

Soren felt the breath whoosh out of her. He knew their plan, which had to mean someone betrayed them.

"Don't think so hard on it, Sora," Kronos mused as the door opened behind her. "A child could have thought of my plan. It's a shame dear Nyx doesn't vet her servants more closely."

She turned to see a man with dark skin and a head of golden curls stride into the room, dragging along a young girl. He let her go, pleading on her knees and kissing his boot-clad feet. His silver gaze flicked down as if she were a mere nuisance.

"Hello, my darling, trouble-making niece," Sol sneered with a cold smile, plucking a speck of dust from his gold-threaded black tunic.

Behind him, two more principal gods filed in. Bella, the goddess of war, wearing thick leather armor, flashed a sneer Soren's way. With her high cheekbones, cropped black hair and sharpened nails, she looked like a blade personified. Next to her stood Janis, the god of duality and Juno's brother. He looked downright bored, tipping his head back and sighing at the broken ceiling.

"Trouble is right," he muttered. "This will take days to fix."

Kronos chuckled, shifting so Vane grunted in pain.

Bella snorted softly. "*That* is Vulcan's heir? Pitiful."

Soren kept her face blank, a mask for the rising panic inside her as Kronos drawled, "So, here we are again. Your plan was foolish, though I do commend you for getting this far. Now, the game is done, and you and I have a rather lengthy ceremony to attend. Though…you cannot wed me with a living husband. So," he glanced down to the blade in his hand, "I better remedy that."

Vane met her eyes across the room. *I love you. I'm so sorry. I had to try.*

Kronos' hand jerked, and Soren screamed Vane's name as the room plunged into an impenetrable darkness. The remaining ceiling and the stained glass windows lining the hall shattered, and a howling whirl of shadows swept up the pieces.

By the time she let the darkness clear, Soren was already running.

At the bottom of the dais, Vane took slow, uneven

breaths, holding the dagger in his chest as he bled out. Kronos was crumpled across the throne, his head hanging off the side and his unconscious body limp—for now. She didn't even look back to see where the other gods were, not as Vane began to choke on his own blood.

She reached him and fell so hard and fast to her knees, they cracked against the marble.

"Sora," he choked out. *Finish Kronos. Leave me.*

"We said together, you *eejja*," she snapped. "Just breathe and let me focus."

His eyes fluttered shut, his breaths growing more uneven as she grasped at every hand Death wrapped around him. But Vane was crowded by the pull underneath the surface, where Death lingered.

"Father," she rasped. "A little help, please?"

She swore she felt Death smile as he eased off, just barely, just enough for her to yank Vane free and shove him into the corner of one of those locked cells deep inside of her. Vane gasped as she pulled the dagger from his heart, pressing her hand to the wound to staunch the bleeding as it closed.

When he was breathing evenly again and fresh blood stopped coating his lips, she grasped for his hand. He took her offered palm, his grip strong.

"Incredible," Janis murmured behind her, but she ignored him as Kronos stirred in the throne.

"Vane," she whispered, turning her palm upward as Kronos pushed himself up, groaning and muttering. "I need you to trust me."

Behind them, Bella muttered, "Oh, *fuck*."

Sol reached for Sora, and she sent a wave of shadow at

the gods, throwing them back as Kronos slowly lifted a hand to his forehead. His fingers were stained as he lowered them, coated in ichor the shade of darkest night.

Vane's breath caught at the sight of the waning moon slicing directly in half by a curved Misean war sword. Not Nyx's mark, but *her's*.

"Together?" she said softly, touching his face with one hand and pulling a dagger from her belt with the other.

Kronos rose to his full height, blasting apart the shadow she tried to cage in him without a thought as he roared, "You are *mine*."

Vane met her eyes as he grabbed the bloody dagger Kronos had shoved in his chest. "You are my beginning and my end, my love. You know I will follow you into whatever oblivion brings."

Kronos lunged as she kissed him, whispering against his lips, "Oblivion can wait. I'll find your soul when we wake again."

Thessilnn. Heles. Kill him.

Vane's eyes widened at the realization as the two largest Vemon dragons to ever exist crashed into the throne room. Anabeth's dagger, thrown from atop Thessa's back, caught Kronos in the shoulder before he could reach Soren and Vane. He staggered back, buying them just enough time to whisper goodbye.

"I love you," she whispered, kissing Vane hard while thrusting her dagger into his hand.

He angled it at her chest, the cold tip pressing against her sternum. "Always. My heart is yours to take, as is my soul."

Thessa reared back her head, flames gathering in her throat. *We will wait.*

We will hold on to your souls with honor, Heles agreed with a roar.

Soren took the dagger covered in Vane's blood and pressed it to his chest. "I am not afraid."

Their lips met at the moment each blade pierced skin and bone. She gasped but kept her eyes open wide, looking into Vane's steady gaze as the dagger tore through her heart. As the light began to leave his eyes and Death's arms welcomed her home once more, her mark appeared on Vane's forehead.

"*Sora,*" he gasped one final time before his breath shuddered and held.

Death enveloped her as dragonfire surrounded them.

Kronos screamed as he died.

But Sora only smiled.

32 YEARS AFTER THE REEMERGENCE OF MAGIC

Cion Livii was a woman of the sword. She had been since she was four years old and Sir Gellings had placed a wooden replica in her hands. But in the face of magic, the blade was much less useful. It had made navigating such a world rather difficult, ruling it even harder. But with a demi-god at her side and a magic-wielder for a younger sister, she had managed rather well. After all, she had peacefully brought a bloody war longer than her lifetime to an end and been crowned queen of the realm's largest kingdom, all at the green age of twenty-two. It had all made her a rather calm person. If she could handle a war and the return of the gods, with all the chaos they brought, she could handle most anything.

But today, as Valhamnor circled over a thick forest at the northern end of Mise, she found herself wondering if this was one task she might not be able to conquer.

Two Vemon dragons had been spotted nearby three days ago. When Ana read the scroll, she had turned pale as a sheet and begged Cion not to make her go. She insisted it was Cion alone. Ana dealt with the nightmares of the past by moving forward and never looking back. She had never returned to Arcadia again once magic returned, had only ever spoken of that day in the former god king's palace once.

Warm air whipped Cion's braids around as she scanned the horizon and then the tree line. Perhaps the sightings had been a mistake. After all, the war-torn villages in this part of Mise had been abandoned decades ago. Ana wasn't the only one who ran from ghosts.

But just as she thought it, a pale flash in the trees caught her attention.

Valhamnor?

Her dragon dropped altitude slowly, still circling as he replied. *There is someone nearby.*

Dragons?

He neared a clearing a few hundred feet away from the flash. *You should investigate, princess.*

He had never called her queen, insisting she was still the young girl she had been when they had met that day at the Choosing Ceremony. She pretended it didn't bother her, but she had always known dragons were the wiser race.

His landing was quiet, and she slipped from his back with the ease and stealth of a practiced warrior in their prime, despite her aging mortal body. "Wait here for me."

Each step through the trees was a battle, perhaps one of the hardest she had ever fought.

"In another life, perhaps we could have been sisters. But in this one, you were simply my captor."

She smelled woodfire smoke, and the tenor of a man's voice carried from the clearing as she approached. Her heart was in her throat, her breath audible in the warm, humid summer air. When she heard the screech of a child's laughter, she nearly turned around, sure she had been wrong.

But then, a small figure darted out of the house, and she nearly stopped breathing.

"Papa! There's a lady in the trees!" a girl called, her brow creased as she pointed to where Cion stood. The child couldn't have been older than five, her face a striking mix of Misean and Arenean features, her silver hair pulled back into tiny braids.

Cion didn't move, simply watching as a ghost wearing the face of Vane Evva hurried out of the house, heading for the child and pulling a long knife from his belt. He didn't look older than perhaps twenty-five, his dark hair free of gray and his eyes rimmed with silver ether as he scanned the area.

When his gaze landed on Cion, he tucked the knife away and the ether faded. "Nya, love, is that her?" he asked the child gently, pointing.

The girl bobbed her head. "She looks like the queen in the painting but old."

Vane's lips curved. "Are you going to just stand there while my four year old daughter insults you, Cion?" he called. "Or will you defend your honor?"

Finally, fingertips tingling and head light, she stepped into the clearing. "My honor is fine. The child is right, and age is nothing to scoff at, not amongst us mortals."

His smirk softened. "No, it is not. You've made quite the name for yourself, my queen."

"We're in Mise," she said, scanning the area. "So I'm afraid you're wrong, I am no queen here."

Vane took a step closer, the child clinging to his leg. "She's on dragonback, Cion. You might have to wait a little while if you wish to see her."

"And the other dragon?"

He chuckled. "Heles is rather good at hiding—and napping. She won't wake unless we're in dire danger, I'm afraid."

"She snores really loud!" Nya said brightly. "And her breath smells bad, but you get used to it. Does your dragon have smelly breath too? He's very pretty—for a boy dragon."

Cion took a deep breath and knelt in front of the child, holding out a jeweled hand. Nya glanced up at her father, and Vane murmured, "It's alright, little love. She won't hurt you."

A spark ran up Cion's spine when the girl touched her hand, and she tilted her head. Even though she was not a magic wielder herself, she could still sense it, and this girl was practically spilling over with power. She ignored the warning bells in her head and instead asked her, "How did you know Valhamnor was a male dragon?"

"The size of his head," Nya said matter-of-factly. "And the spikes by his ears. Female Fesper dragons don't have those."

Cion glanced up at Vane. "You've taught her well."

"I can't claim credit for that part of her education," he said, looking at his daughter fondly. "But she does already have a mean left hook thanks to me. Just don't tell Sora I—"

"Don't tell Sora what, exactly?"

Cion froze, not daring to look past Nya yet. But as the child tugged her hand free and Vane grinned and turned, she could no longer ignore it.

"Mamma, we have a visitor!" Nya exclaimed, running to—

Soren.

Cion hadn't even realized she'd said her name aloud, not until Soren replied, "Hello, princess. I thought you might pay us a visit. Thessa was bound to be seen soon, though I suppose that's my fault for flying so low."

Cion was still on her knees when she rasped, "How?"

"Ana told you, I presume," Vane said quietly, offering her a hand.

She took it gratefully—her right knee had been a bother since she turned forty-five. Then, clearing her throat, she said, "Yes. She only spoke of it once, and when she heard news that Thessilnn was spotted flying, she… Well, I cannot properly communicate her level of shock. She claimed it was impossible, and from what she told me of that day, I agree. It should be."

"Do you want to come inside?" Soren asked. "Sit down or—"

"No," Cion cut in sharply. "I want an explanation."

Vane stepped in front of Soren and Nya. The air warmed with more than the summer heat, and the coals in the firepit flared. "Why do you assume you are owed one?"

"You left me in the mountains with a group of army defects and their dragons," Cion snapped. "Picking up the pieces of what you did, noble as you might have thought it was, was no easy task. The mortal realm was in disarray for nearly a decade. I thought for a long time another war was imminent."

"Apologies, *my queen*," he snarled. "We were too busy being—"

"Vane." Soren's voice was gentle but firm. He turned, his harsh features instantly softening as she searched his gaze. Cion knew they were speaking in the same silent manner she had once seen all those years ago.

"Nya does not know everything, not yet," he said quietly in explanation. "She's too young for the burden of it. But Sora will speak to you if you wish to hear an explanation."

He scooped up a whining Nya, murmuring to her. Almost instantly, she smiled and giggled, throwing her arms around his neck as he stepped into the house.

Cion stood across the yard from Soren, brow raised. "So you took up your old name again?"

She shrugged. "My latest 'mother' named me Marine out of stubbornness, but I never used it. Sora is who I've always been."

"And so these women who birthed and raised you in these last two lifetimes, they are nothing to you?"

Soren sighed. "Nyx handpicked them both from the same bloodline. I think they loved me, in a way, but both were aware of what I was since the moment I took my first breath. I was as much of a daughter to them as they were a true mother to me. But I am grateful to them."

"And Vane?"

"Born two years before me, to a family in your capital city."

Cion began to pace. Movement had always helped her

think. "How did you find each other? Did you remember, or did it take time, like before?"

"My birth mother told me bedtime stories to jog my memory. I knew everything important by the time I was seven and remembered it all clearly by sixteen. Vane's family didn't know, and though he said he was aware he didn't belong there, he only remembered fully when he saw me the first time."

"Which was?"

"Nine years ago. He came to Mise for work as an apprentice in the village I was raised in—or rather, his birth family sent him. There are more fire wielders here, and apparently, his father was growing tired of him almost burning the house down."

Cion did not laugh, instead stopping her pacing. Gods, Soren—Sora—looked just the same. Frozen in time, an immortal goddess borrowing a mortal's body.

"Will you age?"

"No, my body paused at twenty, and Vane's around twenty-four."

Cion shook her head, looking around. "Then why remain here? I am sure Arcadia would welcome you with open arms for your heroic liberation."

Sora's mouth lifted, but her eyes were heavy with sorrow. Quietly, she asked, "Has Anabeth returned?"

"If you know, why ask? She remains here because Arcadia is a tainted place for her. There is too much pain in that place."

Sora raised a brow. "Then you know why we remain here to raise our daughter." She glanced out at the trees. "Someday, when Nya is grown and armed with the knowledge to weather what lies in Arcadia, perhaps we will go. I haven't—" She took a quick breath. "I don't know, Cion. Even in this lifetime, it haunts me."

"Kronos is gone, body and soul," Cion said, the truth stark even as she whispered it. "Why did you not go with him? Ana was sure you had, both of you."

Sora met her gaze again. Beyond, in the house, Nya laughed.

"When Thessilnn and Heles hatched, they both chose not just Vane and I separately, but together. The four of us are linked at a soul level. So, when I claimed Kronos and he was burned in their dragonfire along with our bodies, Thessa and Heles held our souls within them until the fates called us to this world once more."

"No one knows this?"

"I didn't know, not until it was nearly too late to understand. Are you planning to tell others after today?"

Cion took a slow breath, letting all the anger and hurt flow from her. When she reached the source of it, she found only pain, driven by love for a sister who had never been.

"I wouldn't dream of it," she told Sora. "Just promise me one thing."

Sora waited, ether swirling in her once-familiar blue eyes. The firepit flared as Vane laughed inside, and Cion reached into her pocket before holding her open palm out. Sora's eyes widened as she saw the twin gold bands Ana had given wordlessly to Cion just before she departed.

"Live, Sora."

The End

BONUS CHAPTER
50 YEARS POST THE DISAPPEARANCE OF MAGIC, AREN

THE CREEK BED was dry and gone, the stalks of wheat, long dead and carried away like dust in the wind. High altitude farms such as this had been some of the first to go in Aren when magic had ceased to exist, a phenomenon that still puzzled the mortals.

Lying on his back under the branches of a cluster of gnarled balor trees, he stared at the dusk-darkened sky, waiting for the stars to appear. On the ground next to him lay a heavy sword, gloves, and a crude mask that he hated. A handful of paces further, an enormous dragon pretended to be asleep, her midnight-black head resting on the ground.

Heles snored when she was truly slumbering, and she never left him alone on this day.

The first few specks of bright white appeared above him and he lifted his left hand up, reaching for an impossibility. A wayward comet shot across the sky, sparking red just before it faded away. His mouth twitched even as his eyes burned.

"I know I asked you to come back," he whispered. "But things are… bad, Sora. I wouldn't blame you if you wanted to stay up there. I don't know if this world can be mended. I don't know if *I*—"

He cut himself off with a sharp breath, lowering his hand. Thoughts like this were becoming a near-constant, and even though he knew he should try to fight the hopelessness, the will to do so was waning. Some days, he was only held up on two feet by the orders the aged mortal king handed out.

Wind stirred the barren branches above him and he closed his eyes, letting himself slip into a fantasy he only ever allowed on this day—a day he *refused* to be ruled by the horror that had occurred fifty years ago. He would not remember her like that, empty-eyed and still.

Instead, he imagined her lying beside him, silver hair spilling across the ground as she pointed out constellations that made up a celestial map above them. Places she'd say had perhaps once been a home to her mother, before she took a form. She would laugh when Heles snorted in her sleep and smile as he mused how fast fifty years had passed. He could almost hear her voice, asking, *"Did you ever imagine a life so long, when you were a child?"*

No. He never had, because he hadn't known the reality of what he was before her, and, in truth, it wouldn't have mattered without her. He did not want the immortal eternity made possible by his father's blood, not without her in it.

Vane.

He did not open his eyes, ignoring the dragon even as she shifted next to him.

The king will not be happy you are so late. We should go.

A heavy sigh escaped him, fingertips curling into the dry dirt and grass beneath him. *The king is never happy with me. Just give me a few more minutes with her, then we'll go.*

Heles made a low, mournful sound and the earth trembled as she slumped back to the ground. The absence of Sora—and of Thessilnn, who had long-fallen into a slumber where even Vane could not reach her—wore on Heles too. Vane had once questioned why she stayed with him at all and the dragon had merely gnashed her teeth at him and threatened to melt his favorite sword if he ever brought it up again. He *knew* why; knew that the four of them were so deeply bound by fate that even death could not undo the threads. But he also cared for Heles and hated that she was forced to be complicit in his pitiful, cursed existence.

She didn't bother him again until well over an hour had passed, when she nudged at his body with her snout and insisted, *We need to go. I will carry you if need be, but I am aware we would both not prefer that.*

"Fine," he muttered, forcing himself to sit up and look at the field one last time.

Even dry and long dead, it still held a peaceful feeling he could not find anywhere else. Magic had left, taking with it plenty of life, but perhaps some places were always sacred, no matter the passing of time or the change of the landscape.

"I'll be back next year," he murmured to the wind, before donning the wretched mask and mounting the saddle atop Heles.

When he arrived just outside of the palace, Heles let out a screech that shook the cliffside she'd landed on.

"Well, if they didn't know we were here before, they did now," he muttered, patting her scales before sliding off her back.

The king did *request I announce your presence each time you arrive.*

Vane sighed softly. *You probably just woke up half the capital with your roaring.*

You are being dramatic.

Aren't I always?

The dragon huffed and shook her body, obviously irritated with him. Not because he'd scolded her, but because he had risked upsetting King Jonah like this. He wouldn't kill Vane, not for this. The wretched man valued his uses far too much. But that didn't mean he couldn't punish him in other ways for being purposefully disobedient. Jonah hadn't specifically stated when to arrive other than that he required Vane to appear before him in the throne room today. Just before midnight had most definitely not been what the king had in mind, but today of all days, Vane truly couldn't find it in himself to give a fuck.

Guards shifted nervously as he swept past them through the back entrance, and once he was inside the airy hallways that made up the more public areas of the palace, lords and ladies who were lingering in the dim light ogled his arrival. Some of them even wore nightwear covered by silk robes, as if they'd woken up and left their chambers just to watch him meet the king.

People didn't trust what they did not understand. But that didn't mean they couldn't entertain a spectacle.

The king was waiting for him when he strode into the cavernous room, slumped against the throne and fuming.

Next to him, his son and heir, Johannas, lingered. Though the boy wasn't even yet fifteen, Vane was already wary of him. Jonah was cruel, but he was an idiot. For his son, Vane could not say the same. The heir of Aren already had the potential to be dangerous.

"Where have you been?" Jonah spat, his cheeks ruddy.

Vane knelt in front of the throne—a formality that had been insisted upon. If he refused, Jonah would tug the leash of his curse and order it anyways, and the feeling was never pleasant.

"You did not specify precisely *when* I should arrive, my king. Just that it needed to be today."

The king's face deepened into a deep shade of purple, giving him the appearance of a bruised, wrinkled plum. Beside him, Johannas rolled his eyes, though not at Vane. At fourteen, he was already much cleverer than his father and it made Vane uneasy that, someday soon, his chains would be handed off to someone much less likely to make mistakes or create room for error in his commands.

"You!" the king snapped, pointing at a guard stationed a few feet from Vane. "Punish him."

The guard's face paled, his eyes darting from the king to where Vane still kneeled, as if unsure who was more dangerous to provoke.

Vane sighed from behind the mask and motioned to the young man. "Just get it over with so we can carry on with this meeting and be done. I've had a long fucking day."

The guard's brow rose, probably surprised at how nonchalant Vane was when it came to the threat of a beating. What he did not know was that Vane had received far worse from much stronger guards. And he *did* really just want to at least and attempt to sleep for once.

The guard cleared his throat, but jumped as Johannas said curtly, "Well, on with it. Your king gave you a command."

"Right," the guard muttered, approaching Vane slowly.

He gave a pathetic kick that didn't even put Vane in danger of toppling over. The room was thick with a tense silence, the king obviously waiting for more.

"Just pretend I'm someone you hate," Vane said in a low voice. "That's what I do."

Out of the corner of his eye, he saw Johannas smirk, as if pleased, though Vane wasn't exactly sure why. The guard sucked in a sharp breath and, this time, his foot slammed into Vane hard enough to knock the breath out of him. He let himself crumple to the marble floor, mostly for effect so that this whole affair could end for the night. But he'd give it to the guard—he was strong for a mortal. Without proper sleep, the bruises would take a day or two to heal, even with the aid of the ether in his blood.

"Alright," the king barked after a few minutes. "Enough for now."

The guard paused mid-strike, his chest heaving and his eyes wild. But Vane saw the moment the adrenaline dimmed and reality set in. The guard's throat worked at the sight of blood on the marble and his hands shook as he stepped back. He'd probably never hurt someone like that before.

Vane lifted his head, fighting the urge to tear the ridiculous mask from his face and spit blood at the king's feet.

"So," he rasped. "You wanted something, my king?"

The king's nostrils flared, but his son nudged him, obviously trying to keep the old man on track.

"You're to go hunting," the king finally said.

Vane tightened his jaw. "And what exactly are you wanting me to catch?"

"Magic," the king said, lifting his chin. "Anyone who might still have magic."

Vane shifted, returning to his knees and meeting the king's eyes. "You and I are both aware it's a futile task. The demi-gods have all fled and no mortals possess that power, not anymore."

"Yes," Jonah said, his voice lowering. "Not for fifty years now. It was today, yes?"

He barely bit back the wave of heat that tried to break free on instinct at the taunt in the king's voice. Fifty years ago, a young Jonah had stood at the border as Kronos handed him and Ana over like a pair of cattle. Of course, Jonah hadn't been aware that as soon as Kronos stepped back into Arcadia, he'd seal it away and take magic too. Jonah had once been a magic-wielder himself, and though he did not know the whole story, Vane was sure Kronos had told the king just enough to make him hate the two demi-gods he'd 'gifted' him. And enough that Jonah knew what today meant to Vane.

"Ah," the king mused, leaning forward. "So, that's where you were. Mourning?" He snorted. "Despite your uses, you can be quite pathetic."

Vane said nothing. He never did when Jonah taunted him. But these moments, when the king spoke of Sora without even knowing her name or her importance beyond Kronos' former betrothed who'd 'betrayed' him—they were the only times he thought he might be able to actually kill Jonah.

He'd never tried. Maybe that did make him pathetic. But Jonah was stupid, and, if on the off chance he was able to supersede the curse for a moment and attempt to hurt the king, he was sure Jonah wouldn't let him live. The timing of when Sora's soul would return to this world was completely unknown, even to Ana, but he'd be damned if she returned to this mess alone.

So, he kept his mouth shut.

"Nothing to say to that?" Jonah pushed.

He slipped into a mental numbness. "No, my king."

"Fine. You and your beast will depart in the morning. If, within three moon cycles, you've found nothing, you may return for your next assignment."

"Yes, my king."

The king snorted. "Go."

He stood, ignoring the way the guard who'd beat him flinched as he walked past. For a moment, he flicked his gaze up to where Nyx and Thanatos were painted on the ceiling above. Gods who had sacrificed their only daughter to be Kronos' mere property, and for what? Both realms had fallen into chaos anyways. Perhaps Vane was to blame for that. Sometimes he believed it. But the guilt always felt tainted—what he felt for his wife wasn't something he could truly believe was profane. They had not sinned; even the fates had said as much when they were claimed by Heles and Thessilnn.

The fates would not save them, though. That much, he was painfully aware of.

As he rounded the corner to a less-lavish wing of the

palace where his barracks lay, he nearly crashed into someone who was lingering there.

A split second later, he recognized it was Ana by the unnerving buzz surrounding her. Children of Juno carried a visceral sort of feeling with them at all times; a tug in your gut, a thought on the tip of your tongue… a whisper of fate. Most mortals could not sense it anymore, when magic had been gone for so long, allowing her to blend in. Jonah had put her to use in a gentler way, and she spent most of her time in the royal library with her rogue godling brother, staring at scrolls.

"I'm sorry, I didn't mean to startle you," she said hurriedly, placing a hand on his arm to steady him.

He flinched away.

Her mouth tightened as she took in blood dripping down from beneath the mask, her hand still half-outstretched.

"Vane," she said quietly. "You know I'm not going to hurt you."

He said nothing but tugged away the mask, wincing at the sting in his nose. Not broken, thanks to the wretched face covering, but definitely sore.

"Gods, what happened?"

He cleared his throat, shirking off his gloves and gingerly checking the rest of his face. "Nothing. I showed up later than he wanted and he forced some poor guard to—"

"Beat you into a bloody pulp?" she challenged, faint veins of ether brightening in her eyes. "That guard really did a number on you for being forced."

"I told him to pretend I was someone he hated. That it's what I do."

Ana stiffened. It was no secret who he imagined each and every time the king used the wretched curse to force him to hurt someone.

"Well, he still had a choice, unlike you," she said after a moment. "It's different."

"Is it?"

She sighed and opened her mouth, surely to rebuke him, but he cut her off, his voice sharper than he intended as he said, "What do you need from me?"

She frowned. "I don't need anything. I just wanted to make sure you were okay, which you're obviously not so—"

He laughed abruptly, the sound rough and a little wet from the blood still lingering in the back of his throat.

"No," he said. "I'm not."

She lowered her gaze to the floor for a moment, wringing her hands when she looked up at him. "You went out there again, didn't you?"

He slumped against the wall, eyes half shut as he replied, "I go every year."

"You shouldn't torture yourself like that."

This time, his laugh was quieter. Softer. He tipped his head back, staring at the dancing flames of the torch on the other side of the hall.

"I'm not. It's just the only time I can… The only time I *let* myself be with her. I lost track of time today, that's all."

When he looked back at Ana, her eyes were glassy, but she blinked the unshed tears away quickly. "We have to hold on. It's only a matter of time until her soul is reborn into this world."

He caught her eyes and held her gaze as he forced himself to say to her what he'd begun asking himself.

"Don't you think sometimes it might be kinder if she didn't come back?"

He almost expected Ana to get angry, but instead she tilted her head and took a small step forward, her voice soft as she said, "Maybe. But it doesn't really matter what's kinder or what's fair. The fates will always have their way and Sora is a goddess. Her soul never left, not really, and it will return. The same way yours or mine would." She smiled sadly. "An unfortunate effect of having one of the principals as a parent."

"Fucking fates," he muttered.

Ana sighed. "Yes. Fucking fates." She paused, then added, "You have to hold on, Vane. You know as well as I do what Jonah's son is like. The old king will die soon and there's no telling when someone who is just as cruel as him, but much more intelligent takes the throne. I have a bad feeling about it."

"Your 'bad feelings' are never just that."

"No," she agreed. "They are not.'

They both fell silent, time slipping past that neither of them deigned to acknowledge, not until Ana asked in a voice that lacked her usual even resolve, "Do you ever feel… Do you think she watches over us at all?"

"Today, when I was out there, I saw a comet just after dusk. Maybe it's just my own desperation, but I always feel her in that place."

He looked at Ana just in time to see her swiftly wiping away a few tears. She tucked a few wayward strands of hair behind her ear, then cleared her throat. "I should go. I just wanted to check in."

"I'll be gone for a while. An… errand. Stay close to your brother."

She gave a shallow nod and without another word, left the hallway. Once her light footsteps faded, he snatched up the gloves and the mask from where he'd dropped them on the floor. Absent-mindedly, he slipped his thumb over the band on his left pointer finger, over and over as he walked to his barracks alone.

Author Note and Acknowledgements

The process for To Kill a Goddess spanned several years, and for a time, it mostly involved a spiral-bound notebook filled with pages of worldbuilding in my nearly-illegible handwriting and half a prologue that I eventually scrapped. I was intrigued by the world and its characters but they kept flitting beyond reach—more of a hazy concept than a story, if you will. Then, of course, in the usual fashion for me, it all came flooding in and the first draft was completed within a month. As crazy as it sounds, the characters sometimes have minds of their own (inside of my mind???) and maybe Soren and Vane were just waiting for the right time to become clear to me. All of that said, this book was quite a bit different from anything I've written before, from the prose to the story structure, and even the world itself. Whether it appears to you as I saw it my (many) maladaptive daydreams, it's yours now, and that's an incredibly exciting —if not sometimes terrifying—prospect.

Though a romance at its core, the story also explores power dynamics and all the ways a world can plunge into chaos when that power falls into the wrong hands. But as Soren found, the terrifying rules of tyrant kings can be disrupted by just the smallest blip. At one point, Commander Eton claims he 'always knew she was dangerous' and Soren replies, "*Why... because of what I can do or the system I challenge by simply holding any amount of power?"* Their systems are more fragile than they will ever admit. It's why they're so afraid of us, of *any* resistance. Our voices hold power. Don't forget that.

Thank you first and foremost to MK Ahearn for listening to each new story idea I have with the same enthusiasm and support, and for running such a wonderful small press. I will always be grateful to past me for reaching out when I saw Azala was accepting submissions. Thank you to my wonderful editor, Alexa at the Fiction Fix, and also to Whitney for beta reading. And finally, to my husband, Ryan, for always being a supportive partner and never once questioning when I realized my dream career was writing about dragons, faeries, and people kissing.

ALSO BY RACHEL TORK

THE EVENING STAR SAGA

A Fantasy Romance Series

THE LINES WE CROSS

A Contemporary Romance Standalone